Praise for *Forgotten Soldiers*

Warren Martin's debut novel **Forgotten Soldiers** is a compelling story which begins in the Vietnam War and runs through the Cold War period. Warren's documentary style of writing makes this riveting tale more real, more apparently credible and honest, than any other style could possibly create. Warren's voice is Hemmingway-esque. Perhaps this is the voice best suited to military based mysteries, I can't say, but it works... I actually forgot that I was reading fiction until I reached the very end of Warren's **Forgotten Soldiers**. It seemed that real.

This noteworthy and powerful POW/MIA mystery should definitely be on your must-read list.

Pam De Voe — President — Sisters in Crime St. Louis Chapter

Highly recommended! Five Stars!
Fiction? I wonder... Although this is a work of fiction, the story could very well have happened and none of us would have been the wiser. The author uses real events in his story such as the historic U.S. raid on the Son Tay prison camp to rescue seventy American prisoners — a location only 23 miles west of Hanoi, Jane Fonda's infamous trip to the Hanoi Hilton Prison in North Vietnam, and the fall of the Russian empire.

To tell anymore would be a spoiler — you'll have to read this fine story on your own to see how it ends.

Warning: You'll stay up late into the night reading because you won't be able to stop.

—John Podlaski— author, Cherries — A Vietnam War Novel.

A Remarkable Story... To tell a good story you need some kind of narrative device that brings the reader in and then, once you have the reader, to keep them wanting more...
—*Jeffrey Miller*— author, *War Remains* and *Waking Up in the Land of the Morning Calm.*

Clever Thriller! ...All the elements of true suspense. The author has plunged into his rucksack of knowledge and experience and crafted a tale that will keep you in suspense until the final page. I highly recommend it.
—*Bernard Cenney*, LTC (R)— author, *Sparrow's Tears* and *Close Your Eyes and See.*

Won't Be Able to Put This Book Down... At times I found myself wondering if the story could be true...I highly recommend the book for all readers — and not just history or military buffs — but for anyone that has a space in their heart to keep the spirit of our Forgotten Soldiers alive. — *Jen*

Amazing, couldn't put it down! 5+ stars... The story seemed so real...places and events were woven in a spellbinding manner with reality throughout the story...explanations of how and why things happened the way they did during Nam and other wars...I hope the story gets made into a movie. Thank you, Mr. Martin, for writing this story! — *Kindlereader*

Opened to page one at about 2 p.m. and could not put it down. Finished at 11:30 p.m....I would advise anyone who is going to buy it to make sure your schedule is clear. — *Andy*

FORGOTTEN SOLDIERS

What Happened To Jacob Walden?

WARREN MARTIN

Forgotten Soldiers
Copyright © 2014 by Warren Martin

This book is a work of fiction. Names, characters, places, and incidents either are the product of the author's imagination or are used fictitiously. Any resemblance to actual persons, living or dead, events, or locals is entirely coincidental.

ISBN: 9780985472702
Library of Congress Control Number: 2012906322

Published by
Warren Martin Books & Little Elephant Publishing
St. Louis, Missouri
www.warrenmartinbooks.com

Content Editing by Ken Farmer
www.blackeagleforce.com

Copy Editing by Joyce M. Gilmour
www.editingtlc.com

Interior Design by Jera Publishing
www.jerapublishing.com

Cover Design by Digital Donna
www.digitaldonna.com

Cover Photos by Warren Martin

Dedicated to the memory of those who served their nations, sacrificed their freedoms, gave their lives, and who have since joined the ranks of "Forgotten Soldiers"

"Posterity! You will never know how much it has cost us to preserve your freedom. My hope is that you will make good use of it. If you do not, I shall repent in heaven that I ever took half the pains to preserve it." —John Adams

ACKNOWLEDGMENTS

I want to acknowledge those I have dedicated this book to, the Veterans of the Cold War, those who have become what I call the "Forgotten Soldiers." They served, sacrificed, and many never returned. These individuals served under the veil of the Cold War: anonymous, obscure, and unknown to most, and ultimately unrecognized or remembered for their sacrifices. While this book is fiction, its theme and message embodies the heart, soul, and faith of our Forgotten Soldiers. Veterans of the Cold War were a collective group of the Armed Forces and individuals in government service in various intelligence and other government agencies, whose combined efforts contributed to the outcome and winning of the Cold War, preserving the freedoms and liberty we continue to enjoy.

I would also like to acknowledge the collaborative mentoring, support, and assistance I have received from friends, professionals, the Military Writers Society of America (MWSA) and the St. Louis Publishers Association (SLPA).

Special thanks to *Son Tay Raider* Command Sergeant Major (Ret) Pat St. Clair for his insight and assistance. Thank you to Ken Farmer for his mentoring and assistance, and my sincere thanks and appreciation goes out to everyone who has encouraged and assisted me in my writing and publishing endeavors.

A special thank you to my wife Debbie Kay and our children, Shelby, Jessica, and Buddy for their longtime participation in a world traveling career military family, and for their continued encouragement and support.

CONTENTS

PRELUDE

VIETNAM

30 June, 1970

Day 1

"Oh God, oh God, oh God!" Captain Jacob Walden yelled out through his oxygen mask as his ejection seat violently propelled him through the Vietnam sky.

The sounds of his yells were muffled by the mask over his face and the deafening sounds of the ejection seat rockets that just seconds before lifted him out of the exploding aircraft. Over the midmorning sky of Vietnam, the rockets propelling Captain Walden's ejection seat extinguished, his parachute opened, and the ejection seat separated, falling toward the earth almost 20,000 feet below. The entire time from initial ejection to the point where the parachute fully opened took less than eight seconds, but for Captain Jake Walden it seemed like an eternity.

For Jake, this was the first time that he had been exposed to this level or type of danger. The 24-year-old captain had been assigned to Vietnam less than a month, and although he had received training in what to do if he were shot down—the training was still much different from reality.

The previous violent moments were now transitioning to a surreal quietness and peacefulness. The breeze of the air caressed the cold sweat Jake experienced as he drifted under his parachute. As he regained his composure, he looked around and then down to see, what under normal circumstances, any sport parachute enthusiasts would be thoroughly enjoying. It was eerily quiet, except for the slight sound of the air passing through the parachute as he had begun from an unusually high altitude.

During his descent, Jake was transitioning to becoming one more American, falling victim to the Vietnam War. While he already had memberships in several personal and professional organizations and clubs, he was about to join a unique and somewhat ironic privileged membership in three more, one as a prisoner of war and another as a veteran of the Vietnam War. The third one, however, would not receive any real recognition for the sacrifices made by soldiers like Jake Walden. People such as Jake did not receive recognition, memorials, or even a national monument in their honor or remembrance. Captain Jacob Walden was about to take up membership in a fraternity of "Forgotten Soldiers."

CHAPTER 1

MISSING IN ACTION

FOUR MONTHS LATER
18 November, 1970
Day 142

By mid-November of 1970, the fate of Jake Walden and many other Americans who were missing and presumed captured was uncertain. Months earlier in July of 1970, the outcome of the Vietnam War had, for the most part, already been determined, and while the war did not end for almost three more years, President Nixon had already put into place plans and negotiations for ending it. The Vietnam War was highly politicized, dramatized, and in some cases very personalized by the American people. In many instances, Americans were disconnected from the reality of the individuals making the sacrifices—individuals like Jake who had been shot down. Back in the United States, at places like the San Francisco airport, people were spitting and yelling at soldiers who proudly wore their uniforms as they walked through the terminals.

While there was no lack of public opinion and political agendas, one view of the military leadership focused on the recovery and rescue of its own people. In June 1970, discussions began in Washington, D.C. concerning options to conduct rescue operations. President Nixon was quite interested in the possibility of not only rescuing prisoners, but also forcing the North Vietnamese to the peace negotiations.

EGLIN AIR FORCE BASE, FLORIDA
18 November, 1970

Air Force General Leroy J. Manor, his staff, and less than a hundred other military personnel were at a secret operations center at Eglin Air Force Base in Florida. A few months earlier General Manor had been appointed the commander of a secret operation named Task Force Ivory Coast, to research, prepare, and possibly execute a rescue operation of American prisoners of war inside North Vietnam. The second in command was Army Special Forces Colonel Arthur D. "Bull" Simons. Bull Simons recruited Army Special Forces volunteers—Green Berets—from Fort Bragg, North Carolina, to sign up for a mission that they were told nothing about, except it was classified and they may not make it home. Without hesitation, they all volunteered, as did the Air Force crews that would fly the helicopters and other support aircraft on the operation.

Aircraft Training in Florida for Raid 1970

During the midafternoon, another rehearsal of a rescue operation at a mock POW camp had just finished. General Manor, Colonel Simons, and other staff members were going over their daily post rehearsal details, which had become more of a routine than rehearsal. On this day, however, the briefing was interrupted by a knock on the door, followed quickly by a sergeant sticking his head inside the room.

"General, call for you on one. Think you're gonna want to take this one, Sir."

General Manor walked over to the table where the secure telephone was located and got on the phone with the secretary of defense. General Manor listened for a moment and then said, "Thank you, Sir." After hanging up, General Manor looked around the room at everyone and then at Colonel Simons with a smile, and stated: "The President has given his approval. We're a go."

Eager to get the operation going, Colonel Simons cracked an ever so slight smile.

BANGKOK, THAILAND
19 November, 1970
Day 143

After General Manor had received the green light, it didn't take long for the task force to get loaded up on an aircraft headed for Thailand. When they departed Eglin, however, the members of the task force were told they were heading to California for more training. The flight ended up passing through Alaska, Japan, and on 19 November ended up at Takhli Royal Thai Air Force Base north of Bangkok, Thailand, an air base that also doubled as a CIA secret compound.

The following day at 1800 hours the fifty-six men of the ground force were assembled at a theater on Takhli waiting for a mission briefing from Bull Simons. While waiting, the men talked among themselves about the still unknown location of the upcoming operation. During the previous three months at Eglin, the Green Berets and Air Force crews had prepared and rehearsed for the upcoming tasking. During that time, they conducted 170 rehearsals on a mock-up of the POW camp, but they were never told the actual location. The camp was a replica built from a photograph where the mission would take place. The entire operation and training, which included the daily breakdown of the camp and rebuilding of it to prevent pictures from being taken by the daily flyover of Soviet satellites, had to be kept secret. If the satellites had been able to take photographs, they would have passed the info to the North Vietnamese and jeopardized the entire operation.

At 1800 hours, Simons entered the theater where the team had assembled. The men were anxious but eager to get on with the mission and although they didn't know the exact location, they had speculated as to where it could be; however, none of them had anticipated what Bull Simons was about to tell them.

As he arrived, silence blanketed the room and everyone's attention was on the colonel. As a member of the staff uncovered an oversized photo of a camp, Simons started his briefing. "Gentlemen, we are going to rescue seventy American prisoners of war, maybe more, from a camp called Son Tay. This is something American prisoners have a right to expect from their fellow soldiers. The target is twenty-three miles west of Hanoi."

There was complete silence in the theater for a few seconds as the men realized that Colonel Simons just said, *"twenty-three miles west of Hanoi."* They knew without question not only the significance of the operation, but also the real danger and that the mission was also in Hanoi's backyard. The 23-mile distance might as well be in downtown Hanoi. The silence was broken as a few men let out some whistles before the entire group stood up and began applauding. After they calmed down and the applauding stopped, the colonel and his staff continued the briefing. Afterward, the men of the task force prepped for the tasking and at 2030 hours loaded up on a C-130 and took off for Udorn Air Base in Thailand.

Son Tay Prison Camp 1970

UDORN AIR BASE, THAILAND
20 November, 1970
Day 144

Udorn Air Base was a significant base of operations during the Vietnam War and was located just thirty miles west of the Laotian border. The C-130 flight from Takhli was not long and after landing at Udorn, the task force made their final preparations before they boarded the waiting Jolly Green CH-53 helicopters. At 2317 hours on 20 November, 1970, the choppers took off from Udorn Air Base on the estimated three-hour flight to their target.

As part of the overall operation, coordination had been made for over 100 Navy and Air Force aircraft to participate in the mission for diversion and support purposes. Shortly after midnight, the fighter aircraft took off from another air base in Thailand, and shortly after one in the morning, additional aircraft were launched from three Navy carriers: USS *Oriskany*, USS *Ranger*, and USS *Hancock*.

Throughout the Hanoi region, American prisoners were awakened from their sleep by the sound of the diversionary flights, flares, and more so from the noise created by the North Vietnamese launching of surface-to-air missiles, called SAMs. Although the prisoners knew something was happening, they also thought nothing more of it than another operation and were unaware of the significance.

As 0200 hours approached, the helicopters were twenty minutes from the Son Tay camp. The time was getting close, and so far, the diversions created by the air support had worked. The men were ready to execute the mission and rehearsed in their heads their parts of the operation. Finally, the time had come and they were within a minute of the camp.

As the five attack force CH-53 helicopters approached the camp, two moved to a standby position overlooking the camp area. The other three choppers made their approach, as rehearsed, with one using its door-guns to destroy the guard towers. The helicopter, code named Blue Boy, with the main assault force, prepared to make a crash landing inside the walls of the camp, which was part of the plan to get the assault force quickly inside the camp and had been rehearsed without a problem; however, as the pilot made the approach, he immediately noticed that the trees inside the walls were much taller and thicker than anticipated. The higher and thicker trees made it much more difficult to control a crash landing safely, but it was too late to stop or turn around.

As everyone braced inside Blue Boy, the pilot took the helicopter in, shredding the trees as the aircraft violently vibrated and slammed to the ground. Amazingly, the crash was successful with only one injury, a broken ankle—otherwise, the rest of the men were uninjured and exited the craft as planned. They began their assault while one of the men used a megaphone to notify the prisoners that they were being rescued.

The assault group and support group that landed outside the camp immediately engaged in a firefight with the Vietnamese guards while they simultaneously conducted their cell-by-cell search of the prison looking for American prisoners. As the teams made their check of the cells they made a disappointing discovery—every cell was empty. The task force spent twenty-five minutes searching the camp for prisoners while continuing firefights with the Vietnamese guards. During the twenty-five minutes, they had killed an estimated fifty Vietnamese guards inside the prison and another 100 at the nearby barracks.

The teams completed their search, but they did not find any prisoners. After the search of the camp was finished, explosive charges were set inside the crashed Blue Boy helicopter as planned, and then the teams moved out to the nearby clearing where they waited for exfil by the returning helicopters. As the birds landed, loaded up and took off, there was tremendous unspoken disappointment in the hearts of the rescuers as the choppers began the three-hour flight back toward Udorn, Thailand. Although the mission had been a tactical success, the absence of American prisoners, or any prisoners, was depressing. Within a few minutes after takeoff from the Son Tay prison camp, at 0252 hours, the illumination of the explosion and destruction of Blue Boy left inside the camp was seen in the distance, and momentarily broke the silence inside the aircrafts.

Remains of Helicopter Inside Son Tay Prison

THIRTY-SIX YEARS LATER
ST. LOUIS, MISSOURI
21 August, 2006

During an early Monday afternoon in her St. Louis suburban home, Carolyn Jordon, sat at her desk doing some work on the computer. Back in 1970, she was Carolyn Walden, married to Jake Walden—they had two children. After Jake was shot down, his status changed several times over the years, starting as missing-in-action, then to POW status, and later back to missing-and-presumed dead. In 1980, Carolyn remarried, had two more children with her new husband, and for the past twenty-six years had adjusted and accepted what she believed to be her first husband's fate—that he had died in Vietnam.

A knock on the front door got Carolyn's attention. She stood up and when answering it, she was a little surprised and startled to see her former brother-in-law Jerry Walden standing in front of her.

"Hi, Carolyn," he said, a gentle smile on his lips.

"Jerry, what a surprise."

"I'm sorry, Carolyn. I should have called, but I thought it would be better if I saw you."

She invited Jerry inside, and they walked to the kitchen while briefly catching up with each other's life, since they hadn't seen each other for over fifteen years, once when Carolyn remarried in 1980. They met again in 1990 when the DoD issued a death certificate for Jacob and notified Carolyn and Jerry that Jake's death had been confirmed, changing his status from MIA to KIA.

After the end of the Vietnam War and after the return of the American POWs in 1973, there had been no word on Jake other than he was not returned and was reclassified as missing. Although Carolyn adjusted with time and reluctantly accepted that he was dead, seeing his brother was disturbing because they looked like twins, even though Jerry was a year older than Jake. Every time she saw Jerry, his presence bothered her and contributed in part to the families growing apart.

"So, Jerry, what brings you here?"

"I think I'd better show you. Can we use your computer?"

"Of course."

They went to the computer and Jerry typed in a video news link. It took a minute for the link to load.

"So what is this?" Carolyn asked.

"Just tell me what you see."

A video from a news website finally opened up. "Well, that's you," Carolyn said as she watched the video of a man carrying a boy out of a school.

"No, it's not," Jerry said.

He then showed her a picture in a magazine and again she said, "It looks like you, Jerry."

"No. It looks like Jake," a choked-up Jerry whispered.

Upset, Carolyn yelled at Jerry for the suggestion and got up from the table. "You know Jake is dead! He's dead, been dead over thirty years."

"I know, Carolyn, I know, but you have to admit, you thought that was me."

"Why are you doing this, Jerry? We've all moved on."

Jerry was also upset, but after a little more arguing with Carolyn, he convinced her to return to the computer. She sat back down, and Jerry zoomed in on the face in the photo of the man carrying the boy and then pointed to the small scar over the left eye at the edge of the eyebrow.

"Jake had a scar there that I gave him when we were learning how to box."

Seeing the eerie resemblance and the scar, she started to tear up. "I don't understand. How can this be?"

Jerry and Carol tried to understand and make sense of how Jake could still be alive. They had doubts while Jake was in a missing status, but when it was confirmed he was dead, the doubts were gone—until now.

After a few more minutes of studying the video and photo, they were convinced that the man they were looking at was Jake, a conclusion that brought up questions for them. Jerry ranted about conspiracies while Carolyn tried to comprehend the situation.

"Why didn't he come home? Did he turn?"

"Jake would never turn, not in this lifetime...I don't have any answers, Carolyn."

They both wanted to know what happened to Jake, why he didn't come home, and where he had been for over thirty years. They decided that they needed to find someone who could answer their questions—they bonded.

CHAPTER 2

THE JOURNALIST

WASHINGTON, D.C.

5 September, 2006

Day 13,217 — 36 Years, 2 Months, and 7 Days

During the early morning hours, shortly after the sun had risen, Carolyn and Jerry walked along the pathway at the site of the Vietnam War Memorial Wall. They eventually made their way to the section of the wall where Jake's name was located—taking their time as they looked at each of the names. After a few minutes, they found what they were looking for— Jacob Walden. They did as many visitors before them had done; they stared at the wall quietly and said nothing. They just stood, looking at the wall—and remembered.

Vietnam Memorial Wall at Washington, D.C.

A few hours later, they walked up to the entrance of the lobby of the Washington Post. They entered the building, went through security, and then approached the receptionist.

"Hi, I'm Jerry Walden and this is Carolyn Jordan. We have an appointment with Ted Pratt."

The receptionist glanced at her calendar. "Yes, Sir, if you'll just sign the visitors log, please. Mr. Pratt is in Room 222. Second floor, to the right when you exit the elevator. You may have to wait a bit. Mr. Pratt is not always on time."

"Thank you...Nancy," Jerry said, as he glanced at the nameplate on her desk and headed to the elevator.

Carolyn and Jerry got off the elevator and walked down the hallway until they found Ted Pratt's office. They entered and while they waited, they looked around. Ted Pratt, like many of journalists at the paper, scheduled his own time.

Carolyn and Jerry slowly walked around and noticed the extensive display of pictures, awards, and other items on the walls. The appearance of the mementos suggested that Ted had been a successful, accomplished, and awarded journalist.

"Here's the Pulitzer," Jerry told Carolyn, who slowly walked over and looked at the award. Jerry then enthusiastically said, "Wow! This was for that story he did in '93, in the first Iraq War, about those people in that village."

Although Jerry was impressed with Pratt's accomplishments, Carolyn did not display the same enthusiasm. She almost seemed not to want to be there. She remained standing and slowly walked around the office while they continued to wait.

The prestigious Pulitzer Prize received for his story thirteen years earlier was a career maker for Pratt. At the time, he was just twenty-four years old and had the good fortune to be able to do a story covering some of the families in an Iraqi village. The story covered the suffering of the villagers under Saddam Hussein's dictatorship. Pratt's story was one of many similar ones that told what had happened inside Iraq under Hussein's rule. What made Pratt's story unique was not just writing about his observations, but writing an uncensored and unauthorized story obtained from outside of the so-called safe or green zones. Pratt managed to get his story about the abusive tactics of Saddam's regime and the villagers' testimonies published. The story propelled Pratt into a status of being an awarded and independent investigative journalist, the quality and characteristic that had attracted Carolyn and Jerry to him.

In the lobby, an energetic and late-for-work Ted Pratt hurriedly entered the building and headed toward the elevators. The receptionist noticed Ted and yelled at him as he passed by and told him about the couple waiting in his office. The receptionist also took advantage of the brief interaction to flirt with Ted. As for appearance, Ted was physically fit and a handsome man, even what some might have considered a star quality appearance, an asset that had undoubtedly helped him in assignments over the years. Ted acknowledged the receptionist and headed toward the elevators.

As Ted entered, he wondered who was waiting for him, or if he had forgotten an appointment—not an uncommon occurrence. Ted exited the elevator and continued to walk quickly toward his office. As he approached the door, he slowed down and took a few seconds to look at the couple inside. They were not anyone he knew, so he continued to wonder who they might be. Entering his office, he took notice of the couple's appearance and was not sure what to make of them. He thought that they could be a married couple, but then again maybe not. They seemed to be in their middle fifties. The woman was conservatively dressed in a business suit while the man, on the other hand, looked as if he was from the sixties. He had long graying hair tied in a ponytail, and was wearing blue jeans, a T-shirt, and an old army jacket bearing a variety of patches from the Vietnam era. As Ted entered his office, he made a prejudicial assumption that the encounter with the couple would be interesting.

Seeing Ted enter his office, the couple turned toward him, and Carolyn immediately started the introductions and conversation.

"Mr. Pratt?"

"Yes, I'm sorry, did we have an appointment?"

"Not really, but we just need a few minutes of your time, if you don't mind."

Ted paused just briefly, and then with a nod and a smile, he continued the conversation and headed to his chair at the desk.

"So, how can I help you?"

"I'm Carolyn Jordan and this is my brother-in-law, Jerry Walden."

Ted sat in his chair as Carolyn and Jerry each took a seat in front of the desk.

"I was married to Jerry's brother Jake," she said as she took out a magazine from his desk, already opened to a specific page. She and Jerry took their seats.

"I didn't do that story...wish I did, excellent story."

"We know, but you did do a story that won you a Pulitzer."

Ted smiled with pride and agreement with Carolyn as she continued to tell him about the magazine article.

"The man in that picture was my husband, I mean my ex-husband, Jake."

"Really?"

"He's supposed to be dead. He was shot down in Vietnam in 1970, captured, and was a POW...but he never came home. They said he died. It's been thirty-six years, and he just shows up like this."

"There's something going on here," Jerry added.

Carolyn quickly told Jerry to keep quiet, implying with her attitude that nothing he might say would be helpful. Carolyn then looked at Ted. "I know the man in that picture is my husband, Jake Walden." She gave Ted a folder with a few pictures of Jake and copies of other documents, including a death certificate the government had given her. "We had been happily married, had two children...boy and girl. I just don't understand why he didn't come home with the other POWs."

"This looks like you," Ted told Jerry as he glanced back and forth between Jerry and the magazine picture.

"We weren't twins, but everyone thought we were. I was one year older than Jake."

"Well, this could be you, except for the hair," Ted told them, interjecting just a little bit of humor. Carolyn interrupted and brought them back on track.

"I remarried in 1980 because I was told Jake was dead. I've been married to my second husband for twenty-six years, had two more children, and now I find out that Jake's alive. I don't understand, and I'm not sure if I even want to know."

Ted initially was dismissive and explained that there were lots of people who look alike. Jerry interrupted.

"I know that's my brother. You said it yourself, that could be me, and she knows that's her husband. We..."

"Jerry," Carolyn said.

"We don't know what went on or what's going on, but we know this much, that's him. And anyway, again, look at me, and look at that picture, that's me in that picture, but it's not. We're brothers and have always looked pretty much like twins. I realize that what I'm telling you sounds like crazy, conspiracy stuff, hell, I look crazy, I know that, but I'm just a little bit liberal, not nuts."

Jerry and Ted chuckled at the comment; they continued to look at family pictures and the remarkable, almost twin-like similarities between the brothers. Jerry convincingly showed Ted the scar over Jake's left eyebrow.

"The scar on the eyebrow, the picture in the magazine, and even the way he walked in that video we saw tell me that's my brother...even without looking in the mirror...a look in the mirror only confirms it. I know it sounds crazy, but...that's him, I know it."

While Ted listened to Jerry, he had started to get a little interest as he studied the pictures, but he also had understood that time, thirty-six years, and some people do look alike, but a brother who looked almost identical, that was interesting. Ted's dismissive attitude had started to change as he saw the similarities. Jerry continued to rant about conspiracy theories.

"I just want to know why Jake never came home," Carolyn said. "We were the cliché, the high school sweethearts who got married after graduation. Jake went off to the Air Force Academy, and two years after he graduated, he went off to Vietnam. It's kind of surreal, you know. I mean we spent more time together in our high school years than after we married. There is a part of me that doesn't want to know what happened. I was told he was dead, and I grieved, I cried, and I moved on. But as Jerry said, that is Jake. There is no question."

Ted studied the contents of the folder and listened to Carolyn and Jerry. *Damn, there might be a story, even if the man in the photo wasn't Jake.* His attitude became more positive about the prospect as he stood up. "Okay, I'll look into this. Could be interesting. Mind if I keep the folder?"

"Sure, that's why we came," Carolyn replied.

Ted also wrote down their phone numbers and gave them his number as they got ready to leave.

After Carolyn and Jerry left the office, Ted stood in the doorway thinking for a while. He then closed the door, went over and sat at his desk, and got on his computer, eager to get to work.

Ted spent the next several hours researching information about Jacob Walden. He looked up public database information and found that Jacob was listed as shot down June 30, 1970, and a death certificate that was issued in 1990. Ted was curious about the twenty years it had taken to get a death certificate. He made phone calls to his contacts in the Pentagon to get his facts together, but he didn't get much information. Someone did point him in a direction on what office to talk to about Jake's death certificate and where it was issued.

After a few hours of research, Ted headed out of his office and went to see his editor, Kyle Craig, a career journalist in charge of the freelance writers. While Ted had been in the business about fifteen years, Kyle had over thirty-five years and had risen to several high-level editorial positions over the years. His current position in charge of the freelance contract writing staff was not considered a prestigious position; however, it was a position that Kyle had held for almost ten years. He had won too many awards to count over the years, including a few Pulitzers, and although Kyle had been around a long time, the walls of his office did not reflect his career accomplishments. There were a few awards, an American and

POW/MIA flag, a few pictures, and some other items, but still not as many as compared to Ted's office, although Kyle's accomplishments during his career by far overshadowed Ted's.

In contrast to Ted's personality, Kyle was humble and disciplined, and he was what would be called an old-school journalist. His work ethic was dedicated to a level of integrity and truthfulness in the stories he had written, and he had never fallen into the politically correct mode or sensationalism reporting that filled much of journalism in the recent years.

Ted, on the other hand, appeared to be a product of the modern day media and journalism hype. His ambition had propelled him to high commissions based on compensation for his stories, won him awards, and at the same time had earned him a questionable reputation concerning how he got his stories, and, in some instances, the truth and reliability of sources and motives behind some of his stories. For those who knew Ted, it went without saying that he had an ego, and once he set his mind on something, he was going to do it.

When Ted entered Kyle's office, Kyle was on the phone. Ted anxiously waited for him to finish and occasionally interjected a few hellos. Kyle wasn't saying much during the conversation except for a few "yeses" while he glanced at Ted being impatient. As soon as Kyle hung up the phone, Ted quickly got to the point and told Kyle that he wanted to do a story on a presumed dead Vietnam POW. He told Kyle about his conversation with Carolyn and Jerry and how it looked like

Jake Walden had never come home, but was still alive. Kyle dismissively sat back in his seat and looked at Ted as if he was, quite frankly, stupid.

"You serious?"

"What?"

"Are you serious? What's the story?" Kyle asked as he proceeded and then told Ted that there would not be any interest in the story. Ted told Kyle about the eyebrow, death certificate, and the resemblance of the brothers. He went on, passionate about wanting to research the story and insisting that there may even be some hints of cover-ups or something else. Kyle shook his head in apparent disbelief as Ted pled his case. Kyle was not in agreement with this story and told Ted that going after it would be a waste of time and skill and that he should do something relevant to other current issues. Ted became standoffish, and a little bit of his ego and arrogance presented itself as he disagreed with Kyle.

"This is the freelance department. I can do it...freelance for someone else if you don't want me to do it."

"I'm just telling you I think you're wasting your time, Ted. What are you going to accomplish with this? So what if this guy is alive?"

"So what? What do you mean, so what? This is a story, Kyle...this guy never came home, ran away, turned or something. People need to know what happened with him. It's just another thing with the government and that war, just like the one we're in now."

"Sometimes, Ted, there are things people don't need or really want to know about. Like I said, if this guy is still alive it won't matter; it's been over thirty years. Just let it go, Ted. If you want a story that will make a difference, go over to Darfur, Somalia or somewhere, and do a real story."

Ted shook his head and smiled at Kyle. He then headed out of the office and said on his way out, "This could be the story of the year. Maybe it'll get another Pulitzer."

Ted went back to his office and sat at his desk for a moment and thought, but not for long. He picked up the phone and called Peggy at the travel department.

"Peg, Ted here, I need a ticket to Hawaii."

CHAPTER 3

DOG TAGS

HAWAII

19 September, 2006

Ted made his travel arrangements through Peggy to get to Hawaii. Prior to leaving, he did some backtracking research and found through the Air Force's central mortuary, a death certificate for Jacob Walden, issued in 1990. Ted found that the certificate was issued based on the recommendations of the Joint POW/MIA Command, also called JPAC, in Hawaii. He had already convinced himself that there may be a conspiracy, and through some of his connections, managed to get the Defense Department's permission to do a story, start to finish, about how missing service members were recovered including the process of issuing of the death certificates, which was Ted's hidden agenda. He had also toyed with the idea that Jacob Walden may have somehow decided not to return home and figured out a way to disappear. Ted wanted to get as much information as he could before he actually met with Jacob Walden and interviewed him.

Once he was settled in his hotel in Oahu, Ted headed out to his 1:00 p.m. appointment at Hickam Air Force Base where the JPAC Headquarters was located. He wasn't too well received at Hickam, at least that's how he felt. When he arrived at the headquarters, he had to wait about forty-five minutes before he was seen by a marine major who eventually came out to the lobby and introduced himself. Ted was already irritated by the wait and expected some sort of apology, but the major didn't give one.

"You guys aren't big on schedules," Ted said to the major with a touch of sarcasm in his voice.

The major looked at Ted, stone-faced for just a few seconds before responding, "Mr. Pratt, our interaction with you, Sir, is a courtesy, not a mission, or even a requirement."

Ted didn't know how to respond and the brief awkward silence was broken by the major.

"So, Mr. Pratt, this is just the headquarters. The actual facility where everyone works, records, and so forth is over at Camp Smith. If you look outside, you'll see Airman Wallace out there standing by that vehicle. He'll take you over to security and get you a pass so you can get in and out while you're here. He'll then take you over to Camp Smith and turn you over to Master Sergeant Ellis who will be your POC…point of contact, while you do your story."

The major paused for a moment and then handed Ted a folder. "Good to go?"

"I guess," Ted hesitantly replied.

"All right, head on out there to Wallace, get things going, and enjoy Oahu while you're here."

The major didn't really wait for a reply—he turned and walked away while a somewhat frustrated Ted headed outside.

The process of waiting on the major and then getting his security pass ended up taking more time than Ted had expected, and it was almost 3:30 p.m. by the time the driver got him to the parking lot of the JPAC Operations Center at Camp Smith. Ted and Airman Wallace got out of the car, and the airman led the way. Inside the building, after a brief walk down a few hallways, Wallace showed Ted where Master Sergeant Ellis's office was located. Ted thanked the man, and then approached the open office door—he heard typing on a keyboard as he entered the doorway. Master Sergeant Ellis noticed Ted immediately, stopped typing, got up from his desk pleasantly, yet with authority, greeted him.

"Ted Pratt, correct?"

"Yes, Sergeant Ellis, yes," Ted replied reluctantly, while also wanting to say something about his frustration, but Ellis's demeanor seemed to have involuntarily calmed Ted down. Ted was still upset, but the intuitive Ellis seemed to have recognized the frustration.

"It's Master Sergeant Ellis," he said with a grin. "Worked too long to get those rockers...So, Mr. Pratt, you settled in the hotel, got your pass, and Airman Wallace assigned as your driver?"

"Ah, yeah."

"Well, that part's good anyway. I know it probably seems like you've wasted a day, but believe me, we'll make up for it starting tomorrow morning and when we head out to Vietnam."

Ted was in agreement as he thought that he had wasted a day, but at the same time he was really at a loss about how to respond since Ellis had acknowledged the issue.

"Tomorrow then?" Ted asked.

"Tomorrow, 0800, eight a.m. civilian time, unless you want to come in at 0630 out back in the field for reveille and PT, you know, morning exercise. It might give you some more insight for your story."

"We'll see," Ted said with a little reluctance.

Ted and Ellis shook hands, said their goodbyes and then Ted headed outside to find Wallace.

The next morning, Ted arrived at the operations center around 7:45 a.m. and waited in Ellis's office. While he waited, Ted looked at some frames on the office wall, but didn't find anything too personal about Ellis, no awards or anything like that except for a few certificates. The wall did have quite a lot of framed articles and group pictures of recovery trips, which Ted took an interest in until Ellis entered the office.

"Missed you at PT, Mr. Pratt."

"Oh, the jet lag thing got me."

"Not a problem."

Ellis yelled out for Wallace to come into the office and then told Ted about the time constraints over the next two days prior to heading out to Vietnam for a recovery mission.

"You're also going to have to get your shots."

"I don't need any shots," Ted said.

"No shots, no go, plus you'll need your malaria pills and the doc has to check you out and sign off on you going with us. That's the way it is."

Ellis gave Ted and Wallace a list of everyone Ted could talk with, which to Ted's surprise was rather large and with no restrictions about records. Ted seemed to have open access to do his story, but he was also somewhat disappointed because there were not any doors getting shut, except maybe for the marine major he met. Otherwise, everything a reporter wanted, Ted was getting.

During the rest of the day and into the next day, Ted received all the cooperation he wanted for his story. One of the things Ted found out was that the entire operation at JPAC was detailed and precise, and everyone involved appeared to be dedicated to identifying remains and giving closure to families. This dedication was, however, disheartening for Ted who was more interested in finding some sort of red flag for a conspiracy. Because Ted was using the *how-they-do-it* approach for his story, he had to follow the lead of those providing him information and who were genuinely trying to give him what they felt was good information for his story.

On the afternoon of the second day at JPAC, Ted finally was able to get to something in which he had a specific interest. He was taken to a records room where he was shown the record-keeping process and some random records. Ted looked at a list he had brought with him and asked to get the information on what he presented as three random names, one being Jake Walden. The request seemed innocent, and as intended, random. So far he had been given access to everything and still no red flags.

The next day Ted was supposed to get on a plane with the JPAC people and go on an actual recovery operation, a trip he was already considering canceling. Although he had received complete cooperation for his story, Ted had not found anything that led to any evidence toward a conspiracy, and being able to look at the files of Jake and the other two files was just more information for his story and the last interview of sorts before departing for Vietnam. He had also requested, as part of his research, to be able to visit some previous sites where remains had been recovered. That part of his request had not yet been approved, and Ted was hoping that if he requested specific names, particularly Walden's, it may help in getting approval.

The records clerk walked Ted through the process and steps for each of the three files he had submitted. Jake Walden being near the end of the alphabet resulted in his file being reviewed last. The files were detailed with MIA dates, aircraft type, last known location, number of crewmembers, location of crash site, and other pieces of detailed information. Nothing jumped out at Ted to get excited about, and everything seemed straightforward, and from what Ted could determine, accurate.

The lack of anything substantial to give Ted reason to believe there was some sort of conspiracy was disappointing, yet Ted had missed something he wasn't aware of. As the records clerk was putting away the files, she made a comment that suddenly caught Ted's attention.

"These are all pretty typical cases except for the last one. Usually, almost all the time there are actual remains found and processed. Otherwise, everything is the same."

Ted asked about the difference in the Walden file and was told that basically if remains were not found, eyewitness account or other evidence could be used to confirm the death.

"So in that last file, what was it?" Ted asked.

The records clerk took the file back to the desk and opened it up. She told Ted that dog tags were found near the crash site and that there was an eyewitness account, an Air

Force pilot, Lieutenant Colonel Hudson, who made a written statement in 1990. Ted and the clerk looked over the statement of Colonel Hudson, who stated that he was in the Hanoi prison with Captain Walden from November 1970 until January 1973. He stated that Captain Walden had fallen seriously ill in January 1973, and like so many others before him, Captain Walden died in captivity.

"Pretty depressing what happened to those guys," the clerk told Ted, assuming that Ted's depressed look was from the grim details in the files. Ted understood the clerk's remarks and nodded in agreement. But Ted's depressed look was not as the clerk had thought, but from not being able to find any evidence for his conspiracy theory. Ted finished writing up his notes, and the clerk put the file back.

Later in the evening, Ted went back to his room, and after dinner packed up for his morning departure. He sat down at his computer and figured maybe he could still salvage his story and get an interview with Hudson. Ted's hopes were quickly dampened after he did his search and found an obituary for Hudson. After some wishful thinking and some other searches, it still ended up being the right Hudson, and according to his obit, after Hudson was released from the Hanoi Hilton in 1973, he continued his career and rose to be a one-star general, retiring in 1987 after twenty-eight years in the Air Force. This was more frustrating information for Ted as he still could not really find anything to support his conspiracy theory.

Friday, September 22, 2006

When Ted woke up that Friday morning, he was still thinking about the story and whether or not to pursue it, or even if he should make the trip to Vietnam. At that point, he rationalized that maybe he could just make a vacation out of the Vietnam trip and still get a story, at least the original story that the JPAC people believed he was there to do.

At 9 a.m., Airman Wallace arrived at the hotel, picked up Ted and took him to the air base. He dropped him off at the base terminal where the JPAC personnel waited to load the C-17 Globemaster that was taking them to Hanoi. Master Sergeant Ellis greeted Ted and made sure he had everything he needed. Other members of JPAC also made him feel comfortable and part of the group.

Ted was quite at ease with the camaraderie he witnessed. When they loaded the plane, it was obvious to some he had never been on an Air Force aircraft, or at least a C-17. The JPAC veterans of numerous military flights put Ted at ease, which sometimes was difficult for those who had never flown on an Air Force aircraft rigged for passengers. This flight was set up with the forward part outfitted with passenger seats, which faced toward the rear of the aircraft. The back of the aircraft was filled with equipment pallets JPAC was taking for their recovery operations. The handing out of earplugs was also something different. Ted even noticed some of the people put on what looked like earmuffs, the type used at gun ranges or flight lines. The takeoff was a strange sensation for Ted facing toward the rear of the aircraft, as was the noise. He quickly understood the need for earplugs.

After a somewhat long flight and a stop in Japan, the group arrived in Hanoi. Early afternoon on the flight line, the doors and ramp were opened and a voice yelled out, "Smell that heat," which referred to the unique humid heat found in Southeast Asia. Almost immediately after the doors opened, Ted felt the heat and humidity hitting him like a damp blast furnace. He also felt somewhat out of place while everyone went about the task of unloading the aircraft and moving their equipment to a temporary storage area in a hangar provided by the Vietnamese.

It didn't take too long for Ted to mingle with the others as he gave a hand moving some of the bags and equipment. It took less than an hour to get everything moved to the hangar and personal baggage loaded on trucks. Ted found it impressive how everyone worked together, even the Vietnamese. Ted thought it odd that the Vietnamese and Americans seemed to work together so well. It was, in a way, anticlimactic when he saw cooperation between them and took away more of Ted's speculation about a conspiracy.

The rest of the day was spent at the hotel. A few of the JPAC teams had some short meetings, but for the most part, everyone took advantage of some free time. Ted had met a few news people in the lobby and spent the rest of the day and evening with them, sharing stories and getting a short education about Vietnam.

The next morning at 5:30 a.m., a loud knock on the hotel room door woke Ted up. He checked his cell phone to see what time it was and immediately jumped up realizing he had overslept. Ten minutes later, he exited the hotel and headed to a waiting minivan.

As he started to get into the van, one of the JPAC people asked, "Where are your bags?" The lack of an immediate answer and the confused look on Ted's face prompted a second question. "Does that mean you haven't checked out?"

Although the schedule and sequence of events had been covered in a meeting the prior day, it didn't register with Ted that the various JPAC teams had different assignments, and the team Ted was going with was checking out of the hotel and would be traveling to town near the Laotian border where they would stay. Ted headed back inside, got his bags, and checked out around 6 a.m. He was on the minivan heading to the hangar, almost an hour behind schedule and stuck in the Hanoi morning rush-hour traffic.

The ride to the airport hangar took a little over an hour, and as everyone got out of the van, the JPAC people didn't hold back their frustration with being behind schedule. Although the day before Ted had been made to feel welcome, that circumstance changed with a temporary coldness in the attitudes of the JPAC people toward him as they hurriedly loaded their equipment onto the truck. He was allowed only to stand and watch. Another thing Ted missed was that they were taking another flight, and as the truck loaded with the bags and equipment headed out to the flight line toward a Vietnamese Air Force cargo plane, he caught on. They eventually got loaded and took off, almost two hours behind schedule.

After a little over an hour-long, loud, bumpy ride on the cargo plane, they landed at an airfield in Hue, which was a city just south of the center of the country and was also south of the DMZ, the former border separating the old North and South Vietnam. The plane was unloaded, and the equipment and baggage were loaded onto two trucks. Ted, the JPAC people, and several Vietnamese loaded up on four minivans and headed out on an almost three-hour drive into Laos to a town called Dansavan, a border town on the Lao-Vietnamese border. Although Dansavan was where they had to drive to and would spend the next several nights, their destination for the recovery operations was about an hour north of the town.

During the next few days, the recovery operations were put into action, and he took time to document the painstaking efforts of the JPAC and Vietnamese and Laotian personnel at the work site. Ted had also been able to establish a good relationship with one of the Vietnamese guides, Quan, who also doubled as a translator. After several, and at times, persistent conversations with Quan, he agreed to take Ted to Jacob Walden's reported crash site. Initially, Quan was resistant to the request to track down the site location and to the farmer who had found Jake's dog tags, but Ted was persuasive. After he got to know Ted, Quan became sympathetic to his story about Jake and what he had conveyed as closure for the family.

On the fourth day at Dansavan, Quan took Ted south on a three-hour drive to a town called Axinh Na and then east toward one of the border villages where Jake's crash had supposedly happened. As far as he was concerned, Quan had done a good job and everything seemed to be straightforward. Quan found the farmer who turned over the dog tags and who also took them to a crash site. He questioned the absence of any wreckage and was disappointed by the explanation that the crash was thirty-six years old and usually crash sites were salvaged for the metal. Quan confirmed that it was common for nothing to be left at the sites that had been salvaged.

The absence of wreckage made sense to Ted, but then still looking for something, he questioned the farmer's seemingly first-hand account of taking the dog tags off of Jake's body before he was buried and why the farmer couldn't remember the exact burial location. The somewhat standoffish farmer told

Quan that just like the crash site, the body was buried thirty-six years ago, and he couldn't be expected to remember an exact location in the jungle, especially when he was just twelve years old at the time.

The answers Ted had gotten only created more questions and he started to wonder how or why Jake Walden could have died twice. The conflicting account of Jake's death sparked Ted's curiosity and gave him his first set of conflicting facts. Ted suddenly regained some excitement about doing the story and felt that there might be something to it.

Ted had wanted to find a reason to suspect a conspiracy—and while there was no wreckage, no body, and a story from someone who was twelve at the time seemed questionable, it also seemed likely it could be the truth—except for one thing. If Jake Walden ended up alive in a Hanoi prison, how could the farmer have taken the dog tags off Walden's body?

On the ride back to Dansavan, Ted reviewed everything he had been able to get for his story and decided that at the very least had enough to do the story about JPAC, but he was still unsure about a conspiracy. Even with two different accounts about Jake's death, the only thing Ted had was two confirmations about Walden's death. Even if one was false, it still meant that Jake had died.

At Dansavan, he said his goodbyes to the JPAC people, and then Quan took him back to Hue. When they arrived, it was near evening and Quan offered to take him out for dinner.

On the way back to the hotel where he would stay that night, they stopped at a street vendor's stand.

"Got you a souvenir, Ted," Quan said. "Be back in a moment." Quan got out, walked to the stand and spoke to the vendor whom he appeared to know.

Ted looked at the vendor's stand and noticed the variety of items for sale. What caught Ted's attention though was the array of what looked like American military souvenirs and memorabilia from the Vietnam War. Just as he looked closer at the merchandise, Quan returned to the car and handed Ted his gift.

"For you, my friend. I had this especially made for you. I thought you might want something to remember your Mr. Jacob."

"Why, thank you, Quan."

Ted looked in his hand and saw he was holding a set of dog tags. At first he was pleased, but as he looked closer at them he saw the name Jacob Walden. The tags also had all of Jake's information, blood type, social security number, religion. They even looked old, like they were the actual tags from thirty-something years earlier.

His expression changed as he looked at the stand and saw dozens of other dog tags for sale.

"Quan, where did you get these?" Ted asked as he held up the dog tags.

"I special ordered them for you...What's wrong?"

Ted took a moment to study the dog tags and the vendor stand, and turned his attention back to Quan.

"Nothing's wrong, Quan, you did nothing wrong, but tell me, how did he get these?" Ted asked as he held up the tags.

"Tourism...the foreigners buy them, and it's easy to get special orders, just give him a name and they can make for you like your Walden."

"But how do they get the information?"

"The internet," Quan answered as Ted looked at the vendor stand and then back at the set of dog tags he held in his hands.

"The internet?" Ted said with a smile.

"The internet...you can get anything on the internet."

"Thank you, Quan, I assure you, you did nothing wrong."

They said their goodbyes and then parted ways at the hotel.

The tags had caused him to question what he thought he had learned about Jake and the crash site. He changed his mind and believed that the original dog tags from the crash site were probably fake, and as Quan had just told him, there was an incentive in the form of reward money for farmers who could provide information on missing Americans.

When Ted got back to his hotel room, he turned on his computer and pulled up some research he had previously done and came across the information obtained from the Air Force mortuary. Although he didn't notice it before, he saw a sharp increase in the number of death certificates issued in 1990 compared to other years. This added fact gave him more to go on as he sat in front of the computer. He thought about the unusual increase in death certificates, the death of the eye witness, the dog tags, the possible sighting of Walden and other facts he had found. *This is what conspiracy stories are made of.* Ted decided to go ahead and pursue his conspiracy story about Jake. He got on his cell phone.

"Hey, Peg. Need to make some more travel plans."

CHAPTER 4

THE INTERVIEW

JAKE WALDEN'S HOME

21 September, 2006

Day 13,233 — 36 Years, 2 Months, 23 Days

As the sound of the departing taxi faded, Ted Pratt walked up the few steps to the large, covered front porch of what he believed to be Jake Walden's home. Ted brought one of the smaller travel bags with him that he propped up against the wall next to the left side of the front door. Before he knocked on the door, he took notice of some chairs on the left side of the porch and the bench on the right side. He also noticed a large dog, a yellow Labrador, lying next to the bench. The Lab noticed Ted and made an effort to be friendly, but Ted was dismissive and not much of a dog person, which the dog seemed to sense as it left and trotted down the steps.

Ted squatted down in front of his bag, unzipped the top flap and took out his folio-type notebook. Then he stood back

—45—

up, pulled a voice recorder out of his jacket pocket, and placed it inside the folio. Ted then knocked on the door; as he waited he could hear the faint sound of a man and woman's voice that sounded like they were arguing, but the sounds were unintelligible and drowned out by the sound of music coming from inside the house. A minute later, the voices stopped and he continued to wait. After about another minute, he knocked again and waited and listened to see if someone was going to answer the door, occasionally putting his ear close to the door trying to hear something.

Finally, after waiting four or five minutes, the music stopped, and Ted heard the approach of footsteps. They were fast and heavy, sounding like the footsteps of someone walking when he was mad and upset. A visibly upset slender fifty-something woman, dressed in hospital scrubs opened the door. At first, Ted was a little shocked by her outward hostility, so he quickly attempted to introduce himself, but was not given a chance as she turned her back to him and quickly walked away toward the kitchen. Ted cautiously stepped halfway into the doorway and looked past the doorframe.

"Hello?"

As he glanced inside the house, he saw a man in the far corner of the living room by a computer desk talking on a telephone. The man did not smile, but he did notice Ted and with some reluctance motioned for him to come inside.

Ted entered the house and slowly closed the door behind him. For the moment, he felt out of his element after the negative attention he had received from the woman and the man. As he looked at the man, he noticed the resemblance to the photos of Jake Walden. He also could tell that this was the man in the magazine photo, although he already knew this from the magazine source that gave him the contact information.

Ted realized that thirty-something years later looks could be deceiving. The man's age seemed to be in the right range. Jake would have been about sixty, and the man seemed to be in good physical condition and could even be younger, maybe fifty. Ted slowly walked into the living room and waited.

"See you in few," the man said and then hung up the phone. He watched as Ted approached and extended his hand. The man did not accept Ted's handshake offer, but instead, with a little hostility in his voice and demeanor, he started to talk.

"You've probably figured out my wife doesn't care for you."

"I did kind of notice."

"Well, don't feel too bad about it...I don't care for you either, Mr. Pratt."

The man then left Ted standing in the middle of the living room as he walked toward the kitchen.

"Gotta wait about ten minutes until a friend gets here before we can start the interview."

"Who's the friend?"

"Just a friend. He'll be here in a few minutes."

After he left the room, Ted was a little concerned about the hostility and the point of waiting for a friend. Now, even before getting started, there was mystery and as he stood in the living room, he wondered if he was going to get anywhere with the interview. Moving around the room, Ted looked at the assorted living room furniture, knickknacks, and what looked like family pictures of the man, his wife, a daughter, and a son. There were no pictures of his first wife or the two children. The living room was nicely decorated, nothing extravagant, but moderate except for the computer desk. If this man were Jake, he had developed a taste for computers, technology, and music. Ted noticed on the computer screen that the man had been researching him, which put a smile on Ted's face.

Ted headed over to the couch near the fireplace and sat down. He fidgeted with his notebook for a few minutes and then looked around the room again. He noticed on the wall what looked like a picture frame with a newspaper or magazine article in it. Ted got up and walked toward the picture and chuckled to himself when he got close enough to see it. The article in the frame was about Jane Fonda and her trip to North Vietnam in 1972 along with the picture of her sitting on a Vietnamese anti-aircraft gun. There was also a framed picture of the World Trade Center Towers on the wall next to the Fonda article and picture. As he looked at the article, the man came back into the room, and walked over to Ted.

"You a fan of Jane Fonda?" Ted asked.

The man quietly gave a sarcastic grunt. At first, he didn't reply and made an expression of disappointment.

"Some people keep things, awards, pictures…you know to show achievements, recognition, pride, a lot of different things, Mr. Pratt, but that there, I look at that picture and the towers to remind me…to remind me to never forget."

Ted detected a distinct sense of resentment, hostility, or something as the conversation was interrupted by a knock on the door. Ted was a little puzzled and didn't fully understand what he meant. Although Ted was there, hopefully, to do a story about someone from the Vietnam War era, except for his brief interaction with JPAC, he was not very educated on the issue including the Fonda visit to Vietnam. He was also not versed about many topics concerning that time, and as of yet, had no idea of what point the man was trying to make.

Hearing the knock, the upset wife quickly came out of the kitchen and walked to the door. She angrily opened it and did not even acknowledge the person at the door, and just as she had done with Ted, she left the door open, turned around, and headed back toward the kitchen. Ted saw a man cautiously enter through the doorway. He looked into the living room and gave a knowing smile and shrug toward the man, expressing his understanding that the wife was upset. The new arrival looked to be in his late forties or early fifties and was dressed appropriately for the September weather, in jeans and a flannel shirt.

"Hey," he called out.

"Hello, Charlie," the man replied.

Hearing the greetings, Ted became a little excited with what he believed may be a confirmation that the man was Jacob Walden, although up to this point there had not been any acknowledgment by anyone that the man was actually Jake Walden. When Ted talked with the man on the phone, he denied being Jake Walden and insisted he was Robert Makarova. At Ted's insistence, Jake, or Robert, agreed to the visit.

As for Charlie, Ted had no idea who this was; however, his demeanor was somewhat relaxing, and his overall appearance, dress, and manner were nonthreatening, even likable. His initial mannerism came across as a friendly and upbeat individual. As they watched Charlie enter the living room, they also noticed that he had left the front door open. Charlie noticed their observation.

"Oh, my driver's coming in. He's got to change a tire so he'll be in and out."

As Charlie finished his sentence, the driver entered the house, closed the door, and headed to the kitchen. Charlie made his way into the living room and placed a folder on the coffee table. Then he looked at Ted.

"You must be Ted Pratt?"

"Yes, Sir."

"Sir! I like that. See that, Jake, he called me sir, and I'm calling him Jake since that's who you think he is, right?"

Jake ignored Charlie's remark and drew attention back to the Fonda article on the wall.

"Ted was wondering why I had this on the wall, Charlie."

Charlie looked at Ted and started up the conversation. "So, Ted, you know the story behind that picture and the significance of it?"

"Not really. I never knew she went to Vietnam."

"Haven't done your homework, have you, Ted?" Charlie said with a little sarcasm.

Ted got a little defensive. "I know enough to find out why Jake never went home."

"Don't get cocky, Ted. My point is you've come here to do an interview about someone from the Vietnam War, and if you're to do a story about him, you should also know about Vietnam, what was going on back then, the Cold War, demonstrations, all the other things, and not just about this guy, or Jake, that's all."

"I know about the war; I know it was a war we shouldn't have been in, just like the Iraq War."

Charlie looked over at Jake with a sense of disappointment.

"There you have it, Jake. We shouldn't have been there. Already has his mind made up."

As Ted started to respond, Charlie interrupted him. "We better get started if Ted here is going to make his flight."

"So who are you?" Ted asked Charlie.

"Interesting that you should ask that." Charlie reached down to the coffee table, got his folder, and pulled out a piece of paper. "I'm Charlie, and that's all you need to know, Charlie Smith if it makes you feel better. Before anything happens here, you need to sign this. You can read it if you want, all it says is that the unnamed government employee, that's me, present at today's interview cannot be referenced to in any manner. I'm here to fill in any blanks about the past thirty-five or so years, and you're not to mention me. No reference to a source or anything like that."

"I knew it!" an excited Ted yelled out. "A conspiracy, cover up, right?"

Charlie looked at Ted with a grin, without replying.

"Can I..." Ted started to ask.

"You can use anything I tell you or anything he tells you, but you just can't mention *me*. If you do, treason, jail, Patriot Act, and all that stuff, that simple."

"I knew it, I knew it," an excited Ted mumbled to himself. At first, Ted was reluctant to sign the paper. He inquired again about what he could and could not do, and then went ahead and signed the paper. Charlie took the paper, put it into his folder, and then sat down at the end of the couch closest to the fireplace. Ted sat at the other end of the couch, and Jake sat in a recliner on the other side of the coffee table facing the fireplace.

"Ted, I really hope that after you hear the story...you'll decide not to write it," Charlie said.

"Mr. Smith or whoever the hell you are, the public deserves and has a right to know why people like Jake went to that war in the first place and then deserted their families."

"So, Ted, I guess if you're going to insist that I'm Jake Walden, I should probably start where Jake Walden was shot down...you think?"

"June 1970, right?"

"That's right, 30 June, 1970, a long time ago...thirty-six years, two months, twenty-three days ago, or 13,233 days."

"You kept track of the number of days it's been?" Ted asked, and with that question, Jake gave a look of disdain and hate.

"Yeah, I keep track...kept track. It's a long time, and frankly the difference between guys like me and everyone else is that we're never allowed to forget. Everyone else can forget and move on with their lives, wives, families. They can move on, but not us..."

A confused Ted interrupted, "I don't understand..."

Charlie took notice of Ted and Jake's building hostility toward each other.

"I suggest we keep to the subject at hand," Charlie interjected.

Sitting in his chair, Jake started to think back to the morning of 30 June, 1970. Charlie likewise sat back and also studied the unaware Ted whose focus was on both Jake and the recorder he had double-checked and then positioned on the coffee table. Jake and Charlie looked at each other, somewhat amazed and amused, with a sense of poking fun at Ted's eagerness and apparent naiveté. Ted placed his notebook on his lap, ready to listen. Jake looked toward the fireplace, a blank stare on his face, and said nothing at first, then turned toward Ted with a depressed look—even his tone of voice sounded depressed.

"I guess it all started with the ejection...yeah, that was it, the ejection."

Chapter 5

Capture

"Oh God, oh God, oh God!" Captain Jacob Walden yelled out through his oxygen mask as his ejection seat violently propelled him through the Vietnamese sky. The sound of his yells were muffled by the mask over his face and the deafening sounds of the ejection seat rockets that just seconds before had lifted him out of the exploding aircraft. Over the mid-morning sky of Vietnam, the rockets propelling Captain Walden's ejection seat extinguished, his parachute opened, and the seat separated, falling toward the earth almost 20,000 feet below. The entire time from initial ejection to the point where the parachute fully opened took less than eight seconds, but for Captain Jake Walden it seemed like an eternity.

For Jake, this was the first time that he had been exposed to this level or type of danger. The 24-year-old captain had been assigned to Vietnam less than a month, and although he had received training in what to do if he were shot down, the training was still a much different reality.

The previous violent moments transitioned to a surreal quietness and peacefulness. The cold sweat Jake experienced was caressed by the breeze of the air as he flew through the sky under his parachute. As he regained his composure, he looked around and then down to see what, under normal circumstances, any sport parachute enthusiasts would have thoroughly enjoyed. It was eerily quiet, except for the slight sound of the air passing through the parachute as Jake began the slow descent toward the ground from an unusually high altitude.

After a few minutes, Jake remembered he had to turn his radio on for the distress beacon to transmit his location. Trying to locate the radio, Jake anxiously wrestled with the parachute harness as he tried to reach under it to get to the radio. It took maybe a minute of struggling, but he finally was able to touch the dial and turn on the radio.

After about five minutes in the sky, Jake was still very high up. As he looked around, everything still looked peaceful. There was nothing except for blue sky, some white clouds, and the jungle terrain he could see in the distance. When he looked toward the ground, there too he only saw the jungle and countless rice paddies spread throughout the country-side. It was peaceful and beautiful, but Jake was thinking about the reality. It was difficult for him not to think about what would be next. He had been trained for and felt he was prepared for this moment, but he also remembered comments he'd heard others say about never really being ready for it. As Jake descended toward the ground, he was not thinking about his family, his home, or anything other than praying and hoping that a rescue helicopter would pick him up as soon as he hit the ground.

Fifteen minutes after he ejected from the aircraft and continuing to descend toward the ground under his parachute, Jake scanned the horizon and estimated he had about another three to five minutes before landing. He thought back to his training about parachute landing and the options of landing in the dense jungle and trees or landing in an open area. One of the problems with the jungle and tree landings was injury, getting caught in the trees, and not being able to get down.

As Jake surveyed the area below, he had to decide if he was going to head for the rice paddies or the jungle. He was also distracted by the numb feeling in his legs and arms caused by the combination of the parachute harness and the constant holding of the parachute risers above his head used to steer the canopy. Jake was attentive to the ground below and did not see anyone moving about. As he struggled to make a decision, Jake was aware of the possibility that the Vietcong or farmers who were communist sympathizers might be nearby.

As a rule, usually rescue helicopters could reach downed aircrews anywhere from a few minutes to somewhere under an hour, and by the time Jake would hit the ground, twenty minutes would have passed. Not seeing anyone on the ground, he believed and hoped in his heart that rescue helicopters would reach him quickly, so he made the decision to head for the rice paddies. At the time, his logic was that if he landed in the trees and jungle area he could have been injured and that it would have been more difficult for the rescue helicopters to find him. Landing in the rice paddy seemed like the best choice, and Jake believed it would improve his chances of rescue.

As he descended and approached the ground, he was about a thousand feet in the air passing over a large section of rice paddies. The area was rather large with about twenty paddies in each section, and each paddy was square in shape surrounded by about knee-high dikes on all sides. From the air, the paddies looked something like a giant checkerboard.

The direction he had taken was beyond turning back, so he would land in the northeast part of the rice paddies. As Jake got closer to the ground, Vietnamese farmers slowly emerged from the wood-line along the east side. He was shocked by their sudden appearance. In desperation, he pulled on his left parachute riser and changed his direction slightly. Instead of landing in the rice paddy closest to east wood-line, his last minute maneuver took him some distance from the natives.

Jake passed over the second row of paddies near the east wood-line. The ground quickly came up as he hit the rice paddy, splashing into the water and collapsing onto his side. His adrenaline was pumping, and his anxiety was also working overtime. Jake quickly pushed his body up just a little and looked toward the farmers on the east side of the paddies. He quickly, or what he believed to be quickly, unbuckled his parachute harness and got out of it, took off his helmet, sat upright and looked around again. Jake was not aware of it at the moment, but the combination of his anxiety, the adrenaline, humidity, and, through no fault of his own, his inexperience, were working against him. The almost twenty-minute parachute ride to the ground and the humidity had already started to dehydrate him and as soon as he hit the ground he was, without knowing it, exhausted and operating on adrenaline. He was soaked from his own sweat, and landing in the water-filled rice paddies only made his clothes and boots more difficult to maneuver.

When he had unbuckled his parachute harness, his hands, as well as the rest of his body, were shaking. He was sweating and out of breath, breathing like he had just finished a race. As he attempted to stand, he stumbled and fell down, his legs still experiencing numbness and needing a little time to get the feeling back. He stood up again, staggered for a second, and attempted to get his footing in the uneven ground under the ankle-high water. He looked at the farmers and saw that a few had rifles and the rest held farm tools and were standing on the bank of the paddy.

Jake looked around and decided to get as far as he could from them. Because they were on the east side of the paddies, he headed west. The decision, however, meant crossing four paddies, each about two hundred yards wide. He moved out, clumsily and heavy-footed, splashing across the rice paddy.

He pulled out his radio and made a distress call. He was excited when the call was immediately answered and he was told that the rescue choppers were about fifteen mikes out. Jake's spirits were somewhat dampened by the fifteen-minute wait, but he was also encouraged, and despite his exhaustion, he felt confident.

As Jake moved across the paddy and was about twenty yards from the dike, he glanced back toward the farmers and saw them walking on the dike to his left, on the south end of the paddy. Suddenly he realized that he should have headed to one of the dikes and then run instead of wading across the paddies, but now it was too late and the farmers were walking almost parallel to him. He started running through the paddy, but movement was awkward and time consuming. Meanwhile the farmers came to where the dike intersected and turned, heading north toward where he was heading.

Jake was not aware of it at first, but the farmers were systematically directing him toward the north end of the paddies. As he got to within about 100 yards of the northeast road, he heard the distinct sound of an approaching Air Force single engine Cessna 0-1, known as Bird Dog. Jake looked to the north, started to jump up and down, and yelled with adrenalin-induced excitement. He shouted as the plane flew from north to south over him. The pilot of the plane waggled the wings back and forth in a rocking motion, to let Jake know he had been seen.

"Yeah! Yeah! You guys will get it now! Yeah!"

He followed the plane and watched it fly south, his eyes fell upon the farmers who were now just about fifty yards in front of him—they watched Jake with amazement. Jake turned around and did not see anyone on the road, so he made an exhaustive sprint toward it while the farmers slowly followed him as he splashed through the paddy.

As Jake made his way to the edge of the paddy, he was so exhausted he had to crawl up the knee-high incline to the dike, but as he made his way onto the road, another group of farmers walked out of the tree line blocking his escape. Frustrated, Jake looked around in disbelief. He struggled to stand up straight and catch his breath as he looked around at the farmers. When he could stand, he paced back and forth. Jake tried to analyze his situation, but all he could think of was getting away long enough so that the Cessna pilot could tell the rescue helicopter where he was located.

As Jake paced inside the circle of farmers, he noticed that about half of them were older men and the rest women and teenage children. He momentarily saw the absence of enemy soldiers or young men as a good omen and assumed that old men, women, and children may not be much of a threat. He decided that he would work his way through the farmers and head into the jungle. They had other plans and did not intend to let Jake get away as he made an attempt to push his way through them. Exhausted as he was, he was easily pushed back and to the ground as some of them started to yell at him. Jake got up and tried a few more times to force his way past them, but with no success.

He began to panic, and in desperation he took out his pistol, pointing it at the farmers, which didn't help. The move only incited them, and they began to brandish their farm tools. One of the farmers knocked the pistol out of his hand with a shovel. They overpowered and tackled him. They started to beat him and continued until one of the farmers yelled for them to stop and told them that the American helicopters were coming.

As the farmers stopped beating Jake, he could hear the distinct *whump, whump, whump* sound of the approaching

helicopters—a sound that gave him added strength and deter-
mination to keep fighting as the farmers physically picked up
the resistant American Air Force captain. He continued to
fight despite being repeatedly hit. Another group of farmers
quickly pulled up with an ox cart. They did not take time to
tie Jake up, but quickly threw him into the two-wheeled cart.
Four farmers climbed in on top of Jake as other farmers covered up the back with a tarp.

As Jake continued to fight with the farmers, he could feel
the sensation of the cart being pulled. Soon the sound of the
two approaching rescue helicopters caused the farmers to
hurry, and Jake felt the cart speed up. While some of the group
pulled the cart down the dirt road, the others ran into the jungle and disappeared as the helicopters began their approach
over the rice paddies. Jake heard the sound of the Hueys as
they passed overhead. He struggled to get free, but he was
held down.

The ride in the ox cart continued for several minutes
while overhead the choppers orbited in their search for Jake,
who was able to tell by the sound of the birds and by the yelling of the farmers who pulled the cart that the rescue crews
had not given up. The helicopters continued their rotation
above, and Jake believed that their attention was on the ox
cart. Judging from their tone, the farmers were obviously upset and worried. Their concern was taken out on Jake as they
repeatedly beat him and angrily yelled at him.

As one of the Hueys passed overhead, Jake heard machine guns firing in what he believed were apparent warning shots toward the ox cart. He did not understand what they were saying, but the farmers panicked as the ox cart moved faster down the dirt road. As a helicopter passed overhead again, he heard another burst of machine-gun fire; this time it was louder and closer; the bullets impacted and whisked through the cart, hitting and killing one of the farmers holding him down. The ox cart suddenly stopped when farmers outside of it cried out. There was intense arguing between the farmers inside the cart. They started to panic while holding him down as he struggled to get out. One of the farmers looked outside and angrily yelled. Jake assumed he was telling them that the helicopter had shot the others pulling the cart.

While the helicopter passed over, moving away to make another turn, another group of four farmers came out of the jungle wood-line onto the road. Three of this new group were younger men—the fourth was much older. They quickly grabbed Jake, jerked him out of the cart, and dragged him into the wood-line where he was thrown onto the ground. Taking him from the cart and into the jungle only took a few seconds. Another group of farmers then took the cart and continued to pull it down the road. The new group of farmers had no problem overpowering Jake, although he tried his best to resist. They quickly tied his hands in front of him and then attached a long rope to his wrists and used it like a leash as they headed down a trail, pulling Jake with them.

The four farmers moved out quickly on a jungle trail, dragging him with them. At first, Jake held back trying not to walk with his captors, but with each attempt to resist, he was hit with a bamboo stick on his back and legs, which inflicted intense pain. He still wanted to resist, but the pain and physical exhaustion had taken its toll on him. He could still hear the helicopters in the distance, but the farmers who had continued pulling the cart down the road had apparently succeeded at drawing the helos away, and for the moment, took away any immediate chances for Jake's rescue.

About ten minutes down the jungle trail, Jake's surreal perception of what had happened was becoming more real with each passing moment. The reality of his circumstances and the dwindling hopes of being rescued began to panic him. He reluctantly realized that the possibility of an immediate rescue had passed and began to change his thoughts toward overpowering his captors.

Jake continued to resist—he struggled with his captors and tried several times to pull the rope holding him away from them. His resistance irritated the farmers. They tried to move quickly down the jungle trail, but Jake's resistance slowed them down. He managed at one point to pull the rope away, but they quickly got it back.

His continued to resist, finally getting the attention of the older farmer, the leader of the group, who angrily walked up to Jake, took out his pistol, pointed it toward him, and without any hesitation fired off a round past his head. Initially Jake thought he was going to be shot and instinctively fell to the ground when the shot was fired. The sudden gunshot and ringing in his ear startled Jake as he looked up at the farmer, who calmly, but sternly talked to Jake. He did not understand the Cong, but he understood the message and reluctantly knew he had to cooperate with his captors if he wanted to live and hopefully find an opportunity in the future for escape or rescue.

In just over an hour, Jake's life had changed, and despite everything that had happened up to that point, the experience continued to seem surreal and unbelievable. His mind was racing, looking for opportunities to escape, somewhere to run and get away, yet he kept telling himself that the situation he found himself in couldn't be happening.

The pace of the farmers was quite fast, and after about half an hour, Jake was struggling to keep up and sometimes stumbled and fell. The farmers didn't allow him to rest or stay on the ground when he fell—they simply picked him back up and pushed him forward. The overall pace of everything so far, the trek through the rice paddies, being beaten by the first group of farmers, the ox cart, and now what felt like a race through the jungle, had, up to this point, gone by quickly considering it had only been over an hour since he hit the ground.

As they continued to move quickly through the jungle, time began to catch up with Jake. With the continuous and already repetitive pace through the jungle, Jake's mind was slowing down. He tried to keep thinking to figure out a way to escape, but the task of keeping up the pace was distracting. His mind started to lose focus on escape. He took a glance at his watch and saw that it was 11:40 a.m., but he had thought that it was just 10:05 a.m. when he was shot down. Jake also had just realized that with the exception of taking his radio and pistol away, they hadn't taken the time to search him, a thought that gave Jake some reassurance that maybe he could still get away. He figured out that the probable reason for the fast pace was that they were trying to get out of the box, the particular region and operational area he had last been located in, and out of range of any rescue efforts or encounters with other forces.

His mind started racing again as he plotted and made mental notes of where he had been shot down, the direction he traveled while under the parachute, for how long and where he landed. He took note of the northwesterly direction they had been going since his capture. When he was shot down, he knew he was northwest of Hue in South Vietnam, and knowing that location, he was able to calculate this location to be about 300 miles or so from the North Vietnamese border, maybe 350 or 400 miles from Hanoi. Jake couldn't even imagine that they would be taking him to Hanoi, but he also had jokingly thought, *they can't be planning on walking to Hanoi?* The not-knowing factor started to bother Jake as he caught himself making light of his situation, which quickly brought him back to reality.

There seemed to be no letup on the pace through the jungle as he approached a point of exhaustion. He continued to stumble, fall, get up, and move on. The leader of the group looked back toward Jake from the front of the line, noticed his condition, and realized that they needed to stop. The older man stopped the group and immediately started giving orders to the others. Jake fell to his knees, but he kept an eye on what was going on.

Although he had not realized it yet, the farmers were more than just ordinary farmers. They took prisoners for a living, for the money, and turned them over to the NVA. The group leader was older than the other three and appeared to be a very serious person. Jake had already coined a name for him: Happy. Jake noticed his lack of focus when he found himself giving his captors nicknames. He immediately forced himself to concentrate and look for a way to escape.

His exhaustion did not help. Still kneeling, he glanced around and noticed that no one was actually holding onto the rope tied around his hands. His lack of attention was short-lived as one of his captors walked over and yelled at him as he handed him a canteen of water. Jake didn't have to think about accepting the water. While he drank, he became aware that one of the captors had been standing behind him, which scared him as he realized that he had been watched the entire time, reminding him that he needed to be more careful and pay better attention.

The thought of paying attention quickly became secondary when Jake started getting dizzy. The water was good, but he drank it too fast and then noticed that he was feeling chilled and clammy as he moved from kneeling to sitting. He told himself over and over to stay awake. He tried not to lie down, but within seconds, he found himself growing dizzier. He fell over. Even lying down, Jake was still dizzy, and as he looked straight up through the jungle canopy at the sky—everything was spinning. He could hear some yelling and he even saw Happy standing over him, but the spinning in Jake's head had gotten worse as he tried to keep telling himself to stay awake.

His dreams were interrupted by a kick on the feet. Jake woke up slowly and cautiously as he looked around at his surroundings and heard Happy yelling at him. The brief escape from reality after passing out lasted maybe half an hour, or at least that's the best estimate he could make. He instinctively looked at his watch, which was gone as were the rest of the things he had in his pockets and vest. Two of the captors helped Jake up off the ground, quickly tied a rope around his neck, and then attached it to a long piece of bamboo. A sudden depression hit Jake because with the addition of the bamboo leash, it would be much more difficult to escape. The bamboo pole was about eight to ten feet long with Jake attached to the center and a captor at each end.

As they began to move out, he became aware of the sudden pain throughout his body, more so in his feet. His muscles ached and the blisters that formed on his feet made walking painful. Jake's pain did not allow him to keep the pace the guards had set, but they forced him to keep up. After a few minutes, he noticed that the pace was not as fast as earlier and thought that if not for his feet and aches, the pace would be somewhat slow. It was, in fact, much slower, and Happy and the others had experience in moving through the jungle and understood the need to pace themselves. The speed they were now setting would be the norm as they settled into their march through the jungle.

CHAPTER 6
NEVER-ENDING TRAILS

7 July, 1970
Day 8

Seven days had come and gone since Jake had been captured. As he and his four captors made their way north along the dense jungle trail, he continued the daily struggle to keep going and was already visibly worn down. His Air Force flight suit was dirty, torn, and smelly—his feet had already passed the sore and tender stage and had toughened up from the walking. Every step was still somewhat painful, but the pain has eased a bit from the week before.

His captors had provided plenty of water, but food was less than what Jake had been accustomed to having. Every day had become a lengthy routine, which began before sunrise when he was awakened, untied from a tree, and given a cup of rice. The sequence was reversed in the evening when they stopped and gave him another cup of rice and tied him to a tree. Sometimes they added a piece of meat, what kind Jake didn't know, but it was meat. The little food, humidity, and moving all day through the jungle contributed to his physical and mental fatigue.

The psychological strain took its toll as each day passed. Although he had been with the four VC for a week, he felt isolated. With the exception of general sign language and trying to understand what his captors were saying, Jake felt alone and was descending into a drone state as they moved through the jungle at what had become a routine pace. He had not been given any indication of how long it would be until they got to wherever it was they were heading, but despite the negatives, Jake managed to make a point to keep track of the days and committed each one to memory. An occasional sound of aircraft in the distance and far-off sound of bombs exploding gave Jake some inspiration and hope that something could still happen and that he could escape or be rescued.

The continued routine slow pace drudged on as two of the farmers walked ahead of Jake, and the other two followed behind. During the first three days, his hands had been tied while they walked, but on the fourth day they untied him, although they still kept him attached to the bamboo leash. He noticed that after they freed his hands, his ability to move through the jungle trails improved, thereby allowing them to maintain the pace.

Daily life for Jake's captors also had a routine pace; to Jake, they seemed to stay focused on getting to where they were going. Jake wasn't really sure about their motivation, whether it was the glory of Ho Chi Minh, the people of Vietnam, or the reward money, but they were serious, at least most of the time. As the days passed, he came to believe and understand that his captors had in fact transported American prisoners in the past. They seemed to know where they were going and went through the daily motions as a well-established routine. It became obvious to Jake that they probably escorted prisoners for a living and that it was an important point that he be delivered alive, although his condition may not be as important.

Another thing Jake noticed was that the leader of the group, Happy, was not a happy person at all. He was serious, always alert and directing the others. He did interact, however, it was always as the leader or father figure. The other three seemed to be less serious at times and as Jake observed them over the days, they reminded him of normal acting kids or young men who talked, joked, complained, and carried on like everyone else. With time for his mind to drift and observe, Jake studied his captors and noticed each of their personalities. He wondered how these normal behaving people could be doing what they were doing. He found himself drifting from being in a war to studying his captors outside of a war environment. This perception of his captors, however, would repeatedly be disproved when their attention was drawn toward him. They appeared, or it seemed to Jake, that with all their hearts, they hated Americans, a scenario that he had difficulty understanding.

Unfortunately, Jake had only been stationed in Vietnam two weeks before he was shot down. During those two weeks, he had spent most of his time inside attending orientation and training classes and had only been on one other mission. For the most part, he was fresh out of school. He graduated the Air Force Academy and went on to his training, followed by attendance at survival school and then off to Vietnam. The combination of the brutal humid climate, the jungle, and lack of opportunity to adjust, had taken a toll on Jake, although at this point, it probably would not have made much of a difference.

14 July, 1970
Day 15

Fifteen days of walking through the jungle had turned into endless repetition. He still kept track of how many days it had been, but the days had developed into a continuous and monotonous journey of unchanging jungle and the company of four Vietnamese captors who hated him. While the routine continued, Jake became more anxious as he counted the days and estimated the distance they had traveled. He knew they had been moving north, that they walked about fourteen or fifteen hours a day, excluding breaks and afternoon rains. Jake also estimated that they were traveling about twenty miles a day and figured the distanced covered to be around 200 miles and assumed they were close to or already in North Vietnam.

As they moved ahead through the jungle, there was nothing significant or different about the days as they traveled. Most days, it rained and usually they stopped during the heavy rain and waited an hour or two for it to stop before they got back up and moved out again.

As the afternoon progressed and the overhead clouds filled the sky, Jake and his captors approached an intersection in the jungle trails. Happy was in the front and yelled out, his voice breaking the normal routine. Jake looked up toward the front of the trail to see what the yelling was about, and although not sure, he thought it sounded like he was yelling out to someone. As they got closer to the intersection, his suspicion was confirmed when he saw two other Vietnamese standing in the trail. It was apparent that they knew each other and that there were also three more Vietnamese in the other group—a total of five.

The Vietnamese greeted each other and took Jake toward a tree; he was surprised to see another American already tied there. As Jake was tied, he assumed the stern mannered talking from the captor tying him up was telling him not to talk. As soon as the captors walked away and started talking with the others, his excitement overtook him as the other man spoke.

"Hey there, young captain, you doing all right?" the other American whispered to him. Jake told him he was fine as he noticed the older, self-assured soldier displaying a sense of confidence and experience.

"So, how long have they had you?"

"Fifteen days."

"Just three for me…I'm Brad."

"Jake."

"They've had you for two weeks? I'm probably not going to be that lucky."

"What do you mean?"

"No disrespect, okay, but you're an officer, and me, I'm enlisted. My platoon was ambushed, most everyone was killed, but they kept me."

"Green Beret?"

"That doesn't help with them…probably hurts…they'll get paid something, but not much for me. They haven't figured out I'm not an officer yet, and when they do, they'll be pissed. They get paid more for officers sometimes…not all the time, but sometimes."

Jake's uplifted spirits from seeing an American had dropped in just ten seconds of conversation. Jake could see that Brad was experienced, probably ten years his elder too, but he also had concern for him, knowing that Happy was not stupid and might notice that Brad was not an officer. Jake told him his concern, but Brad had other plans.

"Listen, Captain, I know it's a matter of time, so my plan is to get away. You just need to be ready when it happens, understand?"

Jake hesitantly questioned Brad about the plan, and Brad reassured him by telling about another time four years earlier when he and one of his friends were captured. Brad told Jake about how they had been guarded by three Vietnamese and on the second night, they overpowered and killed all three of them.

"You understand, Captain, the only way this will work is we have to kill them, if not, they'll just find us, got it? We have to kill them all, and you're going to have to kill some of them too. You understand that, right?"

Jake was still hesitant, but he agreed.

"I'll get you out of here, you just have to be ready to move when it's time," Brad told Jake reassuringly.

The late afternoon rains lasted a little longer than usual and didn't subside until almost evening. A big part of Brad's plan was based on an assumption from something he overheard the Vietnamese talking about, that their escorts were turning over one of them and that group would take both. That would be good because that meant that there would only be four or five Vietnamese guarding them instead of nine and the others would be long gone when Brad and Jake made their escape.

During the passing hours, they talked quietly. Brad told Jake that he spoke and understood Vietnamese and had spent about six years in Vietnam. He talked about some of his work with the Montagnard hill people of Vietnam and expressed a sincere love and concern for the fate of the Vietnamese. Brad's experiences and views of Vietnam were a sharp contrast to what Jake had seen back home prior to his arrival in country. Brad seemed to be talking about a different Vietnam. His perspective about the war amazed Jake, and even though he understood the concept of the war against communism in Vietnam, Brad's version of the war was different and made it sound not only justified, but also necessary. The conversations with Brad were educational and provided another point of view, which contrasted to the negative views back home. It was also good to have company and at least a temporary feeling of relief.

Although they had only spent a few hours together, Jake had already developed a feeling of friendship for the other man. It may have been due to the absence of contact for two weeks or because Brad's sincerity and belief for what he was doing. Regardless, Jake felt a sense of security with the older soldier. Even the traditional evening cup of rice seemed more fulfilling with Brad being there.

The anticipated continued movement after the rain stopped never came. The longer rain period and the Vietnamese apparently reminiscing and relaxing seemed to present a decision to stay the night where they were. It was still not clear when one of the groups was going to leave, which started to concern both men. If that didn't happen, escape would be more difficult, and Brad felt that it had to be that night or never. He knew that their destination was probably within a few more days, and felt it may have even been the next day— if they did not escape that night, the opportunity would be lost.

A few hours into the evening, the time came when Jake and Brad were moved to a tree and tied. For Jake it was a couple of hours later than usual, thanks to the socializing of the Vietnamese who sat around the cooking fire, talking, and smoking cigarettes. Jake and Brad continued to talk in whispers until they eventually fell asleep.

15 July, 1970
Day 16

A slight shake and hand over his mouth awakened Jake from his sleep. Brad managed to untie himself and was quickly untying Jake, who was experiencing a strange sense of anxiety mixed with excitement, as he slowly knelt next to Brad.

Before they did anything, Brad put his mouth to Jake's ear and whispered, "You can stay if you want, you don't have to do this, okay?" Jake nodded. Brad whispered again, "I can't promise this will work, understand?"

Jake hesitated a few seconds and then nodded again to Brad. "Let's get out of here."

Brad took the lead and as they started to move, Jake noticed just a few feet away one of the Vietnamese on the ground, dead, already killed by Brad. This sudden discovery made Jake even more anxious as they slowly moved toward one of the other sleeping Vietnamese. Brad quickly got on top of the sleeping man and silently killed him. Jake saw what was happening but not how Brad did it. As soon as Brad killed one, he quietly moved over to another one and again, quietly and quickly ended his life.

Unfortunately for them, as Brad was about to kill one more, two of the captors had sneaked up behind them, yelled, and started to beat Jake on the back with their rifle butts. The sudden surprise of being hit caused Jake to fall to the ground as he tried to protect himself. He could not see what was going on and only heard the yelling of the Vietnamese. The sound of a gunshot stopped the beating and yelling and he cautiously looked up to see Happy holding his pistol toward Brad. Jake's brief glimpse ended when he was hit in the head with a rifle butt.

A few hours had passed and the sun was within an hour of coming up; the pre-twilight morning had begun to brighten up the overnight campsite. Jake started to wake up, with no idea of what had happened other than when he saw Happy pointing his pistol at Brad. Jake realized that Brad had killed another one in a few short seconds—five altogether. Jake looked to the right and saw Brad also starting to wake up.

Brad had been severely beaten and shot in the left leg, and as he sat up, he saw Jake next to him. Their hands had been tied behind their backs, and additional rope had been used around their arms, completing restricting their upper arm movement. When Brad saw that they were being guarded he wanted to apologize for not getting them out of there, but as soon as he started to talk, Happy noticed and got up to his feet and yelled toward Brad and the other three remaining Vietnamese. Happy's ranting went on for about a minute or two, chastising the three other captors while also venting his attention toward the prisoners. Jake didn't understand what Happy was saying, but Brad did. He quickly tried to tell Jake that Happy was blaming everyone for letting the escape attempt happen. Happy was also upset over the death of one of his own men, the one he referred to as *the boy*. The other four dead were from the other group.

The ranting suddenly stopped as he glared at Brad and Jake and quickly walked toward them, a machete in his hand, and started to yell again.

"This is it," Brad told Jake as they were grabbed and then forced to kneel next to each other.

On their knees, fear overtook Jake as he looked down at the ground in front of him. Jake started to pray while still hearing Happy yelling and pacing around.

"Sorry, man…" Brad started to tell Jake, but his sentence to Jake suddenly stopped short as Jake heard an unfamiliar sound, followed by the feeling of a warm light mist hitting his face. Almost immediately he heard a thump hit the ground. He glanced toward Brad and saw his headless torso fall against him. Spontaneity took over for Jake as he yelled out and leaped away from Brad's body, stumbling, crawling, and then getting up to his feet to get away. He didn't get far because he was restrained by the Vietnamese.

Happy motioned to bring Jake over to where the bodies of the dead Vietnamese had been laid next to each other. Convinced he'd be next to die, he was still yelling as he was walked over to Happy. They forced Jake to his knees, but Happy looked at him and motioned him to stand. Jake was still wildly talking until Happy walked up to him and told him to shut up. Jake understood the meaning and the intensity of Happy's voice caused him to stop his yelling. Happy looked at the dead bodies and then back at Jake; he said something and tried to convey something, but several attempts by Happy were not understood by Jake, who just shrugged and angrily looked at Happy. Frustrated with Jake's lack of understanding, Happy, still repeating the same words, held his hands up and through some simple hand signals finally conveyed to Jake what he had been trying to tell him, which was "sixteen." Happy walked over to the dead Vietnamese body from his group, and Jake suddenly understood.

"Sixteen," Jake said to Happy.

Happy understood and could see from Jake's expression that he understood that the one killed from his group was sixteen years old. Happy said a few more things to Jake, but he said them in a manner and tone unlike anything he had previously said. Jake didn't say anything. He didn't have to, for his expression and the realization that a sixteen-year-old boy was killed was clear. It didn't change the fact that the boy was dead or that Brad was dead. Given the way Happy had reacted, Jake thought the dead boy could well have been Happy's son. He and Happy, for a brief moment, seemed to share a mutual remorse. Jake was initially upset to see someone who was so young dead and it confused him, making him start to wonder and second-guess why a sixteen-year-old was out there in the first place. His thoughts started to drift back to Brad, and the image of the beheaded man removed any temporary sense of remorse.

Jake regained his composure. He had started to learn how to survive and to keep his feelings to himself. After a few moments, the quietness was broken by Happy as he yelled instructions at everyone. They broke camp, gathered up their things, untied Jake, and then attached the neck leash to him.

A minute later, they headed out and left the lone Vietnamese behind.

Jake, Happy, and the two other Vietnamese started walking in the morning twilight and without the morning cup of rice, normally eaten the first thing. The absence of not eating breakfast and the change in routine made Jake start to wonder if his captors were close to turning him over to the NVA. If he were turned over, it would be a confirmation to Brad's theory that they were close, but after about two hours of walking they stopped at a stream for a break and began to cook.

Happy said something to Jake and motioned toward him to get water and wash in the stream. A couple of times before he had been allowed to wash, but this time, washing Brad's blood off was something he needed to do, so Jake took advantage of the break and the stream while he waited for the rice to cook. He noticed that his captors were keeping a close watch on him, more so than what they had been during the long previous fifteen days.

After they packed up and moved out, the rest of the day turned into the accustomed routine. They walked all day, and Jake found himself thinking about Brad and everything that had happened. He found it difficult not to think about the Green Beret's beheading. Although he tried, the scene just kept going through his mind. The longer the day went, the more Jake became upset. He found himself hoping that this day was the last day so that Brad's belief in being a day away would be true, and at least their escape attempt had not been in vain. As the day drew toward the end, his daylong fear had come true, for around dark, they stopped for the night, cooked, ate rice, and tied Jake to a tree, just like every other night.

CHAPTER 7

JUNGLE TO JAIL

18 July, 1970
Day 19

"We stop here and rest for fifteen minutes," Happy said.

Jake's captors seemed relieved and very excited about reaching the road. After about a minute, they gave Jake a canteen of water to drink while they were resting and talking. It had been almost three weeks with nothing but jungle, and now suddenly a paved road was in front of them. As Jake glanced around, he even noticed the telephone poles and lines and the passing trucks, scooters, bicycles, and an occasional car.

Happy and the others showed another side of themselves that Jake hadn't seen. They were extremely excited, exuberant, and expressed what he saw as a sense of relief finally to have made it out of the jungle. Jake found it difficult himself not to be a little excited and after the almost three weeks of misery and walking through the jungle, he was optimistically hopeful that a change could only be an improvement. The sight of what looked like a large town about a mile down the road helped reinforce his hopes and gave him a sense of being back in the world, back in civilization.

After the fifteen-minute break was over, the group got ready to move. But, before they started to walk, they removed the bamboo leash from his neck and threw the bamboo sticks off into the tree line. Jake didn't know what to make of being untied as they started walking toward the town, with Happy taking the lead. After three weeks of the leash and being tied, Jake suddenly found himself, for the first time, free of restraints. He thought briefly of running, which was short lived as Happy turned around and said something. The two other Vietnamese also said something to Jake as one of them jabbed him in the back with a rifle barrel.

As they continued to walk, Jake's brief thought of running ended completely when he noticed the two behind him were keeping their rifles pointed at him, something that had not happened before. Although he had been a prisoner, his capture and trek through the jungle had not been at gunpoint, but rather by physical force and restraints. They had the guns, but except for the warning shot by Happy and the shooting of Brad in the leg, Jake at times almost forgot that they had guns.

The change of scenery slowly wore off as the almost hour-long walk toward the edge of town dragged out. The road was traveled by Vietnamese walking, on bicycles, and in a steady stream of vehicles. With each passing civilian, Jake and his captors were either ignored or received expressions of hate directed at Jake. At first, Jake was excited about getting out of the jungle, but as the minutes passed, his mind started to drift. The long walk, the looks from the Vietnamese, and not knowing what was coming caused Jake to become anxious as they drew closer to the community.

As they entered the town, Jake kept thinking about running, the civilians, and the nearby jungle, but he was also very much aware of his own anxiety and the guns pointed at his back. As they continued to walk farther toward the center of town on what he assumed was the main road, they received the same looks from the townspeople. They also heard an occasional unfriendly yell. They walked through town, which took about another half hour. Jake could not help but glance around; he had also quickly learned not to look directly at anyone. The walk took on a somewhat surreal feeling for Jake, and the reality of being a prisoner briefly escaped him as he noticed the normalcy of the town's activities; he even took notice of children in a schoolyard. Jake concluded that the only thing in the town not normal was his own presence there. Being walked through the town was the only distraction to what seemed to be an otherwise normal day.

Up ahead, Jake saw a police station and a few police officers sitting outside. As they approached, Happy started to talk to the police, and by the time they reached the front, another officer came outside, briefly talked with Happy, and then went back inside. As Happy followed the officer inside, he motioned to Jake to sit in one of the chairs outside the door. Jake sat down, seemly almost ignored by everyone as his escorts and the police officers sat and talked with his captors—he could occasionally hear Happy and the other policemen talking.

About half an hour passed as Jake waited. He had no real idea where he was, but he made the reasonable assumption that he was somewhere in North Vietnam. The anticipation of waiting and the unknown caused Jake to not be able to take advantage of the break to rest. He had become very alert and anxious while waiting and again even contemplated trying to run and escape. The thought troubled him as he wondered just where he would go. He knew almost for certain he was in North Vietnam; therefore, his options were limited. He came to the realization that even if he were to run, he had nowhere to go, and given the reception of the civilians, he figured he would not get far.

Eventually, Happy came outside and sat with the others, and as Jake continued to wait, he noticed an older woman approaching. She talked with him for a moment and then nodded his head at her, seemingly answering a question. The woman then turned and approached Jake—she carried a tin cup in her hand. She handed him the cup and motioned at him to eat. Jake took the cup and saw that it was about half-full of rice. His hunger instinctively took over and he quickly ate the rice while the woman watched. When Jake finished, the woman snatched the cup out of Jake's hand and walked away. As an afterthought, Jake said thank you to the woman, but she did not respond as she continued to walk away.

Time passed, Jake was not sure, but it had been at least a few hours as they continued to wait. For what, he didn't know. Conversations continued, and occasionally curious children and passersby stopped to look at Jake. The sound of an approaching vehicle finally broke the monotony. Jake looked and saw that it was some type of a North Vietnamese military jeep. It stopped in front of the police station, and an NVA captain got out along with two soldiers. The arrival of the soldiers drastically changed Jake's emotions as he realized that something was about to happen, and while he assumed they were there to take him away, the uncertainty and his anxiety caused him to become extremely nervous. One thing he had already learned was not to stare, and he was careful to look only briefly at the officer and soldiers and to avoid eye contact. It was obvious that the captain and Happy were talking about him, and he saw that the officer was paying Happy. When the conversation stopped, Happy and his two men began to leave as they said their goodbyes to the police officers and the soldiers.

The soldiers approached, and although Jake didn't understand what they were saying to him, he knew that they wanted him to get up. The soldiers grabbed Jake by his arms as he stood up, put handcuffs on him, and walked him to the vehicle. They then made him get into the back along with one of the soldiers. They said nothing as the vehicle took off through town.

During the next few hours, while the soldiers and captain carried on conversations, Jake found himself drifting as he looked at the countryside and villages. He found himself struggling with the surreal reality of his situation, riding in the back of an open vehicle, as if going on a ride in the country. Sometime later, as the vehicle was moving along a main highway, Jake saw they were approaching another urban area. He had, on occasion, during the ride seen some road signs, but he didn't take too much notice of them. As they drove along, the next road sign he saw was written in Vietnamese and English, which gave Jake a sinking feeling as he read the sign that showed Son Tay 2 km, Hanoi 45 km.

The captain looked back at Jake and in English said, "Almost there."

Jake was surprised by the English, but even more surprised to see how close to Hanoi they were, and made the assumption that they were headed to Hanoi only forty-five km, about twenty or thirty miles away.

Jake remained concerned, but he could not help taking in the view as they drove through the next town of Son Tay. As they drove, the vehicle started to slow down and Jake's assumption of heading to Hanoi came to a sudden end as the vehicle made a left turn. Just ahead, he saw the gate entrance to the Son Tay prison, a former French prison now converted to a POW camp.

As the vehicle approached and entered the prison, Jake saw American prisoners working in a field outside the camp. The vehicle entered through the main gate of the Son Tay prison and pulled up in front of a door by one of the buildings. The captain and the two soldiers got out, stretched, then looked at Jake, and told him in English to get out of the vehicle. Jake got out. Then they waited about a minute until two prison guards came out of the building, walked up, grabbed Jake, and started to walk him toward the building with the captain following.

As they walked toward the door, a faint American voice was heard echoing from one of the cellblocks across the courtyard.

"Hang in there, buddy! Won't matter what you do, just hang in there!"

Jake and the captain both turned their heads, but could not tell where the voice had come from. The guards took Jake inside the building, where they stopped in the hallway as one of the guards called out to someone. A few seconds later, an

Army captain came out of an office, and a discussion between the captain and guards began. The discussion was, of course, about Jake as they talked and glanced at him and his condition. One obvious observation was that Jake reeked from his three weeks of walking through the jungle. He was filthy, unshaven, bruised, and battered. Normally a prisoner was taken directly to interrogation, but for some reason, probably the smell, they decided to let him get cleaned up first.

The guards took Jake out of the building and walked him across the courtyard. One of the guards left, and the other guard escorted Jake over to an outside bath area. As they walked, Jake saw other prisoners in different parts of the courtyard area working, raking, and doing laundry. Jake was not clear about what was going to happen until they arrived at the bathing area. At first, Jake didn't understand what the guard was saying, but the guard motioned at Jake to undress and wash.

Jake was reluctant at first, until he heard an American voice. "There's soap in the bowl sitting on the ledge, and he's probably also given you a razor to shave, but they won't give you much time," the voice told Jake.

The guard yelled at the anonymous voice while Jake quickly began to undress. The other guard returned carrying a prison uniform and sandals and placed them on a bench. No more instructions were necessary—Jake knew he needed to take a quick bath. He stripped down, first cleaning up before shaving. It did take a little while to shave the three-week-old beard, but the guards waited, with an occasional word, but still they waited until Jake finished shaving.

As soon as Jake was dressed in his prison uniform, the guards took him back across the courtyard to a room inside a building, an interrogation room. Although Jake was exhausted, he was also a little refreshed from the cold water bath he had just taken. His brief moments of comfort changed to concern as he sat in a chair at a table, waiting. Nothing was said to him by the guards, so Jake kept quiet. As the minutes went by, the fatigue caught up with him. He started to slouch in the chair and nodded off.

Jake woke up startled. He realized he had fallen asleep and was awakened by the voices of the guards talking to each other. He had no idea how long he had slept; it could have been a minute or it could have ten minutes. He felt refreshed but still could not imagine the guards letting him sleep on purpose or not noticing. He sat up straight in the chair and heard the sound of someone walking down the hallway. Jake's brief break from his nervousness and anxiety quickly returned as he got the impression by the way the guards were talking to each other that whoever was walking down the hallway was coming to the interrogation room.

As he waited, the door of the interrogation room opened and an NVA officer walked in, leaving the door open. The officer and guards talked briefly and then the officer walked to the table, sat down across from Jake, and placed a file folder on the table. The officer was Major Hung, a trained interrogator. He spoke relatively good English, which lead Jake to think that the major was educated somewhere outside of Vietnam. He was average looking and as far as first impressions, there was nothing sinister or threatening about his appearance or actions. He initially even came across as caring and compassionate.

The major introduced himself. "Captain Walden, my name is Major Hung, and I am going to be interviewing you, understand?"

Jake was nonresponsive to the major's initial statement as he tried to remember code of conduct and survival school lessons.

The major had been in the interrogation game a long time, and even though a prisoner may not show it, he knew that it was human nature to be scared and nervous. In an attempt to gain Jake's confidence, the major talked to him in a nonauthoritative manner, attempting to gain his confidence and make him feel comfortable. Major Hung also tried to gain Jake's confidence by telling him that it was already late in the afternoon and that they only had about one hour for the interview before he'd be moved to a cell and fed some dinner. The major pointed out that they had already given him clean clothes and a bath and politely emphasized how important it was that they complete the interview.

"Captain Jacob, the sooner we begin, the sooner we can finish."

Jake gradually did come around to the major's friendly demeanor. He reluctantly sat up a little straighter and looked at the major.

"Relax, relax, we know it's not your fault that you are here... I understand that it was not your choice, I understand. Your name is Jacob, yes... do they call you Jacob or maybe Jake?"

"Captain Walden."

The major smiled at Jake, and the way the major said his next words resulted in a slight, uncontrolled smile from Jake, which also momentarily relieved some of the tension in the room.

"Jake, I am honored to meet you. Of course I believe we both can agree we would have preferred to meet under different circumstances, agreed?"

"Yes."

Outside the interrogation room, the normal late afternoon activity of the prison continued as usual. Guards were on watch, and a few prisoners walked across the courtyard doing their assigned tasks. Business as usual for the prison as the major asked Jake a series of routine, nonthreatening or self-incriminating questions.

After about thirty minutes, the major and Jake were still sitting at the table, and the atmosphere in the room was somewhat relaxed. Jake had become comfortable with the major, and the interrogator seemed pleased. Jake, however, had still not told the man much, although he did respond and conversed with the major. So far, the major was still pleasant toward Jake, but he still needed to get answers and results.

"Jake, I am grateful to you for talking with me. I understand your position, and your orders not to tell me anything, but you must understand my position and my country's position in this matter. You do understand that you are not breaking your orders by telling me what I ask you, don't you?"

"I don't understand."

"Our country is not at war with the United States. The United States is not at war with my country. The Geneva Convention you tell me about would not recognize what your country is doing as a war.

"Jake, we are not at war. Our countries are not at war, and because of that, our country does not have prisoners of war. It is very, very important that you understand. I am trying to help you, but you must understand that in my country you are a criminal and not a prisoner of war. You will be considered a criminal and will go to prison. You understand?"

Jake started to get a little defensive as the conversation progressed. The major continued to stay calm, putting on the appearance that he was trying to be helpful; unfortunately, Jake had become a little too comfortable.

"We're fighting a war, fighting communism, and you guys are trying to take over the world. You can call it whatever you want, but we are at war, Major."

"I am not going to talk politics with you, Jake."

"Well, you know what they say, Major, don't talk religion and politics."

Jake instantly realized that he had screwed up by letting his emotions take over and by becoming belligerent with the major. He then noticed the slight change in the major's demeanor and tone.

"Yes, Captain Jake, we should not talk politics, we should talk about you. I have a proposal for you. Right now, you need to think about you. Not politics, not religion, not if we are or are not at war. You need to think about yourself and the crimes you have committed. You need to sign this confession, confessing your crimes against the people. In exchange for your confession, you will be given a pardon, an amnesty, and will be returned to your home within the next week."

The major's demeanor progressively continued to change, and Jake realized it. He stated that he could not sign a confession and that he had done nothing wrong. The major was insistent.

"At this point, Captain, it is not a point of right or wrong. It is a point of do you want to go home, or do you want to spend the rest of your life in prison, or even be executed for your crimes?"

Jake argued and disagreed with the major, even calling him insane, which was probably not a good idea. The major then took another piece of paper out of the folder and placed it on the table.

"Look! Look at this! These are the names of Americans who have already signed confessions and have gone back to America. You are not the only one. You can sign and go home like these. No bullshit as you say, you can go home."

Jake leaned forward and studied the list of names. The major could see that Jake was fearful and thinking.

Jake was thinking and possibly for a moment considered the offer as he looked at the list and the confession the major wanted him to sign. After about a minute, the major was confident that Jake would agree when the exhausted and scared Jake finally made a decision. Jake sat back in the chair, straightened his posture, and took a deep breath.

"That list, the men on that list who signed those confessions, they weren't criminals...they were traitors, and they are the ones that should be executed."

The major instantly transformed, his demeanor and attitude, changing with Jake's statement. The major looked at his watch. He reminded Jake about the shortness of time available.

"Maybe I can persuade you in the time we have left. If not today, we can try again tomorrow."

In the courtyard of the prison, a group of about twelve prisoners entered the gates walking in formation and carrying farm tools. It normally took a few minutes to walk from the gate to the cellblock, and about halfway across the courtyard the prisoners could hear the faint echoing scream of Jake inside one of the buildings. Although his screams bothered them, they ignored them and continued marching. About thirty seconds later, another scream was heard as the group continued to head toward their cellblock, but one of the prisoners could not help himself and angrily, but quietly, muttered out some profanities about the guards.

About an hour later, a severely beaten Jake was dragged out of the interrogation room, across the courtyard to another building where he was placed into an isolation box. The box was like a small closet—or even a coffin. Jake spent his first night in Son Tay in that box.

9 August, 1970
Day 41

Jake did not sign a confession on his first day at Son Tay, nor did he ever sign one. During the first two weeks, intense pressure was administered through daily beatings, sleep deprivation, prolonged standing, and prolonged kneeling with his arms tied behind his back. The torture did have its physical toll, but it did not make him sign a confession or talk. The torture had actually contributed to his increased feelings of hatred toward the Vietnamese, which he had not previously felt. It also began to provide him with the mental strength to persevere and resist.

Twenty-two days after Jake's arrival at Son Tay, his continued torture regimen suddenly ended. Although it may have been coincidental, the mistreatment seemed to end with the arrival of two new prisoners. Jake was still interrogated and on occasion beaten, but not like before, although he was still kept in a solitary cell.

As the days went by, Jake began a transition process, sometimes being taken out of his cell and put to light work, and gradually transitioning from a solitary status to becoming part of the prison population, although everyone was still kept in individual cells.

29 August, 1970
Day 61

When Jake woke up, he did what he had done every day since his capture and made a mental note of how many days it had been. He made note that it was day sixty-one, just like the day before was day sixty—he kept track. He had now been in the

Son Tay prison a little less than six weeks, which already seemed like an eternity compared to the three weeks in the jungle with the farmers. It had been about ten days since his last severe beating, and he felt as if he was recovering. He also had not had any real interaction with other prisoners other than an occasional nod.

After breakfast, Jake eagerly waited in his cell, just as he had for the past week, waiting for a guard to come and take him outside where he was given a task for the morning. Right on cue, Jake heard the guards getting the other prisoners out of their cells for work, and soon a guard came and opened Jake's cell door. He was on his feet ready, which he noticed seemed to please the guard, who told him to come out of the cell, which he acknowledged and then did as he was told. They went outside the building, and he followed the guard until they reached the toolshed area where he saw a prisoner handing out tools. The guard motioned for him to go to the prisoner giving out tools. Jake stopped for a second, a little confused as he looked at the guard, who then gave him a nod to go.

"Looks like your lucky day," the prisoner handing out the tools told him. Jake gave an appreciative nod to the guard and then turned to the prisoner who handed him a long-handled hoe. As he took it, the prisoner told him to go over to the group of prisoners assembled next to the toolshed. Jake went over to the group of about twenty prisoners who were lined up in two columns.

As the group of prisoners started out across the courtyard, it was now apparent that he had been allowed to transition to work groups. For the first time since his capture, Jake was happy about something. A group of guards escorted the prisoners as they passed through the gates of the prison. Once outside the prison walls, they walked a short distance to a large field where they broke up into smaller groups and went about tending the field. One of the prisoners, Ron, told Jake to come with him and a couple of the other prisoners. The guards took their time as they made their way to the edges of the large field to stand watch.

"You're a lucky son of a bitch," Ron told Jake as they made their way through the field.

"How do you mean?"

"I don't know what the deal is, but normally everyone spends months in solitary. We get interrogated, beaten for months before getting out…and it doesn't even matter what you tell 'em, doesn't matter a bit."

"I tell ya, it felt like months to me," Jake said with just a slight smile on his face.

"I bet it did. My name is Ron, by the way, Captain Ron Meyers, Air Force."

"Jake, Jacob Walden, Captain, Air Force too."

As they talked, Jake couldn't help but feel a bit happy about avoiding what the others had gone through. He found it difficult to comprehend the prospect that the daily torture could have continued.

"You know, there's about seventy of us in here now, too many of us for them anymore, which I guess is good if it means they can't keep up the pace with the torture routine."

Jake thought about what Ron had said and felt fortunate.

During the next few hours, the prisoners worked at a slow deliberate pace in the field, keeping busy enough to stop the guards from bothering them. Jake and Ron kept a watchful eye for the guards and quietly talked while working and passing the time, exchanging personal details. At one point, when the guards were not looking, Jake noticed a few of the prisoners periodically squatting down in different parts of the field. He could tell that they were doing something, but couldn't figure it out and noticed all the prisoners seemed to be in sync, watching for the guards and lining themselves up to obscure the guards' view. Ron could see Jake's curiosity.

"They're moving the code letter," Ron quietly said to Jake.

"What letter?"

"Remember survival school? Putting out the code letter to signal so when our people fly over they see it. We change its position every week to let them know we're still here."

The information encouraged Jake, and it was like turning on a light switch. After almost six weeks in Son Tay, he had suddenly been shocked back to the reality that something else was going on outside his own concerns. He knew that they had the code letter in the field next to the prison and that there was an organized effort by the prisoners.

"You remember the code letter to signal that a downed pilot is at the letter?" Ron asked.

Jake thought about Ron's question for a few seconds as he inconspicuously glanced around.

"K...you're talking the letter K, right?" Jake said with a little excitement in his voice.

"That's it. We got one out here, you can't tell by looking and the guards can't see it, but those IMINT guys, they can see it."

Jake's hopes and his attitude were boosted—his belief that there could be a rescue had also been reinforced.

"Jake, we just have to be careful not to let the guards catch us, understand?"

"Definitely," Jake answered.

The letter itself was quite large and not recognizable on the ground, but from the sky, the trained imagery analysis—or IMINT personnel as they were sometimes called—could see it clearly.

Jake fully understood the situation and continued to work while he went over in his head various aspects of his survival training. He was amazed at how just a small thing like a code letter could make his mind race with memories of survival school. He even started to recount his capture and things he could have done differently. His mind eventually started to stray away from his training and back to the occasional daydreaming while he enjoyed the somewhat limited freedom of working in the field and the conversations with Ron and some of the other prisoners.

2 November, 1970
Day 126

The days, weeks, and the few months had gone by slowly for Jake. The unscheduled interrogation sessions continued, although the intensity of the sessions seemed to diminish. While the prisoners did not know it, the North Vietnamese policy on the treatment of the prisoners had changed after the death of the North Vietnamese leader Ho Chi Minh in September of 1969. Life was still harsh, but the torture had seemed to be reduced dramatically and the prisoners' living conditions were more livable.

The day started out like every other day. The morning and early afternoon were routine. The mid and late afternoon also started out like most others, except for one thing: the rain. On this day and almost every day during the next few months, the afternoons were filled with excessive heavy rainfalls. Most afternoons the rains were so heavy that the prisoners were returned to their cells instead of working. Rainfall was not unusual, especially in the tropics of Southeast Asia, but the amount of rainfall for that time of year was unusual. The excessive rainfall caused flooding throughout the region, and because the prison was located on a riverbank, the flooding also threatened the prison area.

It was not known by the North Vietnamese or the prisoners at the time that much of the excessive rains were actually caused by the secret CIA cloud-seeding operations. All that was known was that it had been raining, and raining a lot. It had rained so much that it had raised concerns by the North Vietnamese of possible flooding of the prison. These concerns prompted the North Vietnamese to make a decision to move the prisoners, a decision that also impacted the results of the Son Tay rescue operation that was to occur 18 days later.

Although it was raining in the late afternoon, Jake and the other prisoners had been called out from their cells and moved outside to the courtyard. The prisoners were told to assemble and wait for the camp commander to address them. The assembly was an unusual event for the prisoners, and there was whispering and speculating about what was going on, but none of the guesses were correct. The camp commander came out from the headquarters building and moved to the front of the formation of prisoners where he made an announcement to them, in English. The camp commander told the prisoners that due to the excessive rains and flooding in the area a concern for their safety had been brought up. The commander told the prisoners that it had been decided that they were going to be transferred. The commander spoke another minute to give instructions to the prisoners and guards, and then the prisoners were told to move out and get their belongings from their cells.

As the prisoners went back to the cells and gathered their things, the rain began to subside. By the time they got back outside the rain had stopped, and sky was clearing. The prisoners waited while a group of about twenty guards also came outside with their gear and waited. Twenty minutes later, two uncovered troop trucks pulled into the camp courtyard; the prisoners were split into two groups and loaded onto the trucks. The guards also had split up and got into two smaller trucks, one in the front and the other at the rear of the troop trucks.

Without any fanfare, the trucks pulled out and drove through the gates, leaving the camp commander and the rest of the staff and guards behind. As the convoy left town, a road sign told the prisoners of their destination as they moved eastward along the main highway toward Hanoi.

Jake and the other prisoners were cramped in the back of two trucks, but despite that, they managed to relax, and strangely enough, tried to enjoy the ride. Many of the prisoners, including Jake, took advantage of being outside of the prison and happily and eagerly looked at the sights as the trucks made their way on the hour drive toward the prison in Hanoi. Jake thought about the surreal impressions he was seeing, for he and some of the other prisoners found it difficult to believe the non-hostile and seemingly peaceful appearance of the locals going about their activities. The tranquil and peacefulness was interrupted occasionally when they passed bomb craters and ruins. The presence of Jake and the prisoners for a while seemed to go unnoticed by the local Vietnamese along the route, except for the occasional group of children, some of whom waved and others who yelled and threw rocks at the trucks.

After about forty-five minutes, the convoy entered the urbanized city of Hanoi, and the demeanor of Jake and the others started to change. The people on the busy streets took more notice of the American prisoners, displayed looks of contempt, and showed hostility toward them. After about fifteen minutes of driving through the city, they saw that they were approaching the prison, which was not like the one they had just left. It was a large full-scale prison—the Hoa Lo Prison in Hanoi—known as the Hanoi Hilton.

CHAPTER 8

WELCOME TO HANOI

2 November, 1970

Day 126

The trucks slowed down as they approached the main gate, and although it was a large prison, one of the prisoners commented that the main gate was not very big. Jake and the others noticed the words on the wall over the gate, *Maison Centrale,* which was the French translation for Central Home.

Hoa-Lo Prision a.k.a. The Hanoi Hilton

As the trucks neared, they drove to a side entrance, entered another gate into a courtyard where the trucks stopped and the prisoners were ordered off the trucks. As they got off, the guards immediately took control of the prisoners, quickly got them into formation and then marched them to the larger courtyard area where they waited. After a few minutes, everyone relaxed and quietly talked, but they were still cautious.

Fifteen minutes later, the prison commander gave the prisoners a "Welcome to Hanoi" speech, which was followed by the guards beginning the in-processing procedures. The prisoners were processed and issued their distinctive red and white vertical-striped prison uniforms. They were then escorted through an array of hallways to their new cells, where some of the prisoners were doubled up while others were placed in separate cells. Jake, at least for the moment, was placed in a separate cell.

After Jake entered the cell, he stood in the middle of it for a few moments, looking around and shaking his head in disbelief as a new realization overwhelmed him. The look on his face was one of disappointment at the thought of being back in a cell. Although he hoped and believed the stay in the new prison would be short-lived, he still could not help but be depressed.

Jake was interrogated several more times during the next three weeks, but interrogations seemed more like a routine for the interrogators rather than an attempt to get any real information. There was also what could be considered light beatings or torture, although it was less intense, it was still torture and painful. It also seemed to him and a few of the other prisoners he managed to talk with that even the torture sessions were part of a routine instead of an attempt to get information or inflict punishment, although violating the rules, which included talking to other prisoners, did result in punishment.

For Jake, life at the Hanoi Hilton developed into a new pattern, with more time in the cell and less time out. Any attempts to communicate with other prisoners were difficult, even though communication between prisoners by use of a code system was in use. The problem for Jake was that he didn't know the code, a system of tapping on the cell walls.

During the next three weeks, he managed to learn bits and pieces and was confident he would learn all of it.

20 November, 1970
Day 144

Around one o'clock in the morning, Jake was awakened by the sounds of air-raid sirens, which were followed a few minutes later by the distant sounds of surface-to-air missiles, called SAMs, being launched. The layout of the prison was in such a manner that some of the cellblock buildings paralleled the outside streets, which enabled Jake to be able to see the outside sky through the small window near the ceiling of his cell. The vantage point also allowed him to see the flashes of light accompanying the launches of the SAMs, and the sounds of the distant exploding diversionary flares the U.S. aircraft were setting off around Haiphong Harbor. One of the prisoners in a nearby cell yelled out, "Something's going on, guys, something big."

"Damm! Listen to that!" another prisoner called out.

Jake and the others knew something was happening, but they had no way of knowing that this was the night of the Son Tay Raid, just twenty miles away at their old prison. They also did not know that if they still had been at the Son Tay prison, they would have been rescued.

In the days and weeks to come, there would be speculation that the Son Tay Raid scared the North Vietnamese Government. The fact that a foreign military force could land twenty miles outside the capital city was said to help speed up the peace talks. Rumors also circulated about the rescue attempt and bolstered the morale and attitudes of the prisoners and gave them some reassurance that they were not forgotten.

Although the prison raid at Son Tay did not result in the rescue of any prisoners, it did actually result in getting the attention of the North Vietnamese. Almost immediately after the raid, the North Vietnamese began to consolidate all the American prisoners from about a dozen prisons to the Hoa Lo Prison in Hanoi and one other prison.

As for Jake, less than a day after the raid, he was moved to another cell with three other prisoners. Suddenly, Jake was now with other prisoners, in a cell where they were not told anything. It took a few moments for the four of them to take in the new living conditions and actually have an opportunity to talk to someone. None of the new cellmates were from Son Tay, and Jake did not yet realize it at first, but for these three, it was the first time they had been in contact with other Americans in years. It was difficult at first for him to comprehend that these three Americans had been in solitary cells, one of them for almost five years. Their excitement was understandable, but as they exchanged their capture dates of "July '65," "March '67," and "May '67," Jake felt depression, mixed with a sense of disbelief and pity—feeling sorry for them and what they had endured. Jake already had an appreciation of how bad it had been, but it was unimaginable for him to think of three, four, or five years. For the new cellmates, they expressed a sense of feeling uncertainty, waiting for the new experience to end.

The experience did not end as they remained in the cell and continued to exchange their personal information and stories. The sharpness of their minds amazed Jake, considering how long they had been isolated. The conversations continued into the evening until they fell asleep.

Although he was now sharing a cell, the influx of prisoners from the other prisons ended the days of individual cells for everyone, except in cases when the cells were used for punishment and isolation. The next day, Jake and his cellmates were still in disbelief and expressed concern about what may happen next. Their concerns gradually ended as they noticed the arrival of more prisoners and saw and heard more groups of prisoners being placed together in cells.

During the next week, more prisoners were brought into the Hanoi prison and while Jake and his cellmates grew accustomed to their new environment, it was also about to change again. It turned into a prison with too many prisoners. As a result, a decision had been made to convert the prison housing and place the prisoners into larger rooms that would hold between 25 and 50 prisoners per room. As the new prisoners arrived, the process began and the rooms filled up. The prisoners were assigned to rooms numbered one, two, three, and so forth—Jake and his newfound friends ended up in room two. Once all the prisoners had arrived in Hanoi and were assigned to their rooms, a slow sense of normalcy started to take over. Chains of command were established in each of the rooms, and a sense of order and hopefulness took hold.

With a new environment in the Hanoi prison, Jake realized that more so for the other prisoners than for himself that there were a lot of changes. The biggest one was the end of single cell isolation. During the first week in the room, Jake learned that the majority of the prisoners had been kept isolated in their cells and that he was one of the rookie prisoners. Except for a few, all the other prisoners had been in captivity anywhere from one to seven years, and the adjustment for many of them was more difficult than it was for Jake.

25 December, 1970
Day 179

After the prisoners had been placed in the larger bay rooms, life at the Hanoi prison had started to take on an odd sense of a new reality and continued to do so with a few exceptions. Christmas 1970 was the first Christmas that Jake had been away from home. Alone, he may have been able to ignore it, but that appeared to be the one disadvantage of living with a large group—everyone remembered Christmas, and for most of them, it was the first one in years that they at least were with someone else and not alone.

After the Christmas and New Year's holidays, a new year of keeping track of the days began for Jake. He and the other prisoners maintained their sanity with companionship, encouragement, and hope. Over time, they were allowed to have some personal items that include receiving mail, but sometimes the Vietnamese would also take away the privileges for no apparent reason other than harassment. Since the Son Tay Raid, the Vietnamese had become concerned with creating and maintaining a positive public opinion; therefore, the prisoners were treated more fairly. On occasion, the Vietnamese brought in foreign press from countries such as France, Sweden, and a few others in the hopes of spreading positive publicity regarding the treatment of the prisoners.

Attempts to create positive publicity aside, life at Hanoi continued, including periodic interrogations accompanied by torture. There would also be the Cuban interrogators, who gained a reputation for being more sadistic without any real logic for what they were doing. Jake was fortunate and was never interrogated by any of the Cubans, but others were not so fortunate, especially the prisoners who were of Hispanic descent. The Cubans seemed to take a particular interest in them, or as told by those who were interrogated by them, more of a personal interest or hatred.

For Jake and the others, life at Hanoi became an uncomfortable routine that progressed one day at a time. Friendships were made along with a chain of command and extensive efforts by the prisoners to keep account of each other and to care for each other. As time passed, some prisoners became ill, a few died, and others had difficulties coping with their captivity. Life at the Hanoi Hilton became what seemed like an endless wait for the next day, always with thoughts of going home.

CHAPTER 9

UNWANTED GUEST

EIGHTEEN MONTHS LATER

8 July, 1972

Day 743

A year and a half after arriving at Hanoi, Jake and the others still waited. Another day at Hanoi filled with what had been mostly the same routines and conversations of speculation filled the days. During midafternoon, an unscheduled disruption to the day occurred when Jake and the other prisoners from his room were called out to the courtyard. This was the second group of prisoners that had been brought out so far. The break in the routine caused many to speculate about what could've been going on, and most of them wanted to believe that this could the day they were waiting for, waiting to be told they would be getting sent home. At least, that was their hope.

Once the prisoners had been assembled, the prison commander and a few political officers entered the courtyard. The prisoners took notice and without any formal command stood to attention. The prison commander watched the prisoners move to attention. Although the act by the prisoners pleased the prison commander and fed into his authority, the prisoners did it simply as a demonstration that they were still soldiers and still operated, even in prison, as part of a military unit and that they had a chain of command. The prison officials were aware of the practice and viewed it as having control over the prisoners. The practice also helped the prisoners maintain their own sense of control and inspired morale.

The prison commander proceeded to tell them the purpose of the assembly and went on to make a politically directed announcement concerning the visit of the American movie actress named Jane Fonda. As the commander spoke, the significance of this announcement became clear to the prisoners as they were told that the visit by the young actress was to show support for North Vietnam and the socialist and communist struggle. The prisoners were then further distressed by the commander's instructions that basically demanded volunteers to meet with the actress during her visit.

The prisoners maintained discipline during the camp commander's speech. They did not make any comments that could be heard by the guards or commander—most kept their thoughts to themselves. They patiently waited for the commander to complete his speech, at which time he then asked for volunteers. His first request was ignored, as was his second and third requests. Not one of prisoners raised his hand to volunteer, which made the commander furious as he looked at his political officers. Then the senior-ranking American officer, or SRO, spoke out and told the camp commander that there would not be any volunteers from room number two.

The camp commander yelled at his staff and the guards as he stormed off the courtyard. What was not known at this point was that the previous group had also refused to volunteer, and the second group's refusal just added to the prison commander's frustrations. It was obvious by their expressions that the guards and staff were not happy, and whatever the camp commander said to them had upset them. One of the prisoners whispered that the commander told them that he was going to send all of them back out to the war. "I'll go back," another voice jokingly said, generating some quiet laughter.

After the SRO made his statement, two of the guards immediately took him away and the rest of the guards began to yell at the prisoners as they started the process of sending them back inside. As they got back to the room, the guards yelled and pushed the prisoners through the doorway. Jake and three of his friends, Gary, Hal, and John, gathered around Jake's bunk. After everyone was back in the room and the door closed, there was initially mostly silence as concern for the SRO temporarily took over, that was until Hal broke the silence.

"So, who's Jane Fonda?"

The comment generated spontaneous laughter through-out the room. "Damn, you've been here too long," John told Hal, his words getting a few more laughs.

After the laughter quieted down, Hal looked at them smil-ing, but also serious, and then said, "I still don't know who Jane Fonda is."

"Henry Fonda's daughter, dipstick," John finally said.

John's comment about Hal being there too long was not too far off. Hal McConnell was not typical of the majority of the prisoners. Most of the prisoners were pilots from the Air Force, Navy, and some Army. There were also some civilian prisoners, but Hal was neither of these. He was a master ser-geant in the Army Special Forces, a Green Beret. At the time he was captured, he had already been in the Army sixteen years. He had been sent to Vietnam in an advisory role in 1962 and was captured in late 1964.

The thought that Hal had been a prisoner since 1964 de-pressed Jake for several reasons. One was that Hal reminded Jake of the other Special Forces Sergeant, Brad, whom he had met in the jungle. They both seemed to have the same de-meanor, personalities, and view of why they were in Vietnam. The other reason was that since first meeting Hal two years earlier, Hal had been a prisoner almost eight years. By com-parison, Jake had only been in prison two years, and it already felt like an eternity, so it was difficult to imagine staying in the prison for eight years.

The other two cellmate friends of Jake were John Freely and Garry Shreve. John was the Navy man in the group, a pilot. He was shot down in 1969 and had been a prisoner for three years. The third cellmate's story was a little different. Gary Shreve was one of several civilians held prisoner. He had been employed by the State Department, and his job was in the agriculture field helping local farmers. Unfortunately, being a civilian did not help Gary when he was captured in 1967. Gary's situation was unique in that even when he met Jake and the other prisoners, they all assumed he was CIA. When Gary told them his story, they still suspected he was, which was also what the North Vietnamese had believed and apparently still did.

Throughout the rest of the day, the remainder of the prisoners from the other rooms went through the same process of being taken to the courtyard and refusing to volunteer. By the end of the day, all of the prisoners had been requested by the prison commander to volunteer to meet the actress, and all had refused except three. The three volunteers did not ease the prison commander's anger, who was hoping to be able to parade a large group of prisoners in front of the actress and the accompanying press corps. Later in the day, the quiet conversations in the room were interrupted by the sound of guards at the door. The guards entered the room, stopped for a moment, looked around, and then called out Gary's name.

Gary stood up and walked toward the guards who grabbed him and roughly took him out of the room.

"It's not right," Jake muttered and got some acknowledgments from the room as silence took over.

John and Hal sat on the bunk across from Jake. Hal asked Jake if he knew the story about Gary's capture. Although Jake and John had known Gary a few years, neither of them had ever heard his whole story. Hal made a brief inside joke about maybe he didn't tell them because they were officers, which got a needed smile and broke the tension.

Hal pointed out that Gary's trek to prison was similar in many ways to the rest of them, being traipsed through the jungle for about a month until arriving at a prison. But Gary was unlike them in that he was a civilian, and although he worked for the government as an employee for the State Department, he was not involved in the fighting. Gary was an agricultural specialist working with local governments and farmers, something he loved doing. On the day of his capture, being a civilian did not stop the Viet Cong from taking him and two other civilians in his group. Another difference Hal pointed out was that one of the others in the group was a woman, which got closer attention from Jake, John, and some of the others. Gary had told them how his captors tired of the woman, and after about a week in the jungle, the woman got food poisoning, which ended up killing her within a few days.

Gary sincerely believed that his captors had purposely poisoned her, and with that reason, his hatred for the Vietnamese was forever embedded in his attitude.

During the next few days, the Vietnamese were still upset with the prisoners for not volunteering to meet the actress, and there were many attempts to get them to agree, but with little success. Several prisoners who refused were beaten, and when Gary was returned to the room three days later, it was obvious that he too, had been beaten. Fortunately, Jake, Hal, nor John had been taken from the room, although they were yelled at daily by the political officers and guards and for several days feared that it was a matter of time before it was their turn to be taken.

Eventually the guards did come, however, Jake was the only one they took out. The Vietnamese already had three prisoners who had voluntarily agreed to speak with the actress, and Jake was just one of about a dozen others the Vietnamese selected for the meeting and press conference. In the meantime, Jake was not sure what was going on or where they were going to be taken. Before they left the prison, the Vietnamese gave them new uniforms to wear. Then they were taken through the prison kitchen area out the back where they loaded up in a covered truck and left the prison. In the back of the truck, the prisoners talked about what was going on. Some were hopeful that this was a meeting with some kind of delegation while others brought up the volunteer situation and that maybe they were being taken to meet the actress.

The truck ride lasted only about five minutes, and when the truck stopped, Jake and the others got out and were taken inside a building. A political officer gave them instructions about how to conduct themselves when the American actress and others with her were in the room. With the instructions, the questions were answered, and they now knew they were there for show. It also immediately became clear to Jake and the other prisoners that they were selected for the meeting simply because of their looks, specifically because they had a healthier appearance than most of the other prisoners.

During the days that led up to the meeting, discussions and opinions for the most part branded the actress a traitor. Ironically her visit inspired the prisoners through a newly acquired disdain and hatred for her, which in turn gave some of them the will to persevere. After years of imprisonment, the situation with the actress instilled and reminded Jake and many of the other prisoners about their country, the Cold War facts that they were already familiar with, and a sense of reassurance and justification for why they were in Vietnam.

During the visit by the actress, Jake had the opportunity to actually see Fonda as she talked in length with two of the three prisoners who volunteered to speak with her. The actress had also talked briefly, or rather talked at, Jake and the others as she was ushered through the interview room, but any actual interaction did not occur. Jake could not help but notice, and even in his mind attempted to make light of the situation as he realized that even though Fonda was there for political purposes, she was treated like a celebrity. The Vietnamese surrounded her, catered to her, took pictures, and presented an appearance that they were humane captors. From Jake's perspective, Fonda appeared to be soaking up the attention and seemed to believe what her North Vietnamese host had presented to her.

For just a few moments, Jake found some humor in the spectacle, but only for a moment as he realized what was actually happening. He had to remind himself about how some of the other prisoners had been treated for refusing to participate in the visit. Within a few minutes, he had gone from trying to make light of the situation to a feeling of hatred for Fonda and rationalized that what she had done was treasonous. Jake's agitation had started to build, and he found it difficult to control himself.

Another prisoner who stood next to him noticed Jake's agitation and quietly and sternly whispered to him, "Don't forget about the guys back at the Hilton." The reminder quickly pulled Jake back in focus and in control of his temper. It also got him thinking about the others and showed him that he was still a rookie. His impulse to lose his temper thwarted by another prisoner inspired Jake to have discipline like the others, which also made him wonder how they persevered, given everything they had gone through.

The visit, at least the part that Jake and the others had participated in, lasted about 45 minutes. After everyone left the room, they were taken back outside to the truck and then on the five-minute ride back to the prison. It may have been an oversight, but Jake and the others kept the new uniforms and were taken back to their rooms. Of course, everyone was interested in the event and wanted to hear about what happened. Jake retold the events of the visit and also included the instance of almost losing his temper. He told them about how two of the volunteers had talked to the actress and how they seemed to play their roles well. The room commander made a hate-felt emotional remark about the volunteers, stating that they had disobeyed orders, and that their actions would be remembered when everyone went home. Jake also dispelled rumors about Fonda taking notes passed by the prisoners and turning them over to prison officials. The consensus of Jake and the other prisoners that were at the meeting was that Fonda had no idea what she was doing, and was being guided. They also agreed her actions were wrong, and couldn't help but have feelings of hatred toward her.

With the visit over, life at the Hanoi Prison continued. While the subject of the visit would be a topic of conversation for some, most everyone else wanted to try to forget about the actress and go on with prison life. This initial attempt was short-lived, and the visit was resurrected within a few weeks.

22 August, 1972
Day 785

The prisoners were assembled at various locations in the prison, and the public address system was turned on for a radio broadcast. Just like they had wished a month earlier, many of the prisoners were hopeful that this was the day when they would be told they were going home. Again their hopes were shot down and delayed when the radio broadcast going out over Hanoi public radio and the prison public address system began.

> *"This is Jane Fonda. During my two-week visit in the Democratic Republic of Vietnam, I've had the opportunity to visit a great many places and speak to a large number of people from all walks of life..."*

The radio address was long and the ability for everyone either to focus on it or even remember it in its totality was difficult. There were parts that stood out and parts that totally depressed many of the prisoners. For others, including Jake, it also reaffirmed their will to survive. The visit by the actress, the subsequent radio broadcast, and visits by other activists in some ways had been a morale booster and an educational experience. Many even considered that the actress may have been brainwashed, captured, or that it may have even been an imposter posing for propaganda reasons. Jake and many of the other prisoners, however, chose to believe that she was a traitor.

When the broadcast was over and the prisoners returned to their rooms, intense conversations took place concerning the broadcast, but conversations aside, life at the prison returned to and continued in its routines. Although the visit by the actress had little real or immediate effect on Jake, he could have never imagined that the visit would ultimately have a tremendous impact on his life not too far in the future.

CHAPTER 10

CHRISTMAS BOMBINGS

18 December, 1972

Day 903

The daily routine during the previous months at the Hanoi Hilton had continued to be harsh and long drawn-out misery. What had momentarily developed into a little more relaxed existence in the Hanoi prison abruptly changed on the evening of December 18. A massive bombing campaign on Hanoi began, which generated a thunderous shock wave and lit up the Hanoi sky. The prisoners were drawn to the cramped window areas and looked out at the night sky; many were enthusiastic about the bombing. Others, however, questioned why there was a bombing at all. The prisoners had already known about the peace talks and the efforts that had been made to end the war and get them released. They had already been visited by several international organizations, and a more relaxed environment had taken over inside the prison. The prisoners knew and believed that it was just a matter of time before they would be released to go home.

As evening passed, the prisoners became aware that it was not just another bombing. Normally a bombing could be heard or seen for a few seconds, a minute or two at most, and then it would be over, but this was different. The bombing didn't stop and although there would be a break, it soon started up again. Because many of the prisoners were pilots, they were capable of estimating the size of the bombs and realized that it was a major effort, likely involving hundreds of aircraft. As the bombing continued, the prisoners' discussions changed as they realized the massive damage that had been taking place, redirecting their attention from the bombing to concerns about retaliation and wondering about what happened to the peace talks and their hopes of being released.

The next day, December 19, the bombing continued to be the topic of discussion until that night when the bombing started again and continued throughout the night. Every day and every night, hundreds of B52 bombers and fighter aircraft descended on the Hanoi region. The bombings continued through December 23 and stopped for eighteen hours over Christmas, but they started up again for another four days until it finally ended on December 29.

The concerns of the prisoners grew during the eleven days of the bombing; however, the concerns were also countered by the sudden addition of over thirty new prisoners who had been shot down during the attack. The arrival of a large group of new prisoners initially raised questions about how badly the campaign must have gone, but as the new prisoners came in each day and told everyone what they knew about the operation and its magnitude, morale and spirits grew. When the bombing started, Jake and everyone else had no idea how big a bombing operation it was or that it was said to be the single biggest bombing campaign of the war consisting of hundreds of sorties. When the bombing finally stopped, the spirits of the prisoners were lifted as they assumed the peace talks would resume.

While the attitudes of the prisoners were uplifted, the attitudes of the North Vietnamese were something else. The initial death count in Hanoi was in the hundreds and speculation was in the thousands. The extensive damage and death toll incensed many of the prison staff and guards and although the bombing had stopped, the rescue attempts of those trapped in the rubble in Hanoi continued for weeks.

11 January, 1973
Day 927

A few weeks after what became known as the Christmas bombing and six months after the visit to Hanoi by Fonda, daily life continued to drag on, and for Jake and his friends, anticipation had become the activity. Although the Christmas bombing of Hanoi had contributed to bringing the North Vietnamese back to the negotiating table at the Paris Peace Talks, in Hanoi the bombing was still the topic for many of the prison guards and political officers who took it personally and expressed an increased hatred for the Americans. While tensions within the prison increased, there was an added exception to the routine with the increased rumors and encouraging information the prisoners received from various visiting organizations. This influx of information helped counter some of the efforts of the prison officials and guards to demoralize the prisoners.

In the midafternoon of another day in the confines of the Hanoi Hilton, the prisoners went about their daily routines, which consisted mostly of waiting. The routine of life at the Hanoi prison had developed at times into something like a cruel joke. While the rumors and information circulated about the Paris Peace Talks and an end to the war, many of the Vietnamese continued to be harsh, and unknown to their superiors, even increased their mistreatment of some of the prisoners when they could get away with it.

On the other hand, some of the Vietnamese relaxed their treatment and had grown weary of what had been an endless war, a war that had dated back to the World War II era and had continued with the French and then with the United States. The war had been going on before most of them were born and became a kind of normalcy. The atmosphere inside the prison had reached to a point where Jake could easily recognize and read the faces of the guards, faces that plainly expressed the guards' feelings.

The sporadic taunting by some of the intelligence officers and guards overshadowed the occasional improved treatment. Although things moved ahead, it didn't stop some of the guards and political officers from the psychological harassment of some of the prisoners, including Jake. At times threats were made that they would not be released when the war ended, and reinforced by reminding them about French prisoners who were still in Vietnamese prisons.

Jake and the others ignored the Vietnamese stories and threats and maintained a positive outlook; however, what Jake and the other prisoners didn't know was that the stories they had been told about the French may in fact have been true. It was known that the Vietnamese had kept French prisoners after the French surrendered and left Vietnam in 1954, and although the stories were not confirmed, it was also rumored and reported that North Vietnam had released about a dozen French prisoners in 1971 after 16 years in captivity. Had Jake and the others known any of this information, or chose to believe it when they were told about it, their optimism would certainly have diminished.

Midafternoon of January 11 had Jake sitting on his bed talking with his friends when one of the prison guards, Sergeant Phan, came into the room and yelled out for Jacob

Walden. Fortunately for Jake, Sergeant Phan was one of the guards who had not been abusive toward the prisoners. They considered him to be fair. The calling out for Jake was almost not heard at first or even noticed over the conversations of the prisoners. "See you guys later," Jake told his friends as he got up and started to walk toward the door. As Jake exited the room, he met Sergeant Phan and then followed him down the hallway.

Meanwhile, Hal, John, Gary, and a few other prisoners sat and continued their conversations and did not take Jake's leaving too seriously. Prisoners were routinely called away, taken across the courtyard for questioning, and then returned to their rooms. While Hal and John sat, Gary got up and went over to the window.

"What?" John asked Gary.

"Just curious," a not too convincing and concerned Gary told him.

Gary's concern got the attention of both John and Hal as he continued to look out the window, watching for Jake to be taken across the courtyard.

"So, is he over there yet?" Hal asked.

Gary shook his head "no" as he kept watching. A few more minutes went by and Jake still had not been taken across the courtyard.

Jake had not been taken out of the building; instead, Sergeant Phan had escorted Jake down a series of long hallways in the same building. They turned right and walked for about a minute down a long hallway where at the end there was a room that Sergeant Phan motioned to Jake to enter. He immediately recognized the room, an interrogation room that had been given the nickname Blue Room.

In broken English, Sergeant Phan told Jake to sit and wait in the chair positioned behind a table that faced the door. An immediate sense of anxiety overcame Jake because he already knew what the room had been used for. He maintained his composure as he sat down in the chair and looked around.

Jake tried to focus his attention out of the room. The table and chair were centered in the small room, and he could see directly down the long hallway. There was another chair on the other side of the table, and in the rear right corner of the ceiling was the suspension hook that had been extensively used as a torture device for hanging prisoners by their arms. Jake had firsthand knowledge of this torture method from his first weeks at Hanoi and at Son Tay and hoped and prayed that he was not in for that again.

After Sergeant Phan left the room and stood outside the open door, it became increasingly difficult for Jake not to worry as he tried his best to think about something else, something positive, and to control his anxiety as he waited. He could not help but think about why he had been brought to the interrogation room and rationalized, and hoped, that maybe it could be part of a debriefing process in preparation for release. As far as he knew, no one had been brought to the Blue Room in quite a while, and so he started to think that the room may just be used for more interviews. He thought of many alternate possibilities instead of the possibility of an interrogation session.

The short five-minute wait seemed very long as he sat in the chair looking out the door down the hallway. The structure of the cellblock buildings with its long hallways, open windows, and the manner in which the buildings surrounded the courtyard added to a unique and eerie sound that echoed throughout the building.

As Jake sat and waited, he began to hear the faint echoing sound of footsteps down the distant hallway. The footsteps gradually became louder as they proceeded through the hallways; however, the footsteps had a different sound when they hit the floor. With time in prison, little things like the sound of a sandal, boot, or a leather sole of a boot instead of a rubber sole made on concrete became very distinct. The sound Jake was hearing was not the sandals or the type of boot normally worn by the Vietnamese and as the sounds of the steps came closer, two figures made the turn around the corner of the hallway and started to walk down the hallway toward Jake.

When he first saw the figures of two men, he was relieved and had a momentary smile on his face. He could tell that they were somewhat taller than the average Vietnamese and could also make out that they were Caucasian, not Vietnamese. The lighting and glare in the hallway prevented Jake from seeing clearly, but for about the next thirty seconds he experienced a rush of emotions, feeling a sense of relief and excitement as he made an initial assumption that the two people walking his way were either Americans, international aid workers, or at least someone with good intentions.

As the two figures continued to walk down the hallway toward the room, Jake's mind filled with curiosity as he waited. The unusually long minute finally came to an end as they reached the doorway of the room. They had a brief word with Sergeant Phan who then left the doorway and headed down the hallway to the other end where he would wait.

There was never any reason for Jake or anyone to have conceived of it, or even to have thought of such a possibility, and it definitely had never crossed Jake's mind that the two men at the doorway would be Russians, Soviet soldiers—a major and a sergeant.

CHAPTER 11

THE RUSSIAN

11 January, 1973

Day 927

As the two men came through the doorway, the relief and excitement that Jake had experienced quickly diminished as anxiety, fear, and confusion overtook him. He saw the Soviet Army uniforms, and from the point of view of the Soviets, it would have been obvious to them to see the surprise on Jake's face. They were a total surprise, and for the moment he did not understand why they were there.

In the hallway, Sergeant Phan had made the almost one-minute walk down the long hallway to the other end. The Soviet sergeant inconspicuously made his way to the back of the room out of sight of Jake's focus as he became centered and focused on the major, who did not say anything as he placed some folders and his hat on the table. As the major slowly paced, there was silence in the room, except for the occasional sounds from the hallway and courtyard. As though it had been ironically rehearsed, when Sergeant Phan had stopped walking and took his post at the end of the hallway, the major looked down at Jake and made eye contact.

At this point, Jake didn't know what to think, and although he tried to not show it outwardly, fear overtook him as he tried to conceal his emotions. The major, however, was an experienced intelligence and interrogation officer and already knew and understood human nature and assumed without having to see it, that Jake or anyone in his situation would be somewhat scared and apprehensive. He stared at Jake in what would be considered an awkward moment of silence.

During the time Jake had been a prisoner and even in training he had heard rumors about the Soviet, Chinese, and Cuban advisors in Vietnam and had already seen the Cubans at the Hanoi prison. Years later, the rumors about Soviets, Chinese, and Cubans would be confirmed, but for Jake the rumor had just become reality as the two Soviets stood in the room. Soviet Major Youri Slakve, was an intelligence officer and trained interrogator, and although taller than the average Vietnamese, he was still a man of small stature. He did not project a friendly demeanor, nor did he display much emotion. The Soviet sergeant was a walking cliché, intimidating, standing about six-foot, several inches taller than the major and demonstrated a skill of being able to interact with him.

Jake had done a good job at trying to conceal his nervousness and sat waiting for the major to say something. After about a minute of silence, he finally spoke to Jake, and in fairly good English.

"Captain Walden, my name is Major Youri Slakve with the Soviet Intelligence Service, and you are Captain Jacob Walden, correct?"

Jake at first was reluctant for a brief moment, but the continued eye contact by the major, along with his body language and sudden change in demeanor gave Jake the impression that the major was not too threatening for the moment and just trying to make conversation. Jake also, at this point, still had no real knowledge or understanding about why the Soviets were there.

"Sir, yes, Captain Jake Walden."

"Good, good."

The major then took a seat across from Jake at the table and continued to make conversation with him.

"I understand you've been here about two and a half years now?"

"Yes, Sir, two and a half. I was at the prison in Son Tay at first for about four months before they brought me here."

The major smiled in agreement with Jake's response, and as he continued to talk, Jake had already realized that he had made a mistake by telling the major about being at Son Tay.

One of the many things taught about being a prisoner or undergoing interrogation was to give as little information as possible, even if the interrogators knew the answer, and not to volunteer information. Jake had just done more than answer the question—he had also given the answers to what could have been two or three more questions. Jake had hoped that his cooperation would be appreciated by the major with what seemed to be not too threatening of a conversation.

The major eventually moved on in his line of questioning and went back to Jake's time at Son Tay.

"Son Tay, did you know that right after they moved you from Son Tay, your Special Forces raided Son Tay? A rescue mission."

"I didn't realize," Jake slowly answered, even though he had actually heard the stories and knew about it.

"They killed about two hundred of our Vietnamese comrades and even a few of my Soviet comrades."

"I didn't know that."

"You know that you were almost rescued? You almost went home over two years ago! That must have been depressing to know you almost were rescued."

"I didn't know about that," Jake replied as he tried not to let the major get to him. He also knew and was much aware of how interrogations worked, more than he knew when he was first captured. The major's demeanor had changed and turned into a combination of not only arrogance, but also pity.

"I know what you are thinking because I know what I would be thinking if I was you. You are thinking that this major is making up a story about the Son Tay Raid, and he is just trying to upset you. Am I correct?"

Jake nodded in agreement, and likewise the major agreed as he took out some papers from his folders and placed them on the table. He opened up a newspaper article placing it on the table for Jake to look at. The article was about the Son Tay Raid and showed a cartoon caption with a prisoner saying, "Thank you for trying." Jake had mixed feelings looking at the newspaper and remembering that November night. Still, Jake wanted to disagree with the major, more on principle than anything else.

As the major continued to talk and become more authoritative, he then took out another newspaper and placed it on the table.

"We did not make up that newspaper report about Son Tay. We also did not make up this newspaper story that has a story about a Captain Jacob Walden. That is you, Captain...they have a picture of you from your graduation from the Air Force Academy and a picture of you with your American actress here in Hanoi...you see."

As the major continued talking, Jake glanced at the newspaper and was at a loss. He didn't comprehend what point the major was attempting to make.

"They also say that you are married, have a son and daughter, you are from a suburb of Kansas City, Overland Park, and you attended the Air Force Academy. It says many things about you. You know, Captain Walden, I believe this newspaper. You know why I believe this newspaper?"

"Why?" a reluctant Jake asked.

"Because we checked the information, and we know it is true, and since you never told us this information. How would we be able to make it up if you never told us?"

Jake had started to become aware of where the major was going and sensed a change in his tone.

"You know, Captain, in our country, a newspaper would never tell our enemy about our soldiers like this. An actress who betrayed our country like your actress did would be executed. I don't understand your country, Captain. You fight for a country that will do this to you? I do not understand. If your actress did not come here, and your picture was not taken, this article would have never been written, and you and I would not be having this conversation."

"I don't understand what this has to do with anything. That was six months ago," Jake said while trying to be respectful and not agitate him.

At the same time Jake was becoming more nervous. Looking at the newspaper, the major paused for a moment. He had noticed the slight change in Jake.

"That is true, it was six months ago. Our newspaper monitors only found this article last week… they have been falling behind. However, my point is that my Vietnamese comrades did not know any of these things about you, and thanks to your newspaper we now know this about you."

Not understanding the major's comments, Jake let out a spontaneous short laugh and cracked a slight smile as he replied to the major with a little arrogance in his tone.

"I don't understand. So what if you know I'm married, have children, am from Kansas City, in the Air Force, or went to the Academy? What's your point?"

Just as he finished his sentence Jake realized once again he may have just screwed up. The major became more assertive with Jake as he too cracked what could only be interpreted as the sinister smile.

"My point, Captain Walden, is that we did not know these things about you. I agree these things may not be important for us to know, but what is important to us is that we did not know that you were not a pilot." He reiterated the point and became angry as he continued. "We did not know that you were not a pilot! We did not know that you are in fact an electronics specialist. You call it a communications warfare specialist, an electronic warfare officer. ECW is the short name for it, I believe. We did not know that you were a crewmember of an electronic warfare airplane that was shot down. To us, this is very important information that you did not tell Major Hung! You allowed my comrades to believe that you were a pilot, and now because you did not tell Major Hung that, the sergeant and I have been sent here."

The major paused.

"Now do you understand, Captain Walden?"

Jake did not reply, and a sudden chill came over him as he realized the truth of what the major had just told him.

It was true that Jake was not a pilot. The capture of an electronic warfare officer would have been a valuable asset for the North Vietnamese and the Soviet Union. The fact that Jake was able to conceal his true specialty for over two and a half years was an embarrassment for the North Vietnamese and the Soviets and had caused some unwanted attention for Jake.

As Jake saw the change in the major's demeanor, he became concerned and tried to ignore him. The major got up from his chair and paced around the room as he continued to talk. While Jake focused on not making any more eye contact with the major, he also stayed aware of where he was in the room.

"You know, Captain Walden, it must be very distressful for you, knowing that sometime soon you Americans will be going home. But that's *if* these Vietnamese let all of you go home. You know we have questions for you, questions that you will answer, Captain." The major was silent for about thirty seconds as he continued pacing and then, attempted to make a joke with the cliché, "We can make you talk.

"Your American movies always say that, don't they? But I will tell you, Captain Walden, we don't have to make you talk. Sometimes our prisoners want to talk. We have ways. One is time, Captain, time. I just had the pleasure to spend some time last week with a young French lieutenant, although he is not that young anymore for a lieutenant. He's been with us since, I think it was, 1954. He's always happy to see me and talk. Although I'm not supposed to have emotions, I cannot help but feel pity when I see him."

The major paused and seemed to have a silent emotional moment of pity while he talked about the Frenchman. But the look on his face was somewhat confusing to Jake, since the look could just as well have been one of a memory that someone had when they remembered something that they enjoyed or missed. The major then went back into his interrogator mode.

"You know, if it will help you feel better, I will tell you about the Vietnamese, about when they catch you, they treat all of you the same. It does not matter what you tell them, they will still beat you and treat you the way they did when you were first captured—that is their procedure, and to them you are not important. You're not special to them—you are just another criminal." He paused again, allowing what he had said to sink in. "Now on the other hand, Captain, if I'm here to see you, you can be assured that is another story. If I'm here to see you, you are important, and you are special."

As Jake sat in the chair he looked straight ahead into the hallway as the major continued to pace slowly around the room. His demeanor continued to change and became more threatening and tense. Jake had become aware of the sergeant who had quietly walked up behind him. As the major stopped speaking, he arrived at the doorway and slowly closed the interrogation room door. Sergeant Phan, standing at the far end of the hallway, noticed the major closing the door, but did not think much of it. For about the next two or three minutes, Sergeant Phan stood idly in the hallway smoking a cigarette, everything quiet except for the birds outside, outside, conversations heard from the courtyard, and the faint sounds of the city.

The sudden, horrific scream that echoed down the hallway from the interrogation room caused the cigarette to fall from Phan's lips. Even for the veteran, Sergeant Phan, the scream had startled and shaken him, giving him goose bumps and an instant cold sweat. Sergeant Phan remained frozen for a moment, not really knowing what to do until another scream. Sergeant Phan quickly gained his composure and ran out of the building. Jake's scream had been heard in the courtyard and faintly in some of the prisoner rooms too. As Sergeant Phan ran out of the building, he saw other guards doing their best to make the prisoners go back to work and ignore the screams that came from the Blue Room.

At the window in room two, a prisoner saw Phan run across the courtyard and yelled out, "Something's happening!"

Jake's cellmates rushed to the window and door to see. They also heard yelling by other prisoners in the other prisoner rooms and within a few moments the word spread throughout the prison about the screaming.

Sergeant Phan quickly made his way across the courtyard to the headquarters building where the prison commander, Colonel Minh, was sitting at his desk listening to Captain Phuc going over some prison issues. They heard voices outside the office, which drew their attention to the door where Sergeant Phan came busting in, out of breath and with a scared look on his face. The colonel at first jumped up from his seat and angrily yelled at the sergeant for the disruption, but he quickly saw the expression on the sergeant's face as Sergeant Phan tried to catch his breath when the colonel asked him what was wrong.

"The Russian! He's doing something to the prisoner!"

"What?"

"I've never heard anyone scream like that, never! We've never made any of them scream like that."

The statement by Sergeant Phan caused the colonel and captain to head immediately to the door. Sergeant Phan got out of their way and then followed. As they left the office, the captain yelled at the colonel's assistant to call for guards and send them over to the interrogation room. He also told him to sound the riot alarm.

As the colonel, captain, and sergeant ran out of the head-quarters building, John, Hal, and other prisoners saw them running across the courtyard and became even more concerned. Noticing the prisoners had stopped working and some of them were arguing with the guards, the captain yelled at the guards to take everyone back to their cells.

As the colonel, captain, and Sergeant Phan entered the building about a dozen guards exited another building at the far end of the courtyard and ran toward the cellblock while narration by one of the prisoners at the windows kept the prisoners updated on the activities. When the colonel reached about halfway down the hallway toward the interrogation room, Jake let out another scream, just as gut-wrenching as the first one heard by Sergeant Phan and several others heard during the five minutes it had taken for them to get there. The sound of the screams startled the colonel and caused him to speed up his approach to the interrogation room.

When the colonel reached the room he immediately entered, followed by the captain and Sergeant Phan.

As they entered the room, a dozen guards had turned the corner at the far end of the hallway and run toward the room. The sound of the colonel's entrance stopped Major Slakve in mid-swing with a small bamboo stick toward Jake's bound feet, which were dripping blood. The major angrily turned toward the door, saw the colonel and threw the bloody stick on the desk. An angry colonel immediately noticed that he had a look on his face, a glare, one similar to enjoyment with what he had been doing. The colonel was distressed at the sight of Jake suspended from the ceiling, and although the technique of suspension was also the one used by the Vietnamese, the colonel, just like Sergeant Phan, had never heard screams like that. He was not sure what else the major had done to Jake, but he saw what was obvious.

Jake's hands and elbows had been tied behind his back and he was suspended from the ceiling hook that held him by a rope around his elbows. His feet were also tied together, his sandals had been taken off, and his feet were bleeding. Jake's trousers were pulled down around his thighs and two black wires were leading from his genital area to a small hand-cranked telephone sitting on the desk.

"What is it, Colonel?" the major calmly asked in English.

"What are you doing?" a not-so-calm Colonel Minh yelled at the major.

"I'm questioning the prisoner!"

"How dare you! How dare you do this in my prison! We cannot do this, the war is almost over, and we are under orders to stop this."

As the colonel angrily continued to chastise the major, Captain Phuc directed the guards to take Jake down.

"You jeopardize everything! You already have approval to take him with you and you jeopardize everything so you can do what? What?"

"He is my prisoner!" the major sarcastically told the colonel.

"No, Major! He is still my prisoner. If you are going to take him with you, then take him, but you are not doing this. The prisoner will be taken to the infirmary, and tonight he will be put in an ambulance, and you will take him to the air base with you, and you will leave my prison."

The major became very arrogant, but the colonel maintained control over the conversation and even threatened the major.

"If you say so, Colonel."

"Yes, Major, I do say so, unless you would like to stay here. I can arrange that; I can call Colonel Kiesskof and tell him what you have done, and I am sure he would not approve. You were only supposed to transport the prisoner, nothing else, Major, nothing else!"

As the guards took Jake out of the room into the hallway, the intuitive Soviet sergeant slightly inserted himself between the continued verbal back and forth between the colonel and major and handed the major his hat and folders. The colonel saw exactly what the sergeant was doing. Sensing the major's temper, the sergeant tactfully stopped the major from causing more problems. Jake was in extreme pain and unable to stand or walk when the guards took him out to the hallway. The guards laid Jake down on the floor and waited for another guard with a stretcher, and as the Soviet major and sergeant walked down the hallway the echoing yelling of upset prisoners could be heard throughout the prison.

Through the windows, the prisoners saw the guards in their riot formations entering the cellblocks; however, there was still no sign of Jake, as he was being taken to the infirmary out of sight of the prisoners. Half an hour later, Colonel Minh was in his office and on the telephone with Colonel Kiesskof, in Moscow, telling him about the incident with Major Slakve. Colonel Kiesskof assured him that upon return to the Soviet Union, Major Slakve would be disciplined for his conduct and would never return to Vietnam.

CHAPTER 12

GOODBYE HANOI

11 January, 1973

Day 927

At 2100 hours in the Hanoi prison, Major Slakve smoked a cigarette as he stood by a side door of the hospital where an ambulance was parked with the engine running. A guard came out through the door, walked over to the ambulance, and opened the back door. The guard then went back inside the building and a minute later came back out with another guard carrying a stretcher with Jake on it. They placed him inside the ambulance, closed the door, and then drove off. The major got into another military vehicle, which then drove off following the ambulance out of the prison compound.

HANOI AIR BASE
2130 Hours

The ambulance drove onto the airfield and pulled up to the back of a Soviet—Antonov AN-22 turboprop—transport aircraft. The major and the sergeant got out of their vehicle and walked toward the end of the rear ramp of the aircraft where they were greeted by the crew chief. The Vietnamese guards helped Jake out of the ambulance and then helped him walk to the ramp. Jake could barely walk, but managed to make it up the ramp, grimacing in pain with every step. The crew chief was initially startled when he saw Jake's condition, and noticed the bruised face, badly bloodshot left eye, and the difficulty he had walking. The crew chief was not the only one who noticed Jake as he approached the ramp. Sitting around the ramp area of the aircraft were eight Soviet soldiers who were also taking the flight. They talked among themselves as the major, with a tone of arrogance, told the crew chief to watch the American prisoner.

Before the crew chief could give a response, the major turned away and started to walk up the ramp where his attention was then drawn to a Soviet soldier blocking his way.

"You don't salute officers anymore?" the major yelled out as he glanced around the aircraft looking at the other soldiers.

The sitting soldier—who was in his thirties, wearing a combat uniform, and did not have any visible rank insignia—ignored the major. The other soldiers also ignored the major and projected a seasoned and standoffish element of confidence. When the major started to yell again, one of the other soldiers got up.

"Move," the second soldier told the first as he slapped him on his shoulder and approached the major.

"I apologize for my comrades' behavior, Major. I am Sergeant Kiev, 22nd Spetsnaz. I am very sorry for what has happened."

The major gave Sergeant Kiev a nod, acknowledging the apology, but his attitude changed instantly when Sergeant Kiev said Spetsnaz—Soviet Special Forces—during the introduction. While the sergeant talked to the major, he noticed that none of the soldiers were wearing any rank or unit insignia, and all were older than the typical Soviet soldier. The major knew that the Soviet Special Forces were a well-known elite unit and not someone he or anyone wanted to confront.

"We will watch your prisoner. Since we were rude and unprofessional, we will guard your prisoner for you. We insist, Major," Sergeant Kiev told the Major as he motioned toward him to move to the front of the aircraft.

"Good, good," the major said as he hesitantly accepted—detecting that even though Sergeant Kiev was offering, his tone did not sound like refusing was an option. The major and his sergeant walked up to the front of the aircraft while two more soldiers moved over to the ramp toward Jake and helped him get to a seat.

As the aircraft prepared for takeoff, a few of the soldiers talked among themselves, and although they were speaking in Russian, it was obvious to Jake that he was the topic of their conversations. He found it odd their conversation about him seemed sympathetic, and he could definitely tell from their tone and manner that they were being condescending toward the major.

After Jake was seated, the ramp of the aircraft closed and a few minutes later, the aircraft took off. Just afterward, two of the soldiers along with the aircraft crew chief came over to Jake. One of the soldiers was a medic who began to examine him, being cautious not to alert the major to what they were doing. Jake occasionally glanced around but didn't say anything. The medic worked inconspicuously, and with the help of some of the others examined Jake.

During the exam, they were distressed by Jake's condition. Besides the cuts on his feet and the other visible injuries, when they removed his shirt they saw extensive bruising on his arms from where the ropes had suspended him from the ceiling. He also had bruising and lacerations all over his back, chest, and stomach area. The medic and the others tended to him and dressed his wounds. While they worked on Jake, they talked angrily about the major and what they called "his kind." The Spetsnaz soldiers did not care for the major, his line of work, or what he had done to Jake. Although they were Cold

War enemies, the soldiers did not condone the condition of Jake and the obvious brutality that had been committed.

As they continued to work on Jake, they were infuriated when they saw that his legs had bruising and cuts just like the rest of his body, he had more open bloody sores, burnt areas, and scorched hair on his testicles, which had been caused by the attachment of the electrical wires—they reluctantly held in their anger.

About an hour into the flight, the medic had finished treating Jake, and then with the help of the crew chief laid him down on the seats of the aircraft.

"You sleep, sleep," the crew chief said in broken English.

Jake was reluctant. Although a part of him wanted to sleep, he was still too frightened to take a chance. The brutal treatment at the hand of the major and the previous treatment by the Vietnamese had erased any sense of trust, and the apparent compassion of the crew chief and Soviet soldiers had only confused him even more and made him wonder if there was some other reason or hidden agenda for their help. Although Jake was skeptical of their motives, he noticed that they did seem sincere. He didn't understand Russian, but he could tell in their continued conversations that he was the topic and that they did not care at all for the major.

The motion of the aircraft, lying down, and his exhaustive condition caused from his torture caught up with him, and against his own wishes, he almost immediately fell asleep. Some of the soldiers also slept while others continued to have conversations concerning him and the major while they kept watch over Jake—positioning themselves where the major could not have a view of him—while he slept. Although it was brief, for the first time in a long time, Jake experienced a deep sleep and was unaware of his situation. The motion of the airplane was comforting and something different from what had become the normal Hanoi prison environment. He was briefly able to dream of things not revolving around prison life.

Five hours into the flight, the crew chief shook Jake's shoulder and woke him up. Jake opened his eyes, momentarily confused and not aware of his surroundings.

"Stay, stay," the crew said and motioned with his hands as he sat up in the seat.

When Jake sat up and gained his composure, the crew chief handed Jake some food. He was appreciative and hungry, but he was also still confused about his situation as he took the food from the crew chief and gave him a nod of thanks.

12 January, 1973
Day 928

Shortly after eating, Jake had lain back down and fell asleep again, and slept the remainder of the flight and even during the landing. After the aircraft had taxied and came to a stop, he was shaken and woken up by one of the Spetsnaz soldiers. He was then helped up and saw that the ramp of the airplane has already been opened. He very quickly felt the cold weather, a sharp contrast to the tropical climate of Vietnam. Jake was guided to the ramp where he waited along with the Spetsnaz soldiers, most of whom were standing behind him, blocking Major Slakve from getting near him or being able to exit the aircraft.

The crew chief instructed everyone to wait for the arrival of the processing team before exiting the aircraft. The impatient major waited a few moments behind the soldiers and then in a somewhat authoritative voice yelled out to let him pass. He was ignored and again yelled out, which got him a sarcastic reply from one of the soldiers: "Don't worry, he's not going anywhere," which was followed by a few laughs. The agitated major then placed one of his hands on the shoulder of the Spetsnaz soldier standing immediately in front of him. His action got an immediate and instant unexpected result. As quickly as the major placed his hand on the soldier, he took control and rapidly turned around toward the major and made instant eye contact.

"What is your name, Major?"

The man's demeanor, age, and deep authoritative voice got the major's attention. His face was what could be called battle worn, showing little or no expression and the tint of steel blue eyes that stared right through a person. He had no idea who the soldier was, or if he was a low-ranking enlisted soldier or a general, but one thing was sure, the man was intimidating, so intimidating that he did not respond. The man repeated his question, and the major finally responded to the man who was staring a hole through him.

"Major Slakve, Sir!"

"Major Slakve, my name is Lieutenant Colonel Strazinski. I must tell you, Major, my men and I do not care for you...you work for Colonel Kiesskof, correct?"

"Yes, Sir, Colonel Kiesskof is my superior."

He was now even more panicked, trying to figure out how this colonel knew this information. The colonel just stared at the major a few seconds and then turned around when he heard the sound of the others starting to walk down the ramp. The Spetsnaz officer didn't say anything else as he walked away and down the ramp. The major remained on the aircraft for a few moments allowing everyone else to exit the plane and also managed to keep an eye on Jake as he was taken by a member of the processing team and placed inside a vehicle.

Jake had already become aware of the extreme climate change, the cold, and was appreciative of a little thing like the heated vehicle. The driver and the guard with him were wearing long heavy winter coats while he still had on his Vietnam prison uniform. As the vehicle drove off the runway toward one of the buildings, Jake was still not sure where he was, but he did know that he had to be at least eight or ten hours away from Vietnam and assumed that he must be in Russia. It was still dark, but he saw the beginning of the morning twilight in the distance. When the vehicle stopped, the guard opened the back door, got out and motioned at him to follow. The guard pointed toward a door, and Jake started to walk slowly—hobbled—toward the door as he grimaced and jerked with each step.

When Jake entered what appeared to be a large administrative hall, he noticed two flags hanging on a wall. One flag was that of the Soviet Union and the other he was not sure about, but thought it was a Czech flag. His assumption was correct; the building was a processing point that had been used throughout the Cold War to process foreign prisoners who passed through to the Soviet Union. Since the early 1950s, political and war prisoners from the Korean War, Vietnam War, the Cold War, and other classified captures had traveled through this Czech processing station on their way to the U.S.S.R. Although this topic was not one Jake had any knowledge about, as neither did most people, the Cold War was an era of secrecy, and the fact that American and other prisoners had been shuttled through this Czech processing station to the Soviet Union would not become public knowledge until years later.

Jake waited at one end of the building for several hours while he was processed and his identity confirmed by a Czech Army officer. He was given new clothes including a winter coat and hat, and another meal during the wait. The soldiers from the aircraft and some other people Jake didn't recognize waited in the assembly area at the other end of the building.

At around 1100 hours, his attention was drawn to the soldiers and the others as they started to get up from their seats and stand in line by the door. The group then exited the building while Jake continued to anxiously sit and wait. The wait was only a few minutes until the Czech officer who processed him and a Czech guard came and got him, took him outside and into a vehicle that took them to the same aircraft that had brought him from Vietnam. When they arrived at the aircraft, they got out of the vehicle and the Czech officer handed a folder to the Soviet sergeant who accompanied Major Slakve. Jake did not see the major, who had already boarded and was sitting toward the front of the aircraft, and while the Czech officer and sergeant talked, the crew chief came and took Jake. He walked him up the ramp and seated him near the ramp area. A few minutes later, the sergeant boarded and went up to the front of the aircraft with the major.

The flight from Czechoslovakia to the Soviet air base in Russia would be much shorter than the first flight from Vietnam. Jake was not aware how long the flight would take and was assuming once again his next stop would be the U.S.S.R. During the flight, Jake did periodically nod off and sleep a little, but his nerves and anticipation about what was next, kept him awake most of the time. About three hours into the flight, the crew chief walked through the aircraft and signaled to everyone to prepare for landing.

CHAPTER 13

WELCOME TO
THE SOVIET UNION

12 January, 1973

Day 928

The landing went smoothly, and about five minutes later, the aircraft came to a stop. After the ramp was lowered, the crew chief motioned to Jake to get up and walk down the ramp to two awaiting Soviet prison guards. The two guards grabbed him by his arms and walked him over to a medium-sized bus. Jake got on the bus that already had about a half-dozen people on it and was seated by a guard who then shackled him to the seat. As Jake was seated, he noticed another guard getting a folder from the sergeant getting off the plane. The guard who put Jake on the bus said something to him, but he didn't understand and assumed he had been told not to talk. The other guards from outside got on the bus, and then the bus started to drive off.

As the bus made its way through the Soviet air base, Jake kept a watchful eye on the guards while he also stayed busy looking outside. He was still not sure where he was being taken and assumed he was now somewhere in Russia. A few minutes later, his assumptions were confirmed as he realized he was indeed in Russia and on what seemed to be a large Soviet air base. He also quickly became aware of the cold—the January cold of Russia was very apparent—even though the bus was heated and he was wearing the new clothes given to him in Czechoslovakia.

While the bus drove through the air base, Jake saw countless military cargo and transport-type aircraft. It seemed to take at least half an hour before the bus eventually made it to a gate and left the base. It was close to 1700 hours, and with one time zone change during the flight and the shorter days of the January winter, the sun had already begun to set. As the bus ride progressed, Jake took notice of the conversations of the guards, the flags at the air base, and the road and building signs. Everything confirmed Jake's assumptions about being in Russia.

13 January, 1973

Day 932

Shortly after midnight, the bus slid off the road and got stuck in a snowbank. After the driver and guards determined that they could not get the bus out, they radioed their headquarters and were instructed to remain in the bus for the night.

In the early morning the sun began to come up, which despite the cold, gave Jake more pleasure. Being able to watch a sunrise over snow-covered terrain just added to reviving memories of home. While the sun rose, one of the prisoners asked the guards if they could go outside. The guards agreed, and the prisoners, including Jake, exited the bus and stayed in a group under the watchful eye of the guards. During the night, the prisoners had talked among themselves, which to Jake's amazement did not seem to bother the guards. They even allowed prisoners to go outside during the night for bathroom breaks without being guarded.

Outside the bus, the prisoners were allowed to start a fire, and they talked to each other without any hint of interruption or hostility from the guards. Jake didn't know what to make of the apparent lack of security, but he had already developed an opinion that the Russian guards were not as disciplined as his Vietnamese guards. While standing outside the bus with the other prisoners, the opinion he developed about the guards had been conflicted as he noticed the countryside, and realized as he looked around in the daylight that the lack of concern by the guards may not have been an issue. All he could see was a beautiful, snow-covered, barren countryside, with nowhere to go. The thought of prisoners being allowed outside unguarded had puzzled Jake during the night, but when he saw the vast countryside and nowhere to go, he realized that escape was probably not something on the minds of any of the prisoners. It would be like being free in the Mojave Desert.

Jake didn't enter into any conversations with the other prisoners. While the Russian prisoners did not seem to be too concerned about their status, he still did not know about his future and was afraid to say anything. After some time however, one of the prisoners tried to start a conversation with Jake, but he didn't respond causing the prisoner and then another prisoner to become irritated with him. A guard noticed and yelled at the group of prisoners. "American, he's American," the guard told them in Russian. Jake understood the "American," and the prisoners then, in unison and almost comically, started to nod their heads in understanding and said some other words among themselves. At least one of the prisoners spoke some English and attempted to talk to him.

"You are American, yes?"

Jake looked at the prisoner, and then the others who were all waiting to see if Jake responded.

"Yes, I am American. My name is Jake."

The Russian prisoner then introduced himself as did the others, all extending their hands. Jake went along with the introductions. They continued to talk and relax for at least another three hours while they waited for a truck to come and pull the bus out of the snow. Jake was still amazed at the relaxed environment and how tolerant the guards seemed to be.

Around 1030 hours, one of the guards yelled out something in Russian at the prisoners that drew their attention down the road. In the distance, they could see a large tow truck escorted by Soviet military police vehicles. Without being told anything by the guards, the prisoners quickly put out the fire they had built and got back on the bus. One of the prisoners grabbed Jake by the arm and directed him to the bus. When they sat down, another one of the prisoners looked at Jake and gave him a hand sign to keep quiet. Jake quickly understood as one of the guards then got on the bus, looked around at the prisoners, checking that everyone was in place.

It was odd to Jake when the tow truck and military police arrived. The guards changed their attitudes and authoritatively ordered the prisoners off the bus. The prisoners' demeanor also changed, at least in appearance as they exited the bus in humble prisoner mode as Jake unknowingly had already began his education into the Soviet prison system.

With the prisoners helping to push, the tow truck pulled the bus out of the snow and the last part of Jake's trip was coming to a close. As the bus approached the prison, he was amazed with the size of the place. One of the prisoners whispered to Jake the name of the prison, something that sounded like Inta, but he didn't understand. He did understand from what the prisoner told him that this was the prison and it looked like nothing Jake would have imagined. It was not like an American prison, Vietnamese prison, or anything he had seen in pictures of World War II prisons. The place looked more like a large industrial plant complete with barracks, except for the guard towers, fence, and armed guard at the gates.

When the bus pulled up to a building and stopped, a guard told the prisoners to get off and line up outside. They did as they were told. As they stood in line, Jake started to look around.

"Look straight ahead," the English-speaking prisoner said sternly and with a tone of concern.

Jake was a little startled by the comment, and looked straight ahead. Another minute went by until another guard arrived and told the group to follow him. As the group moved out, the guard from the bus stopped Jake and motioned to him to get back on the bus. He hesitated and was not completely sure about the instructions, but the guard told him again and pointed to the bus.

Jake was the only prisoner on the bus as it slowly drove through the prison complex. The ride took about five minutes until they pulled up in front of a set of fenced-in buildings that looked more like a prison compared to the rest of the compound. When the bus came to a stop, the driver honked the horn. The guard and Jake got off the bus and waited. Soon another guard came out of the building and walked down the walkway toward the bus. The two guards greeted each other, and the bus guard gave a folder to the other guard.

Jake was immediately aware that this new guard was not like the other ones. He immediately yelled at Jake to move, pushing him toward the building, which caused him to fall because of the condition of his feet. The other guard said something that seemed to change the new guard's attitude toward Jake. He got up and started to walk as quickly as he was able, but his hurting feet prevented him from moving fast as he hobbled toward the building. The guard noticed Jake's difficulty in walking, and as they approached the steps, Jake painfully began to walk up them. As he neared the top step, the guard saw Jake's left shoe oozing blood and spots of blood on the steps.

Inside the building, he was taken down a hallway to a central in-processing room where the guard gave Jake's folder to a clerk who started the process of getting him checked into the prison. His picture and fingerprints were taken, and while he sat by a desk, the clerk spent about ten minutes filling out paperwork, which oddly enough he could see was written in Russian and English. The clerk said something to the waiting guard, which indicated he was finished. The guard motioned to Jake to get up, and then he began to walk his slow hobbling walk out of the office.

Jake and the guard made the slow trek through the building and eventually approached the medical ward. He saw the

Red Cross symbols on the doors ahead and assumed the guard was taking him to see a doctor.

"Where are you going?" a familiar voice—Major Slakve—yelled out in English, and then again in Russian.

They turned around to see Major Slakve at the end of the hallway. Jake knew that the guard wanted to take him to the medical ward, but the major had just stopped that as he yelled at the guard and told him to take Jake straight to his cell. The guard reluctantly did as he was told, and they headed away from the medical ward; they spent the next few minutes walking through the maze of hallways of the dim-lighted building until they arrived at his assigned cell. The guard opened the cell door, and Jake entered. The guard closed the door and locked it behind him.

Jake looked around the poorly lighted cell. *Why am I here?* He still did not know a whole lot other than that he was in a Russian prison. So far, the only conversation he had had was the limited ones with the prisoners on the bus and a few words on the plane—otherwise, nothing had been said about what was going to happen to him. The short-lived snow-filled bus ride had suddenly become a distant memory as Jake sat down against the wall in his cell.

He stared at the walls, thought about what had happened to him, and as his eyes adjusted to the light he started to see the walls more clearly and noticed etchings carved on all the walls. He got up and walked over to each wall, rubbing his hands on them and feeling the tick marks. He was able to make out that there were variations of marks representing days, weeks, and years. They were on every wall covering almost every inch of the cell. Within the etchings throughout the cell, there were also other engravings on the walls with names and dates. Some of them Russian, others American names with military rank—one a major, another a captain and dates, October 52, May 56, and June 63—Jake went into a trance as he stared at the engravings on the walls. He found over half a dozen names and dates of Americans, the oldest date being October 1947.

"That's when I knew I was never getting out of there," Jake told Ted and Charlie as he sat in his living room chair with a blank stare—his eyes watered up.

Although not teary-eyed, Charlie was upset by Jake's story. Ted did not know it yet, but Charlie had intimate knowledge about Jake's life and was instrumental in Jake's survival and current status. Ted, however, broke the somber mood, still wanting answers and not showing much concern about Jake's emotions or his fate of ending up in a Russian prison.

"But you didn't stay there forever, you're here, how did you get out...why did they take you there?"

"I had nothing to do with getting out of there. I was still in there until 1989...1989. Sixteen years, Mr. Pratt, I spent there. None of us ever thought we were ever getting out of there, ever."

"What do you mean by none of us?"

"Me and the others…I wasn't the only one there."

Ted was excited about what he heard. He didn't show any concern or feelings for the distress or sadness for Jake's experiences. Instead, he displayed a boyish excitement over the story he was hearing. He was motivated to get more of the story, and now that he learned about Jake being in a Russian prison and also learned that there were others, was in Ted's mind—the scoop of the century. Ted was eager for Jake to continue telling the story, but his apparent lack of sympathy or concern and his almost lustful zeal for the story upset both Jake and Charlie. Jake was more than irritated with Ted's impatience and was ready to stop.

"Let's finish the story, I'll help you, let's just get this done," Charlie told Jake with sincerity in his voice.

Jake took a few moments to regain his composure. "Okay, Ted, as I said, I'm at my new home in a cell in a Russian prison. That's when I knew I was never getting out of there."

As Jake stared at the wall, a wave of emotions rushed over him as he tried to deny the reality of being in a Russian cell. Within a few hours, his period of depression would be interrupted by his first visit by a visibly upset Major Slakve. While Jake didn't know for sure, it did appear that the major was in trouble with his superiors.

"Thanks to you, Captain Walden, it would appear that this is my new home too," the major told Jake with sarcasm and anger.

The major spent about an hour taunting Jake during the first visit, and told him that he was never going to get out of that Russian cell. As the days passed, the major would leave and return frequently to interrogate him, torture him, and continue to try to demoralize him. Jake quickly developed an opinion that the major's visits had become personal and that he had a personal hatred for him.

After the initial shock and continual interrogations, the days turned into weeks, and Jake came to reluctant terms with his new environment and situation. He maintained his mental strength through faith, prayer, and not letting his mind be taken from him. He remembered things other prisoners had told him in Vietnam and made it a point to keep his mind active by developing routines and even played golf, a technique many prisoners had used to help keep their minds sharp. The technique was detailed and revolved around mentally playing the actual game to include the walk through the course. Jake literally spent hours playing a round of golf or a game of chess, all in his mind. Jake even had imaginary interactions and conversation with people he knew, all with the purpose of keeping his sanity. Guards on occasion stood by the cell door and listened to Jake having conversations with himself. The fantasy life inside his mind was interrupted only by the real visits by Major Slakve, daily meals, and the once-a-week visit to the shower room.

2 September, 1973
Day 1,161

Nine months after his arrival at the Soviet prison, Jake continued to spend his days in isolation. He had been isolated in his cell except for what now had become the weekly walk to the bathhouse for a shower. He had a sleeping pad on the floor and a small table and a chair, which he was under the impression was more for the major when he visited. The unscheduled but almost weekly visits by Major Slakve had continued to be brutal, both physically and mentally.

Every time the major visited, he made Jake stand in front of the table, sometimes for ten minutes and other times for one or as many as three hours. On some occasions, he would have the guards hoist Jake up to the ceiling. There seemed to be no rhyme or reason to his interrogations as he asked questions he already knew answers to, and in Jake's mind, beat him more for pleasure than to extract information.

During his numerous visits, Major Slakve gave him various kinds of information, which Jake knew was useless and intended purely as propaganda and psychological torture.

"You know, Captain Walden, that our people in your country are watching your family, your wife, your children. During the summer they went to some place called Branson, to a what you call amusement park. They looked like they enjoyed it...even without you," he told Jake with a smile during one of the visits.

At least they're having fun, Jake thought about saying, but he didn't; instead he ignored the comment.

"The American government is in ruins, Captain; it has gotten so bad that all the Jews and blacks had to be locked up in prisons. They even executed some of them," he said during another visit.

"I didn't know about that," Jake responded, as he did to other remarks, or made similar variations of the response when the major expected an answer during his conversations.

Had it been one or three years earlier, Jake's response to the major would have been much different, confrontational or argumentative, but in just over three years as a prisoner, and nine months with the major, he had learned to interact without really interacting, and control his impulses. Although Slakve's stories were sometimes elaborate and extreme, and even supported with newspapers and magazines, Jake knew that all of the stories were of stereotypes and perceptions that the Soviets had of America. The training classes that he had been given on the Soviet Union had become vivid in his mind.

Almost everything he was told in classes about the Soviet perceptions of the United States and their interrogation techniques were true, except for what appeared to be the extra personal attention by Slakve. This knowledge was part of his saving grace, along with his faith in God. Together, the two helped Jake keep his sanity and his hope alive.

Although he had kept his faith and some resemblance of his sanity, he was at this point, pretty much broken. He still played mental golf every day, but he had settled into a routine of nothingness. He could not help but be frightened every time he heard the approach of footsteps in the hallway. He spent his days and nights in his mind, doing mental exercises, rerunning experiences and trying to keep his sanity.

Jake had adapted to the small portions of food rations he received and had transitioned to substituting his prison food for imaginary back home meals. He tried to recount movies and television shows to pass the time and tried to exercise by walking in circles or in place in his cell. He played golf and chess, but with time, he became bored and started to play other games. Bowling was a game he had played growing up and one he enjoyed more than golf. He used the limited space in his cell to go through the motions of rolling the ball down the lane. Jake thought to himself that he was getting very good at bowling, and even bowled an occasional perfect 300 game.

Mental exercising became the routine of life for Jake; however, even playing imaginary games was becoming difficult as he started to forget what he was doing or where he was in the game. Trying to keep up this system of mental exercise was difficult as he continued to lose weight and became more physically frail as the months passed.

CHAPTER 14

RAY OF HOPE

7 July, 1975
Day 1,834

It was mid-Monday morning just like most Mondays had been during the previous two and a half years in Jake's isolated cell. During that time, he had adapted and learned to tell time, keep track of the number of days in captivity, and the day of the week. The skill of tracking the days of the week was helped by external things, such as different guards who worked different days, the slight differences in meals, sounds of delivery trucks on certain days, and other sounds and events that kept his mind active and aware of the day of the week and time of day.

On Monday, July 7, Jake sat in the chair at the table in his cell. He was in deep thought as he stared down at the table and continued as best as he could to do his mind exercises, although his ability to focus had diminished over the past two and a half years. He would start to focus on one thing but soon lost track of what he was doing. His interrogations by the major were no longer memorable and had become routine, despite the continued torture. Jake's verbal interaction with Slakve was for the most part incoherent. His inability to communicate coherently had not stopped the sadistic officer from conducting his interrogation sessions, which by now, Jake had no idea what he had told the man or if he had told him anything during the interrogations.

As he sat staring at the table, he heard the faint echoing sound of footsteps walking down the hallway outside his cell. While Jake's condition had deteriorated to include loss of weight, his instinctive reactions and awareness or fear of certain things like the approaching footsteps had not diminished. He quickly got up and went to the corner of the cell, sat down with his back against the wall, and pulled his knees up to his chest, waiting and watching the door. This had become the routine for Jake, numb and fearfully awaiting the major.

As it had happened hundreds of times, the footsteps grew louder as they approached and then stopped at the door. The keys jingled and unlocked the cell, the door opened, Slakve walked in and Jake would sit huddled in the corner, but this reoccurring routine had just been disrupted. It was not Slakve or one of the guards entering the cell—and as Jake sat and looked at the door, three Soviet officers entered. Two of them were majors, each carrying stacks of personnel folders that they placed on the table. Then they looked around the cell and at Jake. The third officer was a general who also looked around and then looked at Jake, but unknown to Jake at the time, the general was the new commander of the prison.

The general said something in Russian to one of the majors—Major Divincenzo—who answered and then started to thumb through the folders. The general then looked at Jake and seemed to be a little surprised that he didn't stand up to attention when they entered the room.

"What is your name?" the general asked in Russian.

Jake did not reply, and although he had already spent almost three years in Russia, Jake had not learned Russian—he just looked at the general.

"Are you Captain Jacob Walden?" the general sternly asked.

Jake understood the Jacob Walden part of the sentence and nodded his head as he replied, almost unintelligibly, "Jacob Walden."

The other major went over to Jake and motioned for him to get up and approach the table while Divincenzo pulled Jake's folder out of his stack and began to talk with the general.

"He's an electronics officer, shot down in Vietnam in June 1970."

"How long has he been here?"

"Since January 1973."

"Why is he still here? Why isn't he on one of the work details?"

"It says he is still being interrogated."

"Interrogated for what? What else could he possibly tell us?" an upset general yelled back.

The general angrily grabbed the folder from Divincenzo and looked through it. The expression on the general's face was not a good one as he shook his head while he read the folder.

"Another one of Slakve's!"

While the general read the folder, the distant sound of approaching footsteps in the hallway was heard. With the sound of the footsteps, Jake became anxious again and although he wanted to go to the corner, he nervously remained standing by the table. His anxiousness and nervousness were obvious to the Soviet officers as the sound of the footsteps came closer. As the footsteps arrived at the door, Major Slakve entered the cell, and a frightened Jake, instinctively went back to the corner. Jake's anxiety and obvious fear of the man were immediately noticed by the general.

"Why is this prisoner still here, Major?" the general asked Slakve.

"Sir, we are still interrogating him."

"Who is *we*, Major? You? You're interrogating him?"

"Yes, Sir, but…"

"And what is it that you are trying to find out? We already know everything he has to tell us. We knew everything over two years ago, Major! I don't understand what it is you are doing with this man... or the other ones either!"

Slakve attempted to reply, but the general stopped him and then asked the other major for Major Slakve's folder. The officer looked through the stack, pulled out Major Slakve's folder and handed it to the general. There was distinct tension in the air while the general quietly looked through the folder. Major Divincenzo looked at Jake.

"Why did you run to the corner?" Jake looked confused and looked at Major Slakve as if for an answer.

"Look at *me*, Captain Walden, not Major Slakve!"

Jake looked at Major Divincenzo, but he did not give him an answer.

"How much Russian have you learned?"

"No, none."

"You've been here two and a half years and haven't learned any Russian?"

"No, the only people I see are the major and the guards."

Major Divincenzo angrily called the guard inside and questioned him, confirming Jake's explanation of only having contact with Major Slakve and a few guards. The general then slammed the folder on the table and got everyone's attention.

"Enough! Major Slakve, you're relieved of your duties as case officer for these foreign prisoners, and Major Divincenzo, you will take over these cases, review them, and get them processed as necessary, understand?"

"Yes, Sir!" Divincenzo answered while Slakve stood quietly, but visibly upset.

"Guard!"

"Sir," the guard answered as he entered.

"Take Major Slakve to my office, nowhere else, straight to my office...and if he doesn't listen to you...shoot him," the general sternly told the guard.

The guard understood and immediately motioned at Slakve to move out of the cell.

The general and the two majors left the cell—Divincenzo was last.

"I'll have the doctor come to see you," Divincenzo told Jake as he was leaving.

Jake did not know what to think or say to the major as he left. He didn't understand what was just said by the general and the others, but he was able to figure that it didn't sound good. A visit by a doctor might be good, but what about Slakve? Jake still didn't know that he was just fired and so his mental state had not improved. Wondering about what just happened, he went back to the corner.

Later in the afternoon, the door to Jake's cell opened. He was sitting in the corner when the guard walked in and told him to come out. Jake slowly got up and went out to the hallway. Normally, once a week, Jake took a short walk down the hall to the shower room, but today was not the normal shower day. Jake followed the guard on a long walk through the building.

He passed through parts of the building he had never seen and eventually ended up at the end of the hall by the medical ward where he almost made it to when he first arrived—Jake suddenly remembered.

Jake entered the medical office, and the guard motioned to him to sit in a chair. The guard then walked over to a desk where a young female nurse was sitting, filling out some medical paperwork. The guard briefly talked to her and then left the office. The nurse said something in Russian as she continued filling out paperwork. Jake didn't understand what she said and just watched her continue to write.

Jake was cautiously suspicious. He'd been in a cell isolated from everyone for two and a half years, and now he was in a doctor's office sitting across from a woman. He was experiencing unusual emotions, excited about being out of the cell, even if only for a little while. He hadn't seen a woman in years and being in the room with her depressed him, maybe an unusual reaction for a man who hadn't seen a woman in years.

The sight of a woman, being in an office, being outside of the cell he had been in for over two years, all created a serious emotional conflict for Jake. The nurse brought back memories of home and his family and gave him a rush of emotions as he remembered and missed his wife and children. His emotions were overwhelming as he started to rock back and forth in the chair thinking about the woman, his wife, and about what Major Slakve had been doing to him. Instead of being able to relax, Jake sat and worried as a million thoughts went through his head.

When the nurse finished her paperwork, she glanced over at Jake and noticed his uneasiness. She got up from the desk, grabbed a clipboard with some forms on it, and said something while motioning with her hand to move into an exam room. Jake hesitantly got up and started to nervously walk to the exam room.

"You do not understand Russian?" the nurse asked in Russian, then English.

"No," Jake answered, but almost unintelligible.

"My English is not good, understand?"

"Yes," a nervous Jake answered.

The nurse explained as best as she could that he would be examined, and then she conducted some preliminary procedures, taking his temperature, checking his blood pressure, and filling out some more paperwork. She talked quietly with Jake as she worked and complained to herself about not having a file on him.

"You are the fifth one in here today."

"Fifth?"

"American."

"American?"

"Yes, American. The major did this to you too, yes?"

Jake didn't reply.

"No more. He has been moved. You will not see that major again," the nurse told Jake in an angry tone.

At first, Jake was not sure if the nurse was angry at him, but then the nurse smiled which did get a slight smile in return. Within seconds, Jake felt relief knowing that Major Slakve was not going to bother him again, and as he recounted the general's visit in the cell, he was able to put together what happened.

A rush of relief overcame him, which the nurse could see as he began to shake. Jake's combined confusion and excitement almost caused him to pass out as the nurse grabbed him by his shoulders to stop him from falling out of the chair. The doctor came into the exam room as this happened and helped the nurse, who briefed the doctor while they moved Jake over to the exam table.

The doctor did some minor checking for a minute until he got his composure back and felt a little better. They then had Jake stand and asked him to remove his clothes for the rest of the exam. While the idea of being naked, even for a doctor's exam may be somewhat embarrassing for some people, Jake was not at all fazed and had changed in just a few minutes from an excited state to an almost incoherent one. Living life as a prisoner did not leave room for modesty, and with the passing of time, Jake had lost all sense of modesty, privacy, embarrassment, or intimidation. Even the presence of a woman in the room did not have any effect on Jake as he complied and stripped down.

Jake's demeanor was quickly noticed by both the doctor and nurse as they were struck by his indifference, and an assumption on their part that he would have instinctively covered himself with the gown lying on the table. The doctor started his exam while dictating his findings to the nurse. While the exam proceeded, the doctor and the nurse conversed with each other in Russian—noting the scars, cuts, and bruises on Jake's body— but when they talked with Jake, they talked in English. The doctor had him sit on the table.

"How did you get these?" the doctor asked Jake, referring to the scars and unusual thick calluses on the bottom of his feet.

"Major Slakve," Jake answered.

The doctor was not pleased as he continued to examine Jake. He checked Jake's back and found more scars and several scabs.

"And these also the major?"

"Yes, he used a stick he carried in his bag."

The doctor told the nurse to get the camera and had her take pictures of Jake's feet, back, and legs. The doctor had Jake stand up and checked his genitals.

"And this, how did this happen?" the doctor asked.

Jake paused, hesitant to answer. "Electric wires."

The doctor had the nurse take pictures of Jake's body including his genitalia, making sure to get clear photos of the area where there were scars. On the genitals, there were about half a dozen patches where hair did not grow because of scars caused by the attachment of electric wires.

Jake was numb to what should be a humiliating experience and let them conduct the exam and take the pictures. The doctor and nurse were quite disturbed as they talked about Jake's condition and the condition of the other foreign prisoners they had seen that day. The doctor gave Jake a penicillin shot, and the nurse dressed the open wounds and sores on his body.

After the examination was completed, he was given clean clothes that a guard had brought in. When he finished dressing, he went back to the waiting area while the nurse worked on the paperwork. When finished, she called the guard who came in and motioned to him to come out. Jake got up and headed to the door, where he stopped for a moment and turned to the nurse.

"Thank you."

The nurse looked at Jake, smiled, and nodded at him in response. He left the office and the guard took him back to the cell.

When Jake entered his cell, he sat in the chair, still very much overcome with emotion as his mind wandered and worried. What would happen next was a concern, but he was also still ecstatic about the trip out of his cell to the doctor's office.

He did not stop thinking as his imagination took him away well into the next morning.

By then, the previous day's excitement had worn off and paranoia had set in. Except for the small regular meals he received, nothing had happened since the previous day's visit to the doctor's office. Jake's imagination had gone into overtime with worry. As the time passed, he saw the recent events as mental torture and placed his life in uncertainty, and with the distant approach of footsteps in the hallway, he believed his worries would be confirmed.

The cell door opened and Major Divincenzo entered carrying a file box. Unlike the visits by Slakve, the cell door was left open as the major walked to the table.

"A-2837, come here, sit down."

The major initially addressed Jake by his prisoner number which confused him. The prisoner numbering system was detailed and although Divincenzo never did explain it, Jake would make the assumption the letter "A" stood for American.

"Captain Walden, come sit."

Jake got up and moved to the table, hesitantly sitting down.

"You never sit in the chair?"

"The major always sat in the chair."

"I see."

Major Divincenzo went through the file box, pulled out a piece of paper from a folder, and placed it in front of Jake, who immediately started to think that the "sign the confession" drill was starting all over again. Jake stiffened in the chair and tried to ignore the paper, but the major told Jake to read them as he continued to go through the box and took out some more papers, a magazine, and two small books. Jake noticed the other things he was putting on the table. The paper in front of him did not look like the confessions he had refused to sign in the past. As he looked at the paper he saw that it was not a confession.

"Have you seen this before?"

Jake shook his head "no" as he read the paper.

"Major Slakve should have given this to you, he should have told you, but he didn't tell the others either. Not your fault, Captain Walden."

The document was short and written in both Russian and English. The contents of the document propelled Jake into anger and depression as he became nonresponsive to Major Divincenzo.

"You understand what this tells you? I am sorry, Captain, that the major never told you, but you have been convicted in accordance with Soviet law as a criminal. Your sentence was fifty-five years starting two years ago."

Jake's attitude changed and he believed everything that had happened in the past two days was just part of their cruel ways of torture. Jake continued to be nonresponsive as Divincenzo continued.

"I can understand you not understanding. You have been in this cell too long. You were to go to the work camp two years ago. We will correct this, but first you must get your strength back, and you cannot work at the camp if you do not have your strength and you cannot repay for your crimes by staying in a cell."

Jake looked at the major and thought that what he had said was insane.

"You will stay here for another three or four weeks and then go to the camp. The doctor will see you every week, and starting today, you will go to the dining hall for your meals."

The major seemed sincere as he told Jake about his new situation and even seemed understanding of Jake's reluctance to talk.

"You will also need to learn Russian," he said as he showed him the two books on the table: a dictionary, and a beginner's language book.

"I have one more thing for you. You can keep your conviction papers, but I also have for you this American magazine, *Time*, but make sure you study your Russian, understand?"

Jake still did not reply as he looked at the major, and then looked back down at the table. The major wasn't angry at Jake for ignoring him and gathered up the file box off the table and walked to the door.

"Study your Russian, and I will see you in a few days, okay?"

Jake did not reply as the major left and the guard closed the door.

This can't be happening. A rush of emotion went through his mind as he wondered about what just happened. He looked at the conviction papers in disbelief and then in an effort to avoid reality, tried to convince himself that it was not true and just another trick. He had been in prison for five years and had always had the hope that one day he'd be freed. When he was in Vietnam, he knew about the rumors of the end of the war and assumed he would have been released then, but since being brought to Russia, he had been in virtual isolation. He had assumed the war ended, and the others had been released, but being in a Russian prison he had hoped and assumed that someone knew he was there and negotiations of some kind had been going on for his release. Now, he had been told that was not the case, and he'd been given a 55-year sentence.

Jake continued to sit at the table, just thinking. *This can't be happening.* He glanced at the books and magazine and after a few minutes he resorted to the one thing he had done every day in captivity, he leaned on the table with his arms, bowed his head, closed his eyes, and prayed. He prayed and asked for strength, guidance, and purpose. As many did in times of distress, Jake also prayed for a sign, something to show him the way, to help him cope.

A few minutes later, he took a deep breath and opened his eyes. Signs come in many ways to people in distress, and while the naysayers and pessimists discounted and explained away what others believed to be signs of faith and hope, a sign was still a sign. The sign could be one of the Divine, one of chance or irony, or even one with no logical reason or interpretation except for the one who saw it. For Jake, his head still bowed down toward the table, when he opened his eyes, and the first thing he saw was the *Time* magazine on the table—"What Next?"—was what he saw on the cover. Jake had already earlier seen the Ho Chi Minh cover and the caption on the bottom of the page, "The Victor." But this was not what he saw as he opened his eyes. On the top left corner of the cover, Jake saw the caption, and whether it was a divine sign, irony, or anything else, it was a sign that was an answer to his earlier concerns about *what next*. A question for his question and the entire caption read "What Next in Asia?" But for Jake, the "What Next?" was enough and gave him a new positive outlook.

Jake looked at the magazine, the language books, and then back at the magazine. The cover of the May 12, 1975 *Time* had a picture of Ho Chi Minh with a map of Vietnam inserted. The city of Saigon on the map had been renamed Ho

Chi Minh City, and the caption at the bottom of the page had "The Victor." Although he felt he'd been given a sign, he was still somewhat apprehensive and almost afraid to open the magazine. Was the magazine another cruel trick? Was it a manufactured copy of *Time* just given to Jake as a propaganda ploy? Jake was not sure, but as he looked at the cover he could not help but think so, or else irony itself was cruel and twisted. The cover did interest him, and since he didn't not know what had been happening in the world for the past five years, the idea of what the cover showed was frankly inconceivable or an attempt at satire. The picture of Ho Chi Minh, a map of Vietnam inserted, and the city of Saigon renamed Ho Chi Minh City were not something that anyone back in 1970 would have envisioned.

When he opened the magazine, he thought that it looked authentic and even though at first he doubted its authenticity, it was an actual May 12, 1975 issue of *Time*. As he skimmed through it, he found it full of Vietnam-related stories, all of which initially seemed like a communist propagandist delight in that they projected a victorious North Vietnam over the losing United States. Jake thought that real or not, it was a great example of pro-communist propaganda. It amazed him that the first hint of any news he had received in years happened to be this one issue. Was it on purpose? Or maybe it was a sign. Regardless, he continued to read, and read, and read.

There was a lot that had been going on in the world aside from the fall of Saigon, the last helicopter to leave, the refugees and what would be next for them. There was quite a bit more news and information in the magazine too, and while the issue seemed to be overloaded with Vietnam stories and what at first seemed to be simply a propaganda issue, there were other stories. Jake took in every aspect of every article he read. An opportunity and chance to catch up, or at least to try to catch up on one week's news. He was reading more in just a few hours than he had read in the past five years.

His reading was cut short as his paranoia returned. Jake could hear the approaching footsteps in the hall. He quickly resorted back to his old habits, but first he attempted to hide his new obsession, the magazine, and placed it under his sleep pad. Then he ran over to his corner and waited.

The cell door opened. The guard looked at him and told him to come out. The reluctant Jake moved out to the hall where there were four other prisoners waiting. The guard escorted the prisoners down the hall and through the building where they made two more stops to get two more prisoners, a total of seven. The walk through the building continued until they arrived at a door.

The guard opened the door, and the late afternoon five o'clock July daylight came beaming in. The sudden daylight initially made it difficult to see, but as Jake and the others started to walk, their eyes adjusted, and they got their first view in a long time of what was outside the prison building where they had been kept. They were excited about being outside but also apprehensive about not knowing where they were going. They had forgotten that Major Divincenzo told them they were going to start having their meals at the dining hall. The walk was slow, due mainly to their frailty, which the guard noticed and was understanding of their condition. The walk took about ten minutes and provided the first daylight they'd seen in years.

As they arrived, they heard the noise coming from inside, which was ironically reminiscent of any dining hall and a sharp contrast to the silence of the cell. "Haven't heard that in a long time," one of the prisoners whispered. The guard took them in a single-file line through where the servers filled their bowls, and although not exactly full, it was more than they ever received in the cells. The guard noticed, stopped the line, and said something to the server, who at first seemed to argue with the guard, but then he looked at the prisoners, nodded his head, and added more food. Jake didn't know what was said, but it seemed as if it was required that Jake and the others be given more food, which also went along with what the major had told him about getting healthy. The trip to the dinner had already lifted Jake's spirits, and as he listened to the guard and server argue, Jake jokingly thought, *This is why I need to learn Russian.*

The guard took the seven prisoners to their own table and then left them there while he went to a nearby table with some other guards. None of the prisoners talked and quickly started to eat while they curiously looked around. Suddenly the guard yelled at them. Jake and the others assumed the guard was yelling at them for looking around. The guard continued to yell at them, then got up, and went to their table. None of them understood what the guard had said. Eventually the guard realized that they didn't understand and then with some simple hand signs conveyed the message to slow down. He pointed out to the other tables and the other prisoners at the pace they were eating and showed them his watch, pointing that they had twenty minutes to eat. After the guard figured out that they understood, he went back to his table.

Jake and the others, still somewhat hesitant but also a little relieved, went back to eating and causally looked around. They were amazed at the noise, activity, and given the absence of prisoner uniforms, a strange appearance of normalcy. When they first arrived there were only about fifty prisoners, but within a few minutes, the hall had filled to capacity with over 300. Jake and his table watched the other prisoners talk without restraint, and for the moment, it didn't seem like prison as they watched everyone in the hall apparently come and go freely. He and the others at his table seemed to be the only ones who had a guard, and up to this point, they were also the only ones in the hall who were not talking.

At first, they were all fearful of some sort of retaliation or punishment if they talked, but after the first few minutes passed, one of the prisoners got up the nerve and said something.

"Think it's okay to talk?"

They all glanced back and forth at each other, still reluctant.

"I'm Gary Fuze...Lieutenant Commander," one of the prisoners said quietly.

A few more seconds of reluctance passed as they looked around.

"Nathaniel Jamison," another prisoner said.

The rest, including Jake, took their time with introductions and were careful not to get too excited or too loud. The seven continued to eat and look at each other; a couple of them even cried a little as they attempted to relax while they exchanged some general information until it was time to leave.

21 July, 1975
Day 1,848

During the next two weeks, Jake's life in the Russian prison cell had changed dramatically. He and the other six prisoners had been going to the dining hall regularly during the previous two weeks and had exchanged extensive personal information and attempted to practice their beginning Russian language skills. They also talked in detail about Major Slakve and his treatment and were pleased to have been told by Major Divincenzo that Major Slakve was transferred out of the prison to an advisory group stationed in Afghanistan. At the time, they had no idea of what the implication of being sent to Afghanistan meant, but were happy to have known that he was gone.

Jake's paranoia of approaching footsteps had not completely gone away, but he no longer scurried to the corner when he heard the approach of footsteps. Instead, he stood behind the table at a respectable body position, or military position of parade rest, looking straight ahead. Each time Major Divincenzo entered the cell, he greeted Jake in Russian with a hello, and Jake responded in his beginning Russian. The major then would tell him to sit. Divincenzo and Jake had developed a good rapport during the previous two weeks, and so far he had not made any of the traditional interrogation attempts with Jake.

Major Divincenzo had been making daily visits during which he helped Jake with his Russian and also brought more magazines, which he had been swapping out between the other prisoners. The doctor had also seen him several times and his health had progressed well. He was reminded that he would probably be moved to the work camp in another week or two, which Jake acknowledged—although not without apprehension.

CHAPTER 15

THE GULAG

3 August, 1975
Day 1,861

As the major had told Jake, the day had come for him to leave his cell and move to the camp. Without any real notice or preparations, the guard came to the cell and told him to gather his few possessions. He was then escorted by the guard out of the building where Major Divincenzo was waiting for him next to a vehicle.

"I'll check in on you from time to time."

"Where are we going?"

"Not too far, five minutes."

"What about the others?"

"They too are going, but all of you are going to different workhouses. Some of them are going to different camps, but you are lucky, very lucky, because you are staying at this camp."

Soviet Prison Camp a.k.a. The Gulag

While they drove to Jake's new home, he tried to talk to the major and even gave him a thank-you for the magazines and help with his Russian. Divincenzo just nodded. When they arrived at his assigned barracks, they got out and the major handed Jaked over to the waiting guard.

"Thank you, Major Divincenzo."

"Don't thank me yet, Captain Walden," he said with a stern expression and in a sarcastic tone as he got back in the vehicle.

The emotionally starved Jake was disturbed by the major's remark and did not know what to make of the comment as the guard escorted him inside the barracks. Despite his situation and prisoner status, Jake had gained a professional respect for the major, but then again it could have also been symptomatic of the Stockholm syndrome. Regardless, his remark concerned him as he wondered if the major knew something that he did not know yet. What did he mean? After all, he told him he was lucky to be staying at this camp. As he entered the barracks, Jake's concerns were temporarily postponed as the guard turned him over to someone else in the building, an older, apparently Russian man in his sixties, possibly seventies, who grunted at Jake in Russian to follow him. Jake followed the man to a spot in the barracks where he assigned Jake his bunk area. The old man didn't say anything else, and Jake made the assumption he must be in charge of the building.

Jake sat in the corner, and looked around at the poorly maintained building. He noticed an excessive amount of beds, blankets, and a generally filthy environment, including a slightly mud-caked floor. Based on the closeness of the bunks and the overall condition of the building Jake concluded that the barracks were overcrowded.

As he sat, at least half an hour or more passed and nothing happened; no one came around. Eventually, Jake got up and cautiously walked through the barracks and made his way to the main door—no one anywhere. As he stood by the doorway, he saw a chair and decided to sit and wait there. He looked through the doorway and took in the outside that he had not been able to do for so long. The scenery of the camp was visually dreary, but it was still outside of a cell. Jake remained in the chair for at least another hour, waiting and watching what he considered to be an odd lack of activity, but also an eerie sense of freedom to just sit and watch.

His mental clock ticked as he had become accustomed to a schedule during the previous few weeks. He knew it was near dinnertime but didn't know what to do or where to go. A part of him was apprehensive to go anywhere while he experienced an insecure feeling, which was strange for him given what seemed to be freedom to roam and be outside unsupervised.

Finally, he heard the old man coming out from inside the barracks. He passed by Jake, walked down the steps, and started to walk away from the building. Jake just sat and watched as he walked away, but eventually the old man stopped, turned back toward Jake, yelled, and motioned at him to follow. He then turned and kept walking. Jake got up and quickly followed, caught up with him, and continued to walk until they reached the dining hall. *So far, so good.*

At the steps, they waited. The dining hall was already full, and the group of prisoners was finishing up and leaving through the exit doors at the other side of the building. After a couple of minutes, the old man motioned to Jake and drew his attention to a large group of about a hundred prisoners marching and approaching the dining hall. Jake quickly caught on that the approaching group would be his new roommates. Jake's short-lived optimism about having some freedom was diminished as he observed the slow moving and mostly frail-looking prisoners.

The formation stopped at the bottom of the steps. They were guarded by about ten soldiers who were not very talkative, but they did make some comments to the prisoners that Jake didn't understand. As a sergeant walked to the head of the group, the old man said something to him, which the sergeant acknowledged as he looked at Jake and talked with the old man. The sergeant then went inside the dining hall, and a few minutes later stepped back outside and yelled at the prisoners, which started them moving into the dining hall. Jake was quickly learning Russian; he headed inside the hall, and stayed close to the old man.

After dinner, Jake followed the lead of the old man and the other prisoners and left the dining hall. Outside, the prisoners did not wait for a formation, they simply walked back to the barracks on their own. Jake was apprehensive, but he followed and walked back to the barracks. He felt out of place as he stopped just inside the doorway and attempted to stay near the old man, but the man chastised Jake and wanted nothing to do with him.

He cautiously walked through the barracks toward his bunk and with each step, he grew more apprehensive and paranoid. He made an effort not to look directly at anyone as he walked. When he reached his bunk, he sat in it with his back against the wall and tried to be inconspicuous as he studied the other prisoners and their actions. He had not been talked to or told anything and was reluctant to say anything to anyone. The first impression of the camp, the barracks and the prisoners was similar to culture shock, and he once again started to experience something he didn't know existed.

Although the existence of Russian gulags was known to the world, the actual life experience was not a well-known subject to most people, including Jake. A few books had been written on the subject and stories of life inside the gulags did get out, but the Soviets made an extensive effort to keep the actual activities and conditions a secret. In addition to the secrets, the Soviets also made extensive efforts to keep the occupants and the names of the prisoners a secret, which was not as successful as the Soviets intended due to the massive number of prisoners processed through the gulag system. The policy was also in some ways a contradiction, given their attempts to keep the identity of foreign prisoners a secret although most foreign prisoners were placed into the system with the other prisoners. Over the years, word spread and many of the names made it out of the gulags, generating countless rumors and conspiracy theories.

The first night in the barracks was a long one. Jake found it difficult to sleep and noticed that there seemed to be a constant, low-key level of activity. Prisoners seemed to sleep, but at the same time someone was always coming or going, conversations went on throughout the evening and sometimes arguments. Jake noticed that there was a hierarchy, and after a few nights in the barracks he figured out who to stay away from and who belonged to the gangs. Quickly, he started his education on how to survive in the gulag.

As the days and weeks progressed, Jake adjusted to the routines. The mornings started out early, bread and soup (stew-type) breakfasts and then marching or a truck ride to the work area at rock quarries or sometimes a wooded area for lumbering. Regardless of the work, the daily drill became much the same. It was also apparent to Jake that he had been adopted by some of the prisoners. He noticed that the veteran prisoners and the gang members did not treat many of the new prisoners very well, and some of them even ended up dead. Jake, on the other hand, was not harassed as badly, although he was still harassed occasionally, but still not as violently. Within days he seemed to migrate into a group, a few of whom knew some English, enough to help him to continue to learn his Russian.

It didn't take long for him to realize he was somewhat fortunate in regard to not being harassed too much and asked some of the other prisoners why, but none of them gave him a direct answer. Some of them believed that it was the camp policy that to kill or harm the foreign prisoners was considered treason to the Soviet Union—resulting in death to anyone involved. This explanation was only rumored and no one knew for sure. Jake liked the idea but didn't get too comfortable with it.

While the prisoners seemed to run things within the prisoner circles, the guards still controlled them. At times, even though the work was difficult, life seemed nonrestrictive inside the prison and even at the work sites, but the guards enforced the rules when it came to prisoners staying within their boundaries. The arrival of new prisoners was also part of the routine at the camp and most prisoners, just as Jake had done, conformed to prison culture.

A new prisoner named Karlos—who had only been in the barracks three days—had been a nonconformist to prison culture, gangs, and rules of the prison. Within a few days of being assigned to Jake's work group, Karlos had already attracted the attention of Ambrosii—one of the gang leaders. The chaotic normalcy of the evening dining hall activities proceeded as usual, except for one thing: Karlos made the mistake of staring at Ambrosii.

"What you looking at?" Ambrosii yelled across the hall at Karlos.

Whispers from the prisoners at the table were heard telling Karlos not to say anything, but during the momentary pause, they saw that Karlos was not going to be quiet.

"Nothing, nothing, just a fly on the wall," Karlos answered with a smile and laughed as he said it.

"What you call me?" Ambrosii yelled back, which also generated comments from his gang.

Despite efforts from Jake and the others at the table to keep Karlos from saying something else, the verbal exchange continued.

"I'm sorry, it's a mosquito...that's it, a mosquito, a blood-sucking pest..." Karlos yelled back, but was suddenly interrupted by Ambrosii and his gang who jumped up from their table.

Activity in the dining hall stopped as over fifty gang members stood up. The guards looked on in silence as Ambrosii angrily looked at Karlos. After a few seconds, Ambrosii started to smile as he glanced around the dining hall and relieved the tension.

"You win, you win. That's what you want, right?" Ambrosii told Karlos as he motioned to the others to sit back down.

"Shut up and look at the table before you get us all killed," one of the prisoners told Karlos.

Karlos reluctantly did as he was told and the activity started back up in the dining hall.

The harassment of new prisoners by gang members was something Jake figured out right away as did most prisoners, but antagonizing a gang leader was something else. The practice of allowing gang members to make remarks and harass prisoners was the way to survive in the gulag. Fighting back would occasionally be acceptable if it were a good fight, and the winner of the fight ended up being a gang member. The outcome of the fights was understood, and if a non-gang member won a fight, he would either be invited to join the gang or ended up dead within a few days.

In the barracks, the other prisoners were not pleased with Karlos. Jake had only been there about six weeks, and while he had learned a great deal about how to survive life at the prison, he hadn't learned everything. The other prisoners scolded and chastised Karlos for confronting the gang leader and warned him and worried about reprisal and revenge. Jake was also concerned and upset with Karlos, but not as much as the others as he became more concerned about not under-standing why the others were so upset, but he was told that he hadn't been there long enough to understand. That night was not a typical night as the prisoners in groups of two and three took turns staying up and keeping watch throughout the night.

Fortunately, the night passed without any incidents, and the next morning the prisoners woke up, went to breakfast, and formed up for the march to the work site. Jake felt com-fortable and relieved as he stood next to Karlos in the for-mation of about a hundred prisoners who stood ready to march to work. While marching, Jake's awareness diminished as he daydreamed, just as he had done most days during the forty-minute walk.

Thirty minutes into the march, Jake's attention was broken by the sound of movement behind him. For a second, he heard someone move up behind him and glanced over his left shoulder to see Ambrosii grab the unaware Karlos and push him out of the formation onto the side of the road. Ambrosii then took Karlos's place. When Karlos was pushed out, he fell to the ground. He quickly tried to get back up, but as he got up to his feet, machine-gun fire rang out, and Karlos fell to the ground.

The gun fire caused an immediate, instinctive reaction by the prisoners to fall to the ground. A surprised Jake could not believe what he had just witnessed as he yelled out and tried to leave the formation to help Karlos, but the prisoners around Jake, including Ambrosii, grabbed and stopped him. They tried their best to calm Jake down as they got back up and started to march forward again, leaving the dead Karlos on the ground behind them.

As they began to march again, Jake was filled with emotion and hate as he began a confrontation with Ambrosii, but the other prisoners intervened—they continued to march. This was the first time Jake had been face to face with Ambrosii, and while Jake was filled with anger and wanted to do something, he already knew and saw that the gang leader was nothing but evil. His expression showed arrogance and a lack of any kind of concern or fear. After a few minutes of Jake's venting and the others keeping him under control, the march to the work site was close to its end—Jake regained his composure. Ambrosii talked to Jake in what could be considered fairly good English, which surprised Jake.

"You're the American, Walden, yes?"

"Yes," Jake answered.

"You need to remember something in this place. We don't need to kill you…the guards will do it for us without even knowing it."

The march came to a stop, and the prisoners were told to go to work. They broke formation, and Jake stood in place thinking about what Ambrosii had just said. He had made it clear, the rumor that foreign prisoners were protected from being killed did not mean that they were protected from being killed by the guards, nor that things could happen if someone wanted them to.

Jake unwillingly now understood what the others were so concerned about during the previous night. Jake brooded about the killing of Karlos as the gulag routine became a part of his life. There would be more killings as time passed, but he and some of the others did their part to help new arrivals avoid the same fate. Their efforts would be successful, at least within their work group, but other prisoners in other parts of the prison did not do as well, and during the next few years there would be continued brutality to include killing of prisoners, but not in Jake's group.

CHAPTER 16

A NEW LEADER

FIVE YEARS LATER
18 January, 1980
Day 3,490

Five years after being placed into the camp, Jake was surviving the Russian winter of 1980. He had become a veteran of the gulag, a mentor and sometimes leader for many of the others who struggled with getting by and having a will to live. Jake had never lost his hope, his faith, or his spirit and used them to keep going. He had not climbed the ladder of gang member or any other organization within the prison, but instead managed to become part of, and may have even been responsible for, organizing a close group of prisoners and friends within his work group. For the most part, the work groups and prisoners within a barracks stayed to themselves, and although there was interaction with the other prisoners and barracks—getting to know anyone in other groups was a little difficult and sometimes dangerous.

The rules had not been impossible to follow, and he had quickly figured out how to make life more tolerable. He took to heart the old saying—keep your friends close and your enemies closer—that had been used time and time again. As Jake took stock of his situation, he realized the so-called realities of what life would or could be like for him in the gulag. He developed close relationships within his work group and was able, over time, to persuade many of them to change the way they chose to survive. His basic strategy was not to be aligned openly with the gangs, but he also knew that gangs ran the prison and each gang had their own so-called territory. Ambrosii ran the part of the prison where Jake's work group lived, and Jake knew enough to understand that part of the gang's lifeblood was their ability to trade within the prison. He believed and knew that paying customers who also provided valuable information were less likely to be harmed and more likely to be protected. The plan worked, and the black market trade inside the prison continued as it always had, but with an unofficial alliance that seemed to work for everyone.

The alliance did not change the everyday rigors of the prison, only insured that, for the most part, Jake and those in his group did not have to worry about being pushed out of a formation and killed. The alliance did not protect them from the guards, as one of them found out when he accidentally stumbled and fell out of a walking formation and was shot. That was the only shooting death the group suffered; however, during the past five years there had been around a dozen other deaths from health-related issues such as the cold, flu, and other diseases. The death of a dozen over a four-year period was actually very good and inspiring compared to the averages of the other groups that suffered at least a dozen deaths every year.

The ability of Jake and his group to defy the elements, at least more than most, was a result of his personality and continuing growing leadership skills, which was a unique style he adopted in order to stay unnoticed. He learned that being noticed by the guards or the gangs was not good and could be interpreted as a threat to their controls over the prisoners and internal codes and rules of the prison. Jake gained a respect from many of the prisoners, but still maintained an appearance of being just one of the masses, not an individual or someone to be concerned about. Even some of the guards formed relationships with Jake, although some of the relationships were attributed to an asset Jake possessed. Being an American, to many guards, meant that he was the enemy, and they did not like Americans, but other guards viewed Jake, the American, as a curiosity, not only because he was an American, but also because he was a foreigner. While soldiers were soldiers and guards were guards, they were still people with natural interest and curiosities, and many of the guards grav-itated toward Jake and other foreign prisoners because they were interested in their knowledge of the world outside of Russia.

During his first few years, Jake developed a hatred for the Soviet guards. Over time, as he came to know prisoners and learned to speak and understand Russian, he gained an under-standing of their cultures within the communist system. He began to learn the stories of other prisoners and how they ended up in the gulag, and though many of them were crimi-nals guilty of a whole gambit of crimes, others were political prisoners.

Unlike other countries where it was believed that inmates at prisons were all criminals, the inmates or prisoners at the gulag fell into two categories. One was actual criminals and the other, the political prisoners, like those who protested against the government or others who were perceived a threat to the government. In the case of Jake and others like him, he was in the political category, and the Soviets considered po-litical prisoners criminals and made no distinction between the two groups.

Four and a half years earlier, Jake had been transferred to the work camp and on his first day was taken to the dining hall for the dinner meal. This same routine had been re-peated for all the newly assigned prisoners and at least one or two times a week when Jake and his group returned from work—new prisoners would be waiting at the dining hall.

On January 18, 1980, there was nothing unusual about two new prisoners who had been waiting at the dining hall. They ate their meals, kept quiet, stayed to themselves, and followed the others back to the barracks, where they had been assigned their bunks near Jake. This wasn't unusual because the rotation of prisoners being released was also a constant. There was always space for new prisoners.

The first few minutes back in the barracks the two new prisoners sat back and observed, studied the barracks and other prisoners—a common practice. The advantage they had over most others was that they knew each other. During the evening they didn't talk a lot, but they did have brief conversations, which was more than any new prisoners did when they first arrived. They also did not seem to be as intimidated or scared as an average new prisoner, which seemed strange.

The next morning, everything began as usual as the prisoners got up, went to breakfast, and then formed up to head out to the work area. The two new prisoners kept quiet and to themselves, but Jake and the others by now began to have suspicions about them. Upon arrival at the work site, the prisoners went about their work details; they went to the toolshed, got their tools, and headed out in their groups. The two new prisoners grabbed tools and followed along—as if they knew what they were doing. Jake and the others became more suspicious as they watched the two new prisoners work alongside them. At one point, one of the guards walked by and briefly stopped and talked with the new prisoners, and even though Jake could not hear what they were talking about, their conversation appeared to be friendly.

During the lunch break, discussions broke out about the two new prisoners, as did paranoia, and talks about killing them ran almost out of control. Jake suggested finding out who they were and was quickly elected to be the one to do just that. He was reluctant but realized that it was necessary. He got up and walked over to them. As he approached, he noticed that they did not show signs of fear, nor did they display any traits of a new prisoner. They looked up at Jake as he arrived and paused briefly.

"Alex, or Alexei, but people call me Alex," the less intimidating one said to Jake.

"Major Alex," the other prisoner said in a more serious and authoritative tone.

"Alex will do. This is Sergeant Kresnev, and he goes by Sergeant Kresnev," Alex jokingly told Jake with a smile.

"Soldiers?"

"Yes, soldiers. And you're an American," Alex replied.

"Yes, I'm Jake, Jacob Walden."

Alex extended his hand for a handshake, to which Jake complied.

"We have a little problem," Jake told Alex as he motioned toward his work group.

Alex seemed to understand and was responsive to the concerns. He proceeded to tell Jake why he and Sergeant Kresnev were in prison, and gave a short version, explaining that they were in the Soviet Spetsnaz, stationed in the war in Afghanistan. Then Kresnev told Jake that Alex was his company commander, that they had been court-martialed for questioning strategies of the regional commander, and were sentenced to ten years at the gulag.

"Back to work," the guards yelled out. Jake welcomed Alex and Kresnev to the group, and although the conversation had been broken up, within minutes the tension was eased as Jake passed the word on about the new prisoners. The news gave a sense of relief to everyone.

Throughout the afternoon, Jake, Alex, and other prisoners talked when they could and exchanged information about each other. Although Alex and Jake used to be on different sides, they seemed to have a common connection being military and appeared to have similar personalities that clicked. As the afternoon passed, work ended and they marched back to the gulag. Jake and Alex continued to talk as much as they could get away with and formed a quick bond and friendship.

At the dining hall, the routine went on as usual. During the walk to the barracks, another routine occurred as it usually did with some of the new prisoners when Ambrosii and some of his gang began the customary verbal harassment and intimidation of Alex and Kresnev. Jake and some of the others tried to intervene, but Ambrosii quickly and sternly reminded them who they were talking to and the consequences for interference. They reluctantly stood back as the harassment continued, and although Sergeant Kresnev instinctively wanted to fight back—Alex gave him a look, a nonverbal instruction. Ambrosii and his men took the little money Alex and Kresnev had on them and then moved on. When Ambrosii left, Alex, Jake, and Kresnev kept a safe distance behind Ambrosii while they walked back to the barracks.

Throughout the evening, conversations continued between Alex, Kresnev, Jake, and many of the other prisoners in the barracks. Alex and Kresnev were quick to learn as much as they could about everything inside the gulag, and Alex had learned much more about the activities and who's who of the gulag than Jake had learned about Alex. Eventually their conversations came to an end as everyone went to sleep.

The next few days proceeded as usual. The prisoners woke up, went to breakfast, and formed up for the march to the work area. On the fourth day after Alex and Kresnev arrived at the camp, the group began the march to the work area. The occasional conversations on the way to the work area between Jake and Alex were less substantial during this march than during the previous days—Alex appeared preoccupied. Another thing different was that Kresnev was not marching next to Alex like he normally did and was about ten rows up in the formation.

As the march to work continued, Alex suddenly began to move forward in the formation, he looked at Jake and told him to stay. Jake watched Alex move toward Kresnev. The prisoners in the rows ahead seemed to move out of Alex's way like dominoes—like Alex's movements had been rehearsed. Jake was amazed how quickly he moved up the formation and watched with an uneasy anticipation. As Alex reached Kresnev, he suddenly pushed a prisoner out of the formation and then took his place in the outside row.

The prisoner that Alex pushed out was Ambrosii, who stumbled out of the formation and almost fell, but regained his balance as he angrily turned back toward the formation and began to yell at Alex. Before Ambrosii got more than two words out, he was repeatedly hit by machine-gun fire and fell to the ground. As it had happened before when other prisoners were shot, the prisoners dropped to the ground, then got back up, and began to march on as if nothing had happened. Jake was stunned by what happened, not because someone was shot, but by who was shot and how it happened. The routine Jake had grown accustomed to had suddenly been disrupted and presented questions and concerns.

At the work site, the new routine proceeded as the prisoners got their tools and went to work. It didn't take long for the prisoners to approach Alex.

"You don't have to worry about the gangs anymore," Alex said.

"Worry, they'll kill you!" Jake fired back.

"You don't understand, Jake. The gangs are not going to do anything. We are the gang now and the rest of them now work for me... understand?"

Jake didn't answer, but the other prisoners seemed to know instinctively what had happened—some of them smiling about the news. Jake eventually acknowledged Alex as he realized that there had been a sort of a coup in the camp. It took only a few moments for him to understand fully what the death of Ambrosii meant as his concerns left and he got an unsettling feeling of satisfaction. As he continued to think, another question came to him.

"What about the other gang leaders in the camp?"

"They're gone...all gone," Alex replied with a smile.

Jake didn't know exactly what Alex's words meant. Did they mean they were transferred or killed? Regardless of what happened to them, they were not in the camp anymore.

During the next few days, Jake and the others learned more about Alex. The majority of the soldiers guarding the prisoners, including many of the officers, still had to treat Alex as a prisoner, but they also had a deep respect for him. They learned the story about Alex and the allegations against him as a CC of a Spetsnaz unit in Afghanistan. During an opera-

tion, Alex had changed a plan and was successful in its outcome, which achieved the objective and saved the lives of several of his men. The new regional commander, however, took
Alex's actions as a personal stab at his command skills and had
Alex and Sergeant Kresnev court-martialed. The story of Alex
and his concern for the lives of his men over policy, strategy,
or politics had a positive impact on the soldiers and prisoners.

While life went on in the gulag, and everyone carried out
their daily duties and routines, Alex and Sergeant Kresnev
were looked upon with a hidden respect and as heroes.

Alex took over the inside operations that the former gang
members had run, and within days, he had won over the loy-
alty of all the gulag gang members. As the days passed, Jake,
Alex, and the others continued their daily lives while Alex had
also obtained his role in the gulag running most of the black
market activities. The extremely hard labor routine, however,
was not how Alex intended to pass his time. He was not afraid
or intimidated by hard work, even as a child he had worked
hard, but he focused his attention on getting in a position
where he felt he could better watch over his business activities
while also caring for the prisoners. Alex's new role put him in
a unique position where he would be able to take on the role
of an unofficial leader and caretaker.

Alex was not a career criminal, and in fact, did not deal
in any criminal or black market activities prior to his arrival,

although he did have many childhood friends who were active in the organized crime world. Alex took a different direction in life—his temperament and combination of concern for others combined with a hardened military background and combat experience played right into the opportunity available to him when he arrived at the gulag. It was simply a matter of timing, and the way he was treated by Ambrosii prompted him to take advantage of the opportunity.

During the few short weeks Alex had been in the gulag, he had taken a strong liking to Jake. It may have been their personalities, their military connection, or even a feeling that they were both victims and imprisoned falsely, but whatever the reason, Alex and Jake had become friends. The closeness did not change anything and as far as Jake was concerned, life went on as it had every day for years. He had seen prisoners come and go and die. Having different people to talk to was the only change in daily life.

While Alex did not approve of the attitude that Jake and most of the other prisoners displayed, he did understand why they felt and acted as they did. He understood even more as he had conversations with Jake and learned of his story from his first days in Vietnam through his time at the gulag. Alex clearly and almost passionately understood Jake's trials and also learned the similar stories of other prisoners, both the Russians and other foreigners in the prison. It appeared to

Jake that Alex was a compassionate person and truly showed concern and sorrow.

7 February, 1980
Day 3,510

Almost a month after the arrival of Alex, Jake and his group arrived back from work and waited their turn to enter the dining hall for dinner. Jake and Alex talked while in line and Alex brought up a topic he had discussed with Jake on a few occasions. The topic was getting a different job in the gulag and although the change was something Alex had presented, Jake was resistant to asking for anything or changing anything.

His life so far had been traumatic and to ask or submit to any change voluntarily seemed insane. Alex, on the other hand, looked at a change in jobs differently and saw any opportunity to get off the work details as a positive and even more so for someone like Jake. Although he passed each day surviving and sticking to the routine he had been accustomed to now for five years, he was also a victim of the system, poor nutrition, and the elements. It didn't take Alex long to notice that prisoners were dying every day from poor health and that Jake could be one of them. Jake never complained and always maintained a positive attitude despite the negative events inside the gulag.

"See him, the one at the table in the back?" Alex pointed out one of the workers in the kitchen to Jake as they made their way through the line.

Jake nodded as he looked at the worker.

"His name is Johnnie; he's in charge of the kitchen, he runs this place, but he's also a prisoner like us, an American and has been here since 1952."

"What?" Jake responded.

"And that one over there doing the dishes, the old man, he's a German, been in the gulag since the end of the war in 1945."

Jake didn't say anything as they moved through the line. He had never even noticed who was behind the line, not even the American—a black man.

"Johnnie," Alex suddenly called out.

Johnnie looked up, seemed a little disturbed by the interruption, and angrily walked over to the line.

"What?"

"This man is the one I told you about, Jake the American."

Johnnie looked at Jake and then, in what normally was not heard in the prison, spoke in English to Jake.

"You're American?"

"Yeah," Jake answered quietly.

Johnnie stopped the conversation for a moment, and then back into Russian, he burst out and yelled out for Sergeant Lebedev. The sergeant, an older man in his fifties, walked over toward Johnnie. Jake's concern built as he saw what appeared to be a disturbed sergeant approach an already upset Johnnie.

"Mister Johnnie," Sergeant Lebedev said.

"When am I getting the workers I asked for…how can I run this place if you don't give me the men we need to run the place?" Johnnie yelled out at Lebedev.

His outburst was not intended for Lebedev, which Lebedev knew, and he even held back a slight smile while Johnnie was talking, and then paused and thought about what he had said.

"These two will do," Johnnie said.

Sergeant Lebedev looked at Jake and Alex and back at Johnnie. He did this a few times without responding and then smiled.

"I know what you're doing, Johnnie," the sergeant said.

"You move over to the kitchen barracks tonight, start work tomorrow," he told Alex and Jake and then nodded at Johnnie and left.

Alex and Jake both thanked Johnnie as they took their food, left the line, and went to a table to eat. The moment was surreal for Jake. He had grown accustomed to the exhaustive and endless work detail he had worked the past five years. Although he felt he should be happy, he also felt uncertain and insecure.

As Jake sat and ate with Alex, he reflected on changes he endured during the past ten years since 1970.

"This is great news, great news," Alex said.

"Yeah," a not too enthusiastic Jake answered.

"It is, it is, you'll survive the gulag in the kitchen."

Jake was apprehensive and not focused on the conversation. A part of his concern was about the work group.

"What about the work group?"

"They'll be all right, trust me, they'll be all right."

"And what about Sergeant Kresnev, what happens to him?"

"He'll be okay too; he will be watching over everything in the barracks and will look after everyone. Believe me, this is the right thing to do."

After dinner, Jake and Alex gathered their belongings from the barracks and moved to the kitchen barracks. It was much smaller than their old barracks and was attached to the dining hall building. Johnnie pointed out their bunks.

"Wake up is 0330," Johnnie told them.

The wake up was two hours earlier than their usual time. During some quick introductions, Jake and Alex met the other kitchen workers, a small group of about twelve, not many people for the amount of work they had to do every day.

CHAPTER 17

THE KITCHEN

8 February, 1980

Day 3,511

The next day at 3:30 in the morning, Jake and Alex were introduced to the seven days a week schedule of the kitchen. Initially, Jake had doubts about the new job since realizing that in addition to getting up two hours earlier than normal, the kitchen crew actually had longer workdays that didn't end until late evening, usually after 8 p.m. and sometimes as late as ten. As the first day passed and conversations with the other workers picked up, his doubts subsided as he realized several things, the first being that he was out of the severe cold and was even warm as he worked around the ovens. Long hours aside, he also noticed that despite the hard work, there were periods when things slowed down, and they could take a break. He even noticed some of the workers taking short naps during the day, something he had not been able to do in years.

During the first day in the kitchen, Jake and Alex met the other workers and learned the various jobs. It had only taken half a day for them to adapt to the kitchen tasks, but not without questions.

"Where are the guards?" Jake asked Johnnie.

"Aren't any. Sure, there's Sergeant Lebedev and a couple of guards that check in, but they're not here to guard us."

"Not sure I understand; you're saying there are no guards?"

"That's right, they trust us and leave us alone...no one has ever given them reason to think otherwise. We're like trustees."

"See, Jake, I told you that this is a good job and you're not out there anymore," Alex added.

"That's the truth, no one ever regretted working the kitchen...and you don't die in here either...unless it's from old age," Johnnie said with a smile.

During the first evening after dinner had been served to the camp prisoners and staff, Jake learned about a new routine. The entire kitchen crew would sit and have dinner together at a large table in the pantry area of the kitchen. They would talk, exchange news they'd learned, and even laugh—a completely new environment for Jake.

It was during the first evening dinner that they learned the stories of some of the other members of the kitchen crew.

After they had told their stories, Jake was curious about Johnnie.

"Johnnie, how'd you end up here?" Jake asked.

"Oh...been here twenty-three years...since fifty-seven."

Jake didn't respond, but his and Alex's facial expressions showed their surprised reaction.

"Fifty-seven?" Alex asked.

"Yep, fifty-seven...that's when I ended up here. But I got shot down in 1952 in Korea," Johnnie said and then showed a slight smile.

"You boys knew I was a pilot, right?"

"No," both Jake and Alex responded.

"Common mistake, I was just one of a few black pilots back then," Johnnie said with a bigger smile.

"Before the Korean War I was stationed at Johnson Air Base in Japan, 4th Fighter Wing, but then came the war and they moved us up to Korea."

"What'd you fly?" Jake asked.

"Oh! The Sabre, F-86," Johnnie answered, showing a sense of enjoyment and pride remembering his flying days.

"But...got shot down, captured, spent time in a POW camp. I did escape once but they caught me about a week later thanks to that godforsaken cold in Korea...boys, that's got to be the coldest place on earth, even colder than here. Anyway, when they caught me they shipped my happy ass off to China."

Was there about six months and then off to here...been here ever since."

Both Jake and Alex listened intently and were astonished by Johnnie's story.

"And how's this for a story, you know how I ended up in the kitchen?" Johnnie asked them, to which they both shook their heads "no."

"Racial stereotyping, boys, they needed help in the kitchen and some Russian officer assumed because I was black, I could cook. The guy running the kitchen when I started was a German. He died in 1960. Been running the place since," Johnnie told them smiling and almost laughing.

The evening discussions continued through dinner and cleanup and Jake and Alex also learned about the German—Hans—who had been in the camp since 1945. There was also another American named Robert Romanoff and a Brit named Harry Moore. The American was quick to introduce himself and talked with Jake and Alex. He was also more eager to talk with someone new, which was somewhat understandable since talking to new people helped with life at the camp.

Jake had already learned that thousands of foreign prisoners were in the gulag system. On occasion, he saw some of them in other work groups and heard stories being told about others. Thanks to Alex making the arrangement, Jake was now one of five foreigners working in the kitchen.

As the first few days passed, Jake and Alex learned more about the other workers. The most that Jake knew up to this point about foreign prisoners was that most of them were Germans and some Japanese from World War II. He learned that there were also Americans from the end of World War II who had been in the German POW camps that the Soviets had overrun. Additionally, there were other Americans from the Korean and Vietnam wars, Cold War operations, and aircraft shoot downs. Jake had also heard stories of other foreigners, like the French and British, who had been held prisoner, but their presence was not confirmed until he met some of them.

When Robert Romanoff first approached Jake and Alex, his appearance startled Jake. As they sat at the main kitchen table, they noticed the frail elderly man approach. When he spoke, he was short of breath and at moments seemed distant and forgetful. When Robert told them his story, it puzzled Jake because he was not a pilot. He was an American Army lieutenant colonel working intelligence, assigned to Berlin, Germany, after the end of World War II. In 1948, he was walking down a street in Berlin when he was taken by KGB, a tactic that was used often during the Cold War. Robert was kept in solitary and interrogated for almost three years before he was placed in the camp. An unusual piece of Robert's story was that he was given a military trial, where he was convicted of treason.

"You see, my parents immigrated to the United States from Russia in 1917. I was born in Russia in 1915," he said.

The name Romanoff didn't help, and he was told he was a traitor to the Soviet Union because he did not return to Russia to fight in the war.

The story told by Harry Moore was similar, except for the being born in Russia part. Harry was also stationed in Berlin in 1947 when he was taken by the KGB. Harry and Robert told them about some others who were also taken in Berlin and other places, maybe a dozen or so they estimated, which included some French. Their estimates were based on their paths crossing over the years and stories of them from other prisoners. They also told them that many had been released, but they had no idea as to why some were released and others were not.

Learning about each other was part of the first few days in the kitchen, and on the evening of learning Robert's story, Jake lay in his bed and felt sad for him. His story was heartbreaking to listen to as he reminisced about his wife and children, his life before World War II, and his assignment to Berlin. He had trouble remembering at times and teared up as he talked—it bothered Jake to see Robert the way he was.

Alex saw that Jake was disturbed and tried to encourage him not to let Robert's story bother him, but as Jake lay in his bunk, his mind went in all directions. Robert, who was thirty-eight when he was taken in 1948, was now seventy years old and had spent the past thirty-four years in prison. Jake had difficulty digesting the fact that Robert had been there that long. He glanced down a few rows of bunks and looked at the sleeping German, and then at Johnnie, and the Brit. Jake was almost in a panic knowing how long the others had been there as he tried to make sense of it all.

Hope and prayer had always been there for Jake, and he always believed that at some point, a guard would come and take him away, and he would be released to go home. Hope was the one constant that helped him stay alive, but now, the move to the kitchen barracks and learning about how long Johnnie and the others had spent in prison almost pushed Jake over the edge. He lay in his bunk trembling with anxiety and mumbling to himself.

Alex—in the next bunk—sensed there was something wrong and started to talk, trying to calm him down. Alex had a way about him when dealing with people and he eventually was able to calm Jake down as he told him that there was still hope. He told him about current events in the Soviet Union and the world, and how the old Soviet Union and its ways were changing; changing in a way that he believed would eventually lead to the release of foreign prisoners. Although Alex wasn't really sure, he was trying his best to help Jake as he added other bits of information.

"Ronald Reagan," Alex said to Jake.

"What?"

"Ronald Reagan could be the next President of the United States."

"The actor?"

"Yes, anything can happen, Jake, anything, you got to keep your faith, Jake."

The distraction of Alex's conversation relieved Jake and sparked a renewed interest in what had been going on in the world. Working in the kitchen would also give them access to news, and as Alex explained to him, a new chapter in life in preparation for their eventual release. Jake started to think about what Alex had told him and wondered about what was going on in the world, something he hadn't thought about in a long time. As he said his prayers and just before he fell asleep, he thought of the concept of an actor like Ronald Reagan being President.

The next morning, Jake and Alex got up and joined the kitchen crew. During conversations they learned more about the others and that over the years since Johnnie had been there, there had been seventeen foreigners who had worked in the kitchen. Four of them were just suddenly taken one day, and the others had died. The guards had told them that the four who were taken had been released, but of course there was never any way to confirm what actually happened to them.

It didn't take long for Jake to become accustomed to the new kitchen routine of getting up every day at 3:30 and spending the entire day at the kitchen until late evening. Although the days were longer, the work was not as strenuous. As it was on the work detail, everyone in the kitchen group became close friends and knew each other well.

After serving the meals in the dining hall, the kitchen crew ate their meals and most of the time they could take their time and enjoy the meal without any rush. The meal schedule would sometimes be shortened if the camp staff took longer with their meals, but normally the staff finished on time. The staff eating at the dining hall was something Jake was never aware of prior to being assigned to the kitchen. He also didn't know that a separate menu was prepared for the staff. The menu for the prisoners was generally bread and gruel, a stew or soup type of a meal. The staff was served this too, but also received additional portions of meats, breads, and vegetables when they were available.

During the first few weeks, Jake focused on learning the jobs, but he was still concerned about the kitchen assignment not lasting. As the weeks passed, his concern faded as he became used to the routine and the more relaxed atmosphere, even with the guards and the sergeant in charge—Sergeant Lebedev. Opportunity was also available at times to listen to a radio, read newspapers, and quietly discuss the news. After the experience Jake had gone through the previous ten years of being constantly guarded, he developed a subconscious trait not to trust anything or leave anything for granted. Yet it was still a relief to work in the kitchen and have a small perception of some freedom, even if it was only inside the kitchen.

As the weeks passed, Jake and Alex became fixtures as part of the kitchen crew. Guards and staff came to know them. Alex had particularly become knowledgeable of how the kitchen operated, and just like any business, he noticed that the kitchen received daily, twice, and three times a week deliveries from various suppliers, who brought their delivery trucks into the camp and delivered directly to the kitchen. The delivery people were civilians and were carefully checked upon entering and leaving the camp, and as the scheduled deliveries were made, Jake and Alex befriended the delivery people.

One of the suppliers made their delivery around seven in the evening at the end of the day on Mondays, Wednesdays, and Fridays. One evening the truck showed up as it always did, and the kitchen crew went about their work cleaning and prepping for the next day.

"Karla!" Alex suddenly yelled out.

Everyone looked to see what Alex was so excited about as he ran across the kitchen to the door where one of the delivery truck workers was entering. The female worker also yelled out to Alex as she ran toward him. Jake and the others stood and watched Alex and the woman as they embraced and kissed like long lost lovers. After a few moments, they broke their embrace, and Alex noticed everyone watching.

"This is my wife Karla," Alex told everyone.

This was one of the few times Jake had seen Alex out of his usual character.

Alex introduced Jake, Johnnie, and some of the others to Karla while they unloaded the truck. They realized that Karla worked for the delivery company as she smiled and explained to them that this was her new route. It didn't have to be said, but it was clear that Alex or someone he knew made arrangements for his wife to get the job. While it was obvious, it wasn't completely safe. Sergeant Lebedev was in the kitchen when Karla arrived, and chose to ignore Alex's announcement about his wife. Still, everyone knew that a visit by someone's wife might be a welcomed moment, but they all knew without saying that it also had to be kept quiet.

After they finished loading the truck, they all sat down to eat dinner at the oversized kitchen table that also doubled as a worktable. Karla and the other truck worker joined them, which had already been the routine for the workers even before Karla. Alex and Karla talked and caught up, but Karla also made a point to talk with everyone at the table, even to Sergeant Lebedev who never joined the table but did eat dinner by the entrance of the kitchen. Her personality was pleasant, heartwarming, and everyone took an instant liking to her.

As they finished eating, the crew started to go back to work. Alex and Karla inconspicuously disappeared for a few minutes and were not noticed until Alex was seen working in the stockroom when the delivery truck was heard leaving. Within an hour, all the work had been completed and the crew began to head for the barracks. Sergeant Lebedev grabbed a bag of food on his way out, which was also a routine that Johnnie and the kitchen crew did for years, letting the guards take home any leftover food for their families.

At the barracks, everyone went about their nightly routines and eventually went to bed. As Jake lay in his bed, he thought about Alex and Karla. He was happy for Alex and didn't hold any resentment, but he couldn't help but have feelings about it. The happy reunion reminded him about his wife; he realized he had not thought of her in a long time. At first he was upset, but as he thought more about Alex and Karla, he became happy and grateful for their reunion. It made him realize that he had allowed himself to fall into a complacent attitude and that he had completely stopped thinking about his family. Seeing Karla reawakened a part of him he had not seen or felt in years, and he was happy to have his memories rekindled.

The three times a week deliveries became part of the weekly schedule, but Alex and Karla limited their intimacy. Most days they would have dinner with everyone and talk. Karla always left according to schedule. They were careful not to bring attention to themselves; they also had feelings of guilt, knowing that the others did not have opportunity to be with their wives, and they did not want to cause any hurt to anyone. Alex and Karla did, on occasion, manage to slip away, but their absence was always discrete and unnoticed.

One Wednesday evening, the kitchen crew was sitting at the table eating when they heard Sergeant Lebedev talking with someone at the kitchen door. They heard female voices and then the footsteps of Sergeant Lebedev and two women approaching the kitchen.

"They were late getting out of work and want to know if they can get some dinner?" Sergeant Lebedev explained.

Johnnie immediately said yes and got up to get the two women some food. Jake noticed the women were nurses from the camp infirmary and although he recognized them as nurses, he did not realize that one of the women was the nurse who tended to him five years earlier. When Jake saw Johnnie get up, he also got up and made room for them to sit at the table next to him. Johnnie and Jake got dinner for them and then sat back down with Jake sitting next to the nurse he had first met five years earlier.

Conversations picked back up where they left off, except for Jake who remained quiet for about a minute until the nurse turned to him and smiled. "I remember you from when they brought you to the infirmary...Jacob, right?"

Jake was taken by surprise that he didn't remember her and that the nurse remembered him. Alex, Karla, and some of the others overheard the nurse's comment.

"I can't believe you remember me."

"Yes, I remember...you were the worst one I'd ever seen. The things he did to you...the things he did...unforgivable. I could never forget you, no one could ever forget," the nurse said, her eyes slightly tearing up and voice crackling as she spoke.

Everyone in the kitchen listened. They all thought they knew the story about Jake, and that it was similar to many others, but hearing the nurse say one sentence—in the manner she said it—painted a different picture about Jake, and gave some of them goose bumps and chills when they watched her, and heard her speak.

"I'm Nadya," the teary-eyed nurse told Jake with a smile as she slightly rubbed his shoulder, and then returned to eating.

There was an awkward silent moment at the table.

"I'm Jake," he said to Nadya in an attempt to change the mood as he looked around the table and then to Nadya, which generated a few laughs and another smile from Nadya. Johnnie, Alex, and the others quickly followed up with introductions and changed the mood.

There was no rush to finish dinner and after everyone was done, they started to get up from the table. Conversations broke up as did the primarily one-sided conversation Nadya had with Jake. He was listening, but he was more like a shy schoolboy as the 25-year-old Nadya talked to him while they sat and ate. She said goodbye as she started to the door with the other nurse.

"Join us again for dinner," Alex yelled out to Nadya.

A little embarrassed, Jake looked at Alex and then looked toward Nadya and repeated the request, just not as loudly or enthusiastically. She nodded yes.

Nadya did return, sometimes once or twice a week, and sat and ate with the kitchen crew. Sometimes, some of the infirmary workers including doctors came with her to sit, talk, and eat. Prison guards also came to eat with the kitchen crew. Over time, Nadya formed a friendship with Jake, a platonic courtship that Jake had difficulty understanding. The first meeting in 1975 and then five years later in the kitchen did not add up for Jake. What the connection was, what made Nadya have an attraction toward him was not clear, but it was also an attraction he did not object to or question.

The visits by Nadya and Alex's wife Karla continued for years. The daily schedule of the kitchen became routine and in a way a blessing. The harshness of the working conditions outside the kitchen were well known, and by virtue of working in the kitchen, Jake and the others were fortunate. Prisoners were still dying almost every day from illness, malnutrition, and weather, but for Jake, at least he had a better chance of survival having a job in the kitchen.

CHAPTER 18

TURN THE RADIO OFF

FIVE YEARS LATER

15 April, 1985

Day 5,404

Another five years passed for Jake, five years of working in the kitchen at a job that was long hours, long days, and long weeks. When Jake and the others had a brief moment of self-pity, they only had to look in the faces of the prisoners they served meals to and watch the formations of prisoners who marched out and then back into the camp. While their existence was harsh and difficult, Jake also knew it could be, and had been, much worse.

Fourteen years and nine months had passed since he was first captured in Vietnam where he spent his first three years in prison. Those three years seemed like an eternity ago as life had become an uncomfortable routine that had also developed some brief moments of solitude and friendships.

The small group of prisoners that fluxed in size from ten to fifteen in the kitchen was more like a family or brothers who had formed a unique skill of working together with efficiency and friendship. The freedom of the kitchen, including the trust of the prison officials, provided an independent environment, which gave them slightly more access to the outside world, including news and a radio.

The almost autonomous life for Jake and the others had to be controlled and not made too noticeable. At the same time, their personal bonds had become very close and Karla had managed to keep her delivery job and still visited three nights a week. Occasionally, she brought their three children, including their two-year-old daughter. The visits by the children were therapeutic for the kitchen crew and even for the nurses and Nadya who still came for dinner a few times a week.

Jake and Nadya's close relationship had lacked physical intimacy, although opportunity had been there if they wanted. Their friendship was close and although they had never said that they loved each other, their love for each other had grown and was obvious to Alex, Karla, and some of the others—an awkward and yet romantic situation for them. The reality was that they saw each other maybe one or two hours a week while sitting at a table eating dinner and had known each other over five years. Even the awkward relationship had become part of the routine.

It had been almost two years since any new workers were assigned, even though the kitchen had lost four workers to release from prison and one death, which left eleven. The newest worker that was assigned two years earlier was another American, Jerry Davis. He was a Navy electronics officer and was shot down north of the South China Sea in 1979 and was just one of dozens of listed missing during the Cold War era. Jerry and one other crewman were the only survivors out of an eleven-man crew.

Aside from life inside the prison, life and rumors outside the prison sparked many discussions about problems with the government and the Soviet war in Afghanistan. The discussions were fueled by what seemed to be a shrinking prison population, which had been noticeable by the kitchen considering that the numbers of meals they prepared had dropped by thirty percent during the past year. Rumors aside, information from the outside kept everyone curious about what was happening or what might happen. News aided in giving the Russian prisoners hope that their sentences might end early and for Jake and the other foreigners hope that some event could somehow get them released. The ability to be able to listen to the radio also helped in giving them hope.

Alex had also been a source of information since the day he arrived, and his news reports always seemed to be true. Alex told them about Ronald Reagan becoming President of the United States, the food shortages, and other political events in the Soviet Union. The radio, which sometimes verified what Alex had told them, was a good source of information too. Usually they rotated from local Russian radio stations to the Radio Free Europe and Radio Free Moscow stations for news and music. The radio had been in the kitchen before Jake and Alex came there, and the only restriction was the time of day, generally never when other prisoners were around, and the volume had to be kept low enough that it could not be heard outside or in the dining hall. These restrictions generally resulted in the radio being played only in the evenings after dinner had been served, which meant that it was during dinner for the kitchen crew and being able to listen to music created a more relaxed atmosphere.

On April 15, 1985, a Monday just like any other day, the day was coming to a close. Because it was a Monday, Karla was there for dinner, but even her presence was part of the routine. Nadya only came to dinner a few nights a week, but was not there that night. The radio was on, and the volume turned on low. Everyone was at the table like usual. At one end Alex sat with Karla and some of the others while Jake and Jerry sat at the other end. Johnnie was in his office and little attention was paid to the radio, even the sound of the radio had become part of the routine, on occasion generating remarks about what some of them called "noise" or "garbage" instead of music.

The occasional comments aside, the radio sat on a shelf on the wall and played on, overshadowed by conversations. The station dialed in that night was Radio Free Moscow, similar to Radio Free Europe and other United States anti-communist propaganda stations, but no one really paid any attention to the propaganda, only the music. As one song ended, the radio announcer came on and introduced the next song, which went unnoticed.

At about thirty seconds into the song, the chorus—"Born in the U.S.A."—was repeated several times coming over the radio while table conversations continued. Toward the end of the first chorus, Jake stopped eating and tried to listen. Jerry, who sat across from him noticed and also caught the chorus. Although it had not been noticed by anyone else yet, Jake and Jerry were not sure what they heard or if they heard it right, but for that moment, they were fixed on the sound of the radio. Jerry stayed seated and stared at the radio while Jake slowly got up and walked over to it, still unnoticed by anyone as the—"Born in the U.S.A."—chorus played again. Jake and Jerry heard the words clearly as the song continued to play. Vic, one of the Russian prisoners sitting by Alex and Karla noticed Jake.

"What's he doing?" Vic asked Alex, but not getting a response. "What's he doing over there?" Vic asked again, this time tapping Alex on the arm.

Alex and Karla turned their attention toward Jake, as did everyone else and silence took over the kitchen, except for the radio as they watched Jake standing by the radio staring at it.

"It sounds like noise," Vic said.

"Quiet," Alex told Vic as everyone continued to watch Jake and Jerry.

As they watched, Johnnie slowly came out of the office, stopped at the door, and looked at the radio. Johnnie had come out just seconds before the chorus played again, and as everyone watched, the expressions on Jake, Jerry, and Johnnie's faces said something was wrong as the chorus of the song played. For whatever the reason, the chorus of the song had hit a core in the Americans, and as the chorus played again, goose bumps came over Alex as he let out a sigh, which Karla and Vic both noticed.

"What?" Karla asked.

"It's the song…it says 'Born in the U.S.A.'" It was suddenly clear to everyone at the table that the song had the same effect on all three of the Americans. The fourth American, Robert, was unaware of the words of the song, just that something was wrong. Jake just stood and listened to the song play out, as did Johnnie standing in the doorway.

When the song ended, Alex and the others were not sure what to do or say. Jake noticed Johnnie and turned toward him, and saw tears in Johnnie's eyes. Jake also looked over at

Jerry—the three of them just looked at each other for a few seconds and said nothing. The silence was broken by Johnnie.

"I've been here thirty-three years," a tearful Johnnie said as he turned around and went back into the office.

Jake turned toward the radio and turned it off. Then he turned toward the table, looked at everyone with a blank stare, and said nothing.

"Ronald Reagan," Alex yelled out, breaking the silence and getting everyone's attention, except for Jake.

"Ronald Reagan," Alex yelled out again.

Jake made eye contact with Alex, but did not say anything.

"Ronald Reagan, your President, he will get you all out of here, I know it, I just know it will happen," Alex said.

"Things are happening, just look at us and what we do, the release of prisoners and everyone knows you're here now. They can't hide it anymore...you've got to believe that, you're going to get out of here," Alex went on trying to encourage Jake and the others.

Alex spent the rest of the evening telling them about different political movements and other events that would have an impact on getting all political prisoners, not just the Americans released. The evening ended with everyone going to bed.

"Keep your faith, Jake...keep your faith, you've got to believe that you're getting out of here and not give up," Alex said.

Although Alex tried, his effort did not prevent or stop Jake from becoming depressed.

The next morning at 3:30 a.m., the day started out as usual, and for Jake, a night of sleep and efforts by Alex had slightly helped calm him down. At the dining hall, work went on as usual with one exception: the absence of Johnnie. After a couple of hours, concern for him mounted. Johnnie had never been late, nor had anyone ever been late or not been where they were supposed to be. Everyone was concerned, and even though Sergeant Lebedev hadn't yet noticed, Alex finally told him Johnnie was missing. The reaction from Sergeant Lebedev was not what Alex hoped for. Sergeant Lebedev had witnessed the previous night's incident in the kitchen and had the same immediate concern about Johnnie.

The routine of the day continued as everyone went about their duties. Sergeant Lebedev had not returned all day, and conversations in the kitchen were limited and centered on work-related issues. No one spoke or speculated about Johnnie, not even during dinner. After dinner, everyone got up from the table and began their end-of-the-day duties. It was just a few minutes after they finished dinner that Alex heard someone coming in the side door to the kitchen. When Alex and a few others heard the door, they watched to see who it was—hoping it was Johnnie—it was Sergeant Lebedev. As everyone in the kitchen drew close to see Lebedev, they saw coming in with him the young Lieutenant Rybin, the officer in charge of the dining hall. This was only the second time they had ever seen the lieutenant.

As the sergeant and Rybin entered the kitchen, the old sergeant acted more like a father and was visibly distressed. The young lieutenant attempted to maintain his composure, but it was also obvious given his young age and inexperience that he was also distressed and felt out of place standing in front of the kitchen crew. At first, there was silence as they waited for someone to speak, but nothing was said as Lebedev walked over to the table, sat down, and left the lieutenant standing alone. Alex instinctively knew why they were there. Alex also knew that Lebedev had known Johnnie for almost seven years, and that the young lieutenant didn't know how to say what he came there to say.

Alex approached the nervous lieutenant.

"Major," the lieutenant said.

"Is he dead?"

"Yes, Major."

Everyone in the kitchen heard the answer.

"Do you want to know…" the lieutenant started to ask, but Alex interrupted.

"It's all right, Lieutenant, we don't need to know."

Everyone already had privately suspected Johnnie had taken his own life and knowing the details was not necessary.

"I'm sorry, Major, everyone," the lieutenant said. He followed up by telling them that he knew they all cared for Johnnie and that Johnnie cared for them. The lieutenant told Alex that he would arrange for a truck and have Sergeant Lebedev take them to the burial site. Alex thanked the lieutenant for his kindness and understanding as he walked with him out of the kitchen.

The next day the kitchen operated as usual, but the workers were understandably filled with sadness over Johnnie. While everyone went about their duties, Jake knew that Johnnie had certain duties that still had to be done, like ordering supplies and food. Although he was not told to, he filled in and did Johnnie's job for the next few days. During the evenings, no one had turned on the radio since the night Jake turned it off. On the afternoon of the third day after Johnnie's death, Sergeant Lebedev took everyone to the burial site and allowed them to have their own service. Emotions were strong at the gravesite, and the newest member of the kitchen crew— Jerry—could see that. Jerry broke the emotional silence and began to speak, and gave an improvised eulogy that pleased everyone.

The visit to the gravesite was brief, and the kitchen crew was back at the kitchen within an hour, back at work getting ready for dinner. Jake went about doing his work and Johnnie's—which Sergeant Lebedev had noticed.

"You can have Johnnie's job if you want it," Lebedev told Jake.

"I'm not sure," Jake said after some hesitation.

"Take the job," Alex told Jake.

Although Jake had done the job for a few days, he was still reluctant to take it on, but at the insistence of Alex, the job was his and running the kitchen began another phase of prison life. He had already been working in the kitchen five years, but taking over and running it, like Johnnie had done, at first seemed fatal to him. As Johnnie had said, he had been there over thirty years, and Jake didn't even want to think about being there thirty years, yet he had already been in prison almost fifteen years.

Later that evening as everyone took their place at the table for dinner, Jake walked out of the office and looked toward everyone at the table for a moment. He then walked over to the shelf by the wall, turned the radio on, and then took his place at the table.

CHAPTER 19

END OF AN ERA

11 May, 1988
Day 6,526

On a Wednesday afternoon in May of 1988, life in the kitchen continued. Three years after the death of Johnnie and Jake taking over the running of the kitchen, the routines continued, even the routine of Alex giving Jake pep talks and keeping everyone up to date on world events. Most everyone was aware of current events, including the war in Afghanistan that the Soviets had been in for nine years. They were also aware of the early release of prisoners throughout the gulag system and the closing of hundreds of prison camps. Even the population at their camp had been reduced by half, and every week there was a steady flow of prisoners leaving prison instead of entering it.

The decrease in the prison population also created more idle time for the kitchen crew, and even though they still had to work the same long hours, the daily tasks had diminished, leaving time to think, read, and listen to the radio. It also left time to become depressed and to contemplate their own situations. While it was nice not to have to work as hard, the absence of work left time for the mind to be distracted by thinking of family and a life before the gulag.

With a smile on his face, Sergeant Lebedev came into the kitchen and handed Alex his early release papers. Alex and Sergeant Kresnev had been notified that they were to be processed out on Friday. The news was exciting for Alex, and everyone was happy for him, including Jake. Although Jake was happy, the reality of the kitchen seemed to be changing and with Alex leaving, it would leave only eight: three Americans, the Brit, the German, and three Russians. Alex reassured Jake that they would always need kitchens and that he would be safe as long as he stayed in the kitchen. Alex also reassured Jake that he would soon be released.

By the time Thursday night arrived, the word had circulated throughout the prison that Alex, Kresnev, and about twenty other prisoners were being released. After the evening meal, the kitchen became an unofficial host of a low-key going away party. Alex had made many friends during his stay to include guards and prison officials, and they all made their way to the kitchen to say goodbye. As the evening came to an end, it was difficult to believe that the kitchen was a prison kitchen.

The following morning, Alex said his goodbyes to the kitchen crew. As he said goodbye to Jake, he gave him a hug and told him not to lose hope. He also told Jake that his wife would keep her job and that they would continue to visit, keep in touch, and be lifelong friends, a friendship that Jake felt confident about despite the impending separation by Alex's release. During the next week, the absence of Alex was felt, but they adjusted and continued to adjust as the work requirements decreased. Alex and his wife also visited two weeks later and continued to visit almost weekly while the prisoner population in the camp experienced a steady decrease over the next year.

15 February, 1989
Day 6,806

Wednesday night the delivery truck pulled up out back. Alex and Karla came in carrying supplies and were followed by a few other men carrying more supplies. The presence of the extra people caught Jake's attention as did Alex's upbeat excitement. Alex talked about an historic day and asked the sergeant to pass the word that they would have a quiet celebration in the kitchen.

"The war is over, Jake. Afghanistan, it's over," an excited Alex told Jake.

While the final cleanup of the kitchen continued, the guards and prison staff started to arrive and Alex explained to

Jake and the others that the last Soviet soldiers left Afghanistan, and the war was officially over. Jake noticed how happy everyone was and the atmosphere was contagious, encouraging Jake and the others to join in the celebration. Throughout the evening, Jake saw that at times the mood grew somber as some of the Russians reflected on lost friends. On occasion some of them would look at Jake.

"Afghanistan was our Vietnam," a Russian soldier said to Jake.

That sentiment would be repeated many times during the evening and with it, Jake sensed something he couldn't exactly place, but it was something, and almost seemed like the Russians were expressing a sense of pity or remorse for the American prisoners, while some others expressed the opposite. Those moments never became too serious because Alex or someone else would quickly change the mood and the subject.

As the evening came to an end and everyone left, Alex and Karla gave Jake a hug and said goodbye. The next week they would visit again as would Nadya who had continued to visit every week. The daily activities continued with no significant changes for months, until November.

9 November, 1989

Day 7,083

In the early evening of Sunday, November 9, 1989, the kitchen crew was going about their business when Alex walked in. A

Sunday visit was unusual, and Alex was not his usual self. At first he told everyone nothing was wrong as he turned on the radio, but it was clear that something was going on. Still, Alex seemed reluctant to say anything.

About an hour later, around 7:45, conversations were disrupted when Alex suddenly went to the radio and turned up the volume. A news broadcast had come over the radio from Berlin, Germany. A few minutes later, at 6:53 p.m. Berlin time, an East German official started to make a statement concerning a new lifting of travel restrictions, in which the official stated the restrictions were to go in effect immediately.

Jake and the others didn't know what this announcement meant, but Alex seemed to know as he tried to explain the politics and events that had been occurring during the last few months throughout Europe and the Soviet Union. As the evening progressed, Alex told them about current events while they continued to listen to the radio. A few hours later the kitchen had about twenty guards and staff listening to the radio as well as watching a small black and white television one of the guards had brought in. They listened and watched as news reports were speculating on events in East Germany and its borders. Everyone in the kitchen listened and watched intently as the news reported about massive crowds of East Germans forming at the Berlin border crossings. At 10:30 p.m., the news reported that the gates at the Bornholmer

Strasse border crossing in Berlin were opened and that the crowds of people had started to cross the border.

The mood in the kitchen was mixed, with some expressing their approval and others disapproval, but it was definitely not the same mood as when the Afghanistan war ended. As the hours passed and everyone continued to take in the information, Alex explained to Jake and the others about the concerns of the Soviet government about a repeat by East Germany of countries like Poland and Hungary, that had already separated from the Soviet Union.

Jake and the others got a few hours of sleep that night, and when they woke up, Alex was still there. Alex gave them the latest updates and told them that the crowds were tearing down the Berlin Wall. Alex seemed excited but still concerned, and when he left, he told Jake not to worry and that he would check on him soon. Jake wondered why he was not supposed to worry, and although the Berlin Wall being torn down was significant, Jake wasn't sure how it would impact him or anyone else in the kitchen.

The Berlin Wall – November 9, 1990

12 July, 1990
Day 7,318

Nothing significant happened for Jake or the kitchen since November, although during the past few years the Soviet Union had been going through many internal changes, including the emptying of its prisons, its withdrawal from Afghanistan, and implications of the fall of the Berlin Wall, the impact on Jake and his kitchen crew had been minimal. There were still eight left in the kitchen, but the amount of meals prepared were less than half of what they had prepared ten years earlier. The days were still just as long. There were also new guards who seemed to be rotated more often.

As the evening ended and the kitchen crew entered their barracks, a new sergeant and a few guards were waiting for them. The sergeant explained that the foreign prisoners were being moved to a cellblock and the Russians would remain in the barracks. The foreigners would still be working the kitchen, but they would have to stay in the cellblock. There was no other explanation for the move. The news disturbed Jake and the others, but there was nothing they could do about it.

Jake and the others packed their things and were walked to their new home. He remembered the familiar building where he had spent his first three years. Although he was not put in the same cell, it was the same building he was in when he first arrived almost seventeen years earlier. As they were being taken to each of their individual cells, they were told that someone would come for them in the morning to take them to work. Jake, a little less intimidated than he was seventeen years earlier, reminded the sergeant to make sure they were on time so that the morning meal would be ready. The sergeant acknowledged Jake and even conveyed a sense of understanding. Jake entered his new cell, and the door was closed behind him and locked. He sat down in the chair and looked around the dimly lit cell with a feeling of disbelief and depression about what had just happened.

Every morning, the guards came and walked Jake and the others to the kitchen where they continued their daily schedules. In the evening, the guards did not seem concerned about what time they got everyone back to the cellblock as the new addition of heading to the cellblock was added to the daily schedule, usually around 10:00 p.m. With the exception of the new living conditions, the kitchen duties continued, visits from Nadya, Alex, and Karla continued, as did the continued slow decline in the prison population.

CHAPTER 20

REVOLUTION

MUNICH GERMANY — U.S. CONSULATE
19 August, 1991
Day 7,721— 21 years, 1 month, 21 days

The past year in the gulag prison kitchen had been uneventful for Jake, but in Munich, Germany, Charlie Smith started his day with what had also been uneventful in the basement of the American Consulate—but that was about to change.

Charlie Smith was in his early to mid-thirties and had been working for the government in a variety of assignments the past fifteen years. As Charlie sat at his desk and went over some paperwork, about a dozen people were working and going about their activities outside his office in the agency's operations center. The uneventful day began to change as one of Charlie's assistants, Ryan, brought in an envelope.

"Express courier just delivered this."

"One hour?"

"One hour, sender is Sokoll."

Charlie and Ryan smiled at the name and Charlie quickly opened the envelope. The one-hour delivery and sender name had some hidden importance to Charlie as he read the note inside, which was a request for a meeting. Charlie didn't share any information with Ryan at this point except to tell him to get a car and to call one of the taxis. Ryan acknowledged Charlie's instructions and left the office. A few minutes later, Charlie also left the office and walked through the operations center, and as he approached the door he turned around and got the attention of everyone in the room.

"I'll be back in about an hour, so let's find out if anything is in the works. Don't know what it is yet, but something's up, people, so let's track it down."

A few blocks away from the consulate in a high-rise apartment building, Soviet KGB intelligence personnel had their own smaller apartment-sized operations center from where they watched the American consulate and its personnel. Through the window, there was a direct line of sight toward the front of the consulate and its entrance from where a KGB agent watched while three other agents read newspapers and magazines. On the wall, they had a detailed organizational chart set up of names and pictures of consulate personnel to include Charlie and Ryan. They knew which department or section in the consulate where people worked and knew just about everything about who worked inside the consulate. There were, however, some question marks on some of the pictures and most of the pictures had index cards attached with information about each person, which included if they were an embassy state department employee, military, or other agency, including the CIA. Charlie and Ryan's pictures, and about two dozen of the other pictures had question marks about which agency they worked for.

The KGB agent watching out the window observed Charlie and Ryan getting into a car.

"Looks like Mr. Charlie and Ryan are going out!"

"Together?" one of the others asked as he got up and went to the window.

"Yes, together."

As Ryan drove the car out the entrance of the consulate, a taxi pulled up right behind them and honked the horn. Ryan immediately began to speed off and the taxi stayed right behind them. At the same time two KGB agents were in another car and followed behind the taxi. One of the KGB agents got on a radio.

"They're using the taxi again; do we have anyone else to help?"

In the apartment, one of the agents got the message on the radio and shook his head, knowing he had no one else available to help except to send out a few from the apartment—but he also knew from experience it would be too late by the time they would get there.

"No, no one available, just do what you can."

As Charlie and Ryan drove through the streets of Munich, Ryan drove erratically, not seeming to be going in any particular direction. His erratic driving was deliberate as he drove quickly through the streets, making turns every few blocks. The problem of being followed by KGB operatives was constant during the Cold War, especially for the intelligence personnel. In Munich, throughout Germany, and the world, intelligence operatives spent a major part of their lives on surveillance and countersurveillance, so it was a difficult task to keep the identities of intelligence personnel a secret. It was ever more difficult once an identity was known, for intelligence operatives like Charlie and Ryan to keep their activities secret.

August 19 was not an ordinary day for Charlie. Although the tactics of avoiding being followed and making a meeting was somewhat a normal activity, the upcoming meeting was not scheduled, and the information he would receive would be unlike any information he had ever received—this day was not going to be routine or normal.

The immediate task of avoiding being followed was the first priority. Charlie and Ryan's departure from the embassy was unscheduled and quick, which helped with preventing the KGB from not having enough time or people to follow. Sometimes the simplest and basic methods worked, and the KGB who followed already knew what was going to happen, which was why they called for help. They knew that at a busy intersection, Ryan would probably stall the car long enough for the traffic light to change, and the taxi would block the following KGB car. It was quite simple, always worked, and was frustrating to the KGB in the trail car.

Unfortunately, Charlie and Ryan knew that losing a tail would be short-lived if the KGB were determined to locate someone. Once clear of the intersection, Ryan quickly drove through the streets for a few more minutes, turned a corner, and came to an abrupt stop.

"Know where to pick me up?"

"Twenty minutes, get going."

Checking his watch, Charlie quickly exited the car and then entered a city train station. Ryan kept driving down the street, checking his mirrors to see if there was any trace of anyone following him or Charlie.

Inside the station, Charlie walked toward one of the train platforms, and right on time, a train pulled in, and he got on as the doors closed. He made his way through the train cars, and at one point, as he opened the door to walk to the next car, a man coming from the other direction was also stepping out of the opposite train car. Charlie and the other man acknowledged each other with a smile and greetings, and as their conversation was suppressed by the noise of the traveling train, the other man handed Charlie an envelope.

Twenty minutes later, Ryan pulled up near the exit of a train station as Charlie exited, walked to the car, and got in, and Ryan quickly drove off.

"We have to get back to the consulate as fast as we can," Charlie told Ryan.

"What's up?"

Charlie seemed not to know what to say for a few seconds. He seemed almost giddy and in disbelief about what he was about to share with Ryan; Charlie's temperament was uncharacteristic of his usual calm and unemotional personality.

"There's a coup in the works. The Soviets, they're having a coup...everything's going to fall," he said with a smile.

On the short ride back to the consulate, Charlie told Ryan to get to the ops center right away and to make sure that no one went home, to get everyone to work, alert everyone, notify assets, and to prep escape and evasion plans for inside Russia.

When the car pulled up to the consulate gates there was a line of cars waiting to get inside. The security check and line took a few minutes—Charlie was impatient. He told Ryan that he was going to go see the chief and Ryan should get to the ops center as soon as he got inside.

"Slow down!" Ryan said as he got out of the car—a reminder that the KGB was watching.

Charlie slowly walked to the consulate building.

"They're back," the agent in the apartment told everyone as he watched Charlie.

"Must not have been too important," another agent said.

Charlie made his way to the building and once inside ran to the chief's office. When he arrived, a secretary tried to tell Charlie that there was a meeting going on, but he ignored her and burst into the office.

"Sorry, boss, but I've got to see you right away," the winded Charlie said, and then asked the others in the office to leave. Charlie closed the door behind them.

"Okay, what's up?" the chief asked.

"Just had a meeting."

"And?"

"We got a couple of problems; the Soviets are having a coup, tonight or maybe tomorrow."

"A coup...where did you get that?"

"The meeting was with Sokoll. There's no doubt the coup is going to happen, or at least an attempt at it."

"Always something," the chief said as he sat down at his desk.

The chief thought for a few seconds and then got on the phone to his assistant and told her to get all the department chiefs in for an emergency meeting and to get the ambassador on the phone for him. The chief then hung up the phone, smiled, and was excited about the news of the Soviet Union's potential fall.

"So what's the other problem?"

Fifteen minutes later, Charlie raced into the operations center, which was in a flurry of activity. He headed to his office and called out to Ryan and Nancy to follow him. Charlie sat at the desk and pulled out an envelope from his pocket, got a piece of paper, transcribed some information from the envelope, and then gave it to Ryan.

"Besides everything else, we have to put together an operation, that's the priority, and we only have a few hours. You need to pull up a safe house, preferably a barn...a farm. It needs to have a big enough field for two helicopters and it needs to be along the border close to these coordinates on the paper."

"Is that all?" Ryan asked jokingly.

"No, one more thing. Tonight, we have to have it tonight."

He checked his watch and saw that it was already just past 1100 hours.

"Not much time on this one," Ryan commented.

"No, there's not. I'll fill you in later, but we've got to get started."

Ryan acknowledged the instructions and then left the office. Charlie then told Nancy—who was a senior manager—that she would be left in charge of the op center. After she left the office, Charlie started to look up some phone numbers.

BAD TOLTZ, GERMANY

U.S. Army Special Forces Headquarters

1115 Hours

Inside the headquarters command section, the telephone rang at the staff duty desk. A staff sergeant answered and went through the standard military greeting as Charlie anxiously waited.

"Sergeant, my name is Charlie Smith and I have a priority call for the battalion commander, need to speak with him right away."

"Sorry, Sir, he's out at the training site, actually almost everyone's out there."

"*Anyone* there?"

"The assistant S-3 is here."

"No, no, look, Sergeant, I really need to get the commander. Do you have another number where I can reach him?"

"Sorry, Sir, I can get him on the radio but that'll take a few...Sergeant Major Wilcox is heading out the door if..."

"Stop him!"

Flint Kaserne in Bad Tölz, Germany. Home of the U.S. Army Special Forces during the Cold War from 1953-1991. Former home of the former German Army SS-Junkerschule Officer Training School until the end of World War II.

While Charlie waited, the sergeant put the phone down and ran outside where he found Wilcox. The sergeant major came back inside and got on the phone.

"Sergeant Major Wilcox here."

Charlie and the sergeant major briefly exchanged greetings. Charlie asked the sergeant major to go to his office and call him back on a secure line. Wilcox hung up and went into his office to use that phone.

"Sergeant Major, I'm sorry but we don't have much time. Normal chain of command has been bypassed, and I've got authorization to get two of your A-teams for an operation."

"Charlie, I can't just..."

"I know, you'll be getting a call in a few minutes giving you authorization. As soon as you get that call, I need you to call me back. We're going to need those two teams, and I know you might not have full teams, but we need at least eight men on each for a cross border operation, and they need to be free-fall teams...and will be leaving your location in about three hours."

"Hold on a second." The sergeant major swung around in his chair and yelled out to the staff sergeant while he looked on the wall at his battalion staffing board.

"Yes, Sergeant Major," the sergeant answered.

"Get the CO on the horn and tell him to get back here for a Red Cross emergency...understand?" he said, emphasizing the implied hidden meaning of *red cross*. "And get someone from the comms section over here." The sergeant major swung back around toward his desk. "You said three hours, right?"

"That's critical, three hours, no more than four...and you know your people, so we need guys with experience."

"Understand, Charlie, but since we're talking free-fall guys, it may have to be composite teams."

"That's fine, Sergeant Major, but we need to make sure that whoever's on these teams they have some free-fall infil experience and will be able to hit the target."

"All right, Charlie. We can do that."

"I'll give you more info when you call back."

Charlie hung up the phone and called out for Ryan, and wrote down some notes while he waited. When Ryan came into the office, Charlie had him close the door.

"Okay, Ryan, we've got two operations going on here. We're going to leave Nancy in charge here at the ops center. You and me, separate operation...only us, the chief, and the ambassador know."

"Okay," a little bit excited but hesitant Ryan responded.

"You're going down to Bad Toltz to pick up the special ops guys and take them to the safe house. I'll get to the safe house with security and get set up. And we need to get out of here without our Rooski buddies across the street noticing."

As Charlie continued to give Ryan some more details about the operation, out in the office Nancy and some of the others heard them raising their voices, apparently disagreeing about something and causing Ryan to be somewhat emotional. When Ryan left Charlie's office, he was upset about something. Nancy and some of the others in the operations center noticed that Charlie was also upset, something they had never seen in Charlie before.

CHAPTER 21

THE MISSION

SOUTH GERMAN-CZECH BORDER
19 August, 1991
1830 Hours

As the late summer day began to transition into the evening twilight, Ryan, who drove one of three vans, approached the entrance roadway to the farm being used as the safe house. The vans were loaded with the men and equipment of two Green Beret A-Teams from Bad Toltz. The drive to the safe house had been relatively short, taking only about two hours to reach the isolated farm on the Czechoslovakian border. The vans turned off the main road onto the access road and drove past the main farmhouse, heading toward the oversized barn located a few hundred meters behind the house.

Inside the barn, Charlie heard the vans as they pulled up and walked over to the door, opened it and waved. Ryan and the others exited the vans, grabbed the equipment, and headed inside. The battalion commander, Colonel Sutter, and Sergeant Major Wilcox went inside the barn ahead of the others to check in with Charlie. The colonel, sergeant major, and Charlie greeted each other—it was apparent to those who looked on that the three had known each other a long time. While the Green Berets brought their equipment into the barn, the colonel attempted to inquire about the mission, but Charlie was evasive as he watched and studied the men as they entered the barn. Then he brought his attention back to the colonel as he opened up a folder and took out some papers.

"Colonel, Sergeant Major, first things first. You need to sign these nondisclosure agreements."

The colonel and sergeant major smiled and immediately realized the compartmentalization requirement of the mission, which also stopped any further inquiries. They signed the papers and handed them back.

"Compartmentalization...need I say more? And sorry, but you'll need to get going, you can take a few minutes, but I do need you to get going in about ten minutes."

"Understood. I hope you can understand that part of me that wants to go along," Sutter replied.

"I don't think you'd want in on this one, Sir," Charlie answered.

The colonel was puzzled by Charlie's remark as he and the sergeant major mingled a few minutes while they talked with the men before leaving the barn. Meanwhile, Charlie was still watching the two A-Teams—16 men total—as they interacted and waited. One of the skills Charlie developed over the years was an ability to read people. Ryan came over and gave him a roster of the men and some other paperwork. Charlie looked it over and then called over the two team leaders— Captain Hanna and Master Sergeant McDonald.

As Charlie took nondisclosure forms out of a folder, he had already taken notice of the master sergeant's age, and knew by virtue of the rank and being a Special Forces team sergeant that the master sergeant likely had extensive experience. He wasn't totally sure about the captain.

"Gentleman, I know you don't know anything yet, other than this is a live operation, and with that, you need to know this is a combat operation, but first, you and your guys will need to sign these nondisclosure forms. Then I'll give all of you a mission briefing."

"Sounds good," McDonald said.

"So, Sergeant McDonald, where's your team leader?" Charlie asked.

"Well, it's kind of like a combination of officers getting kicked out, RIF'ed, that reduction in force crap, and shortage of Special Forces officers...so I'm it for my team."

"I'm sure that's not a problem," Charlie said with a smile and tone of knowing reassurance.

"Hopefully guys like Captain Hanna here stepping up will get some of the slots filled; he's been in group a few months now," McDonald told Charlie.

"Okay...good," Charlie responded.

Captain Hanna detected what he thought was a tone of uncertainty in Charlie's remark.

"I know I've only been in group a few months, Mr. Smith, but I'll tell you I know what I'm doing...was a Ranger, Ranger platoon leader in the Panama operation, got 87 free-fall jumps, and..." Charlie interrupted and placed his hand on Hanna's shoulder.

"It's all right, Captain Hanna, it's all right...sorry if I hurt your feelings, but this is not about feelings, it's about experience, and it's clear you got the experience...all right? Some of these guys, even though they have the rank and title, don't have the experience, Captain, and it's natural to question the experience level of a young captain like yourself, but like I already figured out, you got experience, so no problems, okay?"

"All right, sorry. Just thought maybe..."

"Don't be sorry, just focus on the mission. Right now we need to get the forms signed, and I'll be over in a few minutes."

"All right, Mr. Smith," Hanna acknowledged and they headed back over to their teams.

A few minutes later, the colonel and sergeant major wrapped up their conversations with the team members, said their goodbyes to Charlie, and left. Ten minutes later while the men were prepping their gear, Ryan came inside and motioned for Charlie to come outside. One of the security personnel was with Ryan when Charlie got there.

"Little problem," Ryan told Charlie.

"Problem?"

"We caught two of our KGB buddies over by the farmhouse."

"Which ones?"

"Our Munich guys."

Charlie was a little upset as they headed over to the panel van where the KGB agents were being kept. Charlie opened the door and looked at the two agents. Although he didn't know them personally, he did recognize them and focused his attention on the older agent.

"So, where did we screw up?" Charlie asked.

The younger agent kept a stern face, intent on not talking, but the older more experienced agent gave a cooperative smile.

"This main road here is the only main road for twenty kilometers. We just checked everything off the road and got lucky, or maybe unlucky, yes?"

Charlie nodded his head in agreement and looked at Ryan as he thought about what to do.

"You know normally we would probably have to get rid of you," Charlie said to the KGB agent in a semi-serious manner.

"Yes, yes, so what's *not* normal, Comrade Smith?"

Charlie and Ryan smiled and almost laughed at the KGB agent's remark.

"Tell you what. Tomorrow, we'll let you go. Maybe tomorrow you won't want to go, all right?"

"Thank you, Mr. Smith," a grateful KGB agent told Charlie.

Charlie instructed the security to hold the KGB agents as he and Ryan went back to the barn.

"Heads up, everyone, gather around," Charlie announced.

"First, with the nondisclosure statements you've signed, you all realize that this is a classified operation, and likely always will be. Second, this is a combat operation, the real deal, guys, and people are going to get killed tonight, by you, and so I've got to ask, if you're not prepared to do that, because I'm telling you that is part of this operation and there is absolutely no way around it; if you cannot do it, you need to step out right now."

He scanned the group and allowed them to think over the options.

"Let's get downrange," one of the guys yelled out, followed by a few other agreements.

"All right then, I appreciate your enthusiasm, gentlemen. Not sure if you'll still be as enthusiastic when you learn what the mission is, so...last chance, gentlemen."

Charlie looked around the group one more time. "The mission has been named Operation Buried Treasure, and I already know what your first question is, guys: Where do they come up with these names?" Charlie said, getting a few laughs, and then he continued. "You'll figure out the reason for the name of the mission in short order. In twenty-five minutes, two Soviet helicopters will be picking us up... two MI-17s or what you know as HIPs, to be exact." There were already questions on the faces of the men as Charlie spoke. "You heard right, a joint operation. So the plus is you guys get to fly on three Soviet aircraft tonight. The MI-17 helicopter out of here, then we'll board an An-22 fixed wing for our infil, and then exfil on another helicopter, the MI-26, which is ironically known in those aircraft recognition cards you guys got as the HALO."

The prospect of flying in Soviet aircraft generated some positive remarks and enthusiasm from the men.

"So here's a brief FRAG order. Each of your teams will be conducting a joint operation with two Soviet Special Forces teams inside the Soviet Union. One U.S. team with one Soviet team, same mission, two different locations. Distance to targets from here is approximately 1200 miles. We have to be on target in about five hours. Because of the distance, guys, that's why we're taking helos to a Czech air base, which is where we link up with the Soviet teams, and from there fixed wing so we get to the target in time." Charlie paused for a moment while he pointed out with a stick, key locations on the sand-box.

"If you don't know it, the AN-22 is about the fastest transport aircraft in the world, and we're estimating close to a three-hour flight time to travel roughly a thousand miles, and then the fun part, guys, HALO jump from 28,500 feet."

"Hell yeah!" one of the guys yelled out.

"...hell yeah is right. Two drops about five minutes apart. Soviets have different oxygen consoles, which is why you had to bring your own, and will be doing about ninety minutes of pre-breathing.

"Sounds like you've got some HALO experience yourself," McDonald interjected, referring to Charlie's knowledge of military free-fall and tactical operations.

Charlie smiled. "I'd say that. I come from the same background as you guys, and as for HALO jumps, about two hundred or so."

The manner of Charlie's reply and clear understanding of terminology was well received by everyone and conveyed a sense that Charlie knew what he was talking about.

"We'll cover more of the tactical execution a bit later and on the aircraft, but just to give you a little background on what's going on, the big news is that it looks like there's going to be a coup in the Soviet Union..." Positive outburst from the men interrupted Charlie for a few seconds.

"Not so fast, guys. The Soviet team's working with us, they know about it, but not involved in it, and the actual mission...well." Charlie paused as he thought about how to explain what he was going to tell them next. "The Soviets have had a policy of not releasing prisoners. They've kept Germans and Japanese from World War II, some estimates were that 100,000 Germans were never released. Maybe a thousand Americans who were in German POW camps overrun by the Soviets, never released. Kidnapping of intelligence officers and other various Cold War personnel. Americans from the Korean War, Vietnam, and some of the aircraft shoot downs...kept by the Soviets and never let go," Charlie said as the mood in the barn changed.

The information got the attention of the men, but also created some doubts—Charlie's story sounded more like a Hollywood conspiracy movie than an actual operation, and the expressions on some of the men's faces were of doubt concerning the truthfulness of what he had just told them.

"Believe me, gentlemen, it is true. Documented, former Soviet and American prisoners interviewed who've provided names, dates, places. Keep in mind that the Soviets have always tried to be careful not to let the ones they kept get out, unless it was an exchange, and that's one of the ways we've found out. It's pretty simple, they do not let them out, and they cannot allow it to be known that they, quite frankly, imprisoned these guys, ours and others from countries such as England and France."

"So what is this about? Are they letting them go now or what?" a disturbed McDonald asked.

"No, they are not. Like I said, gentlemen, they cannot, and will not allow any of them to be released. Regardless of the outcome of a coup or takeover, the same people will be running things, and those people are not going to allow what they did to become public knowledge."

"Don't like where this is going," McDonald said to Charlie.

"Agreed, I don't like it either, but like it or not, we have a job to do, a job with a bigger picture than our emotions or feelings. There are a lot more details we need to cover, but the mission objective is the prisoners. Part of our mission is to make sure that there is no evidence, no record, no trace of the existence of prisoners kept by the Soviets, and that is also the mission of the Soviet Spetsnaz who are going with us tonight. These prisoners did not exist, do not exist, and after tomorrow…they still will not exist."

Charlie looked over the faces of the men and could see disappointment and disagreement as he was getting ready to go over more details of the operation.

Inside the barn, Charlie spent the next twenty minutes continuing his briefing while outside the barn the security force maintained watch. As Charlie finished his briefing, the distinct sound of the two approaching Soviet transport helicopters could be heard in the distance. Charlie and the two A-Teams, carrying their parachutes and equipment, exited the barn and walked toward the open field behind the barn. They made their way and waited for the helicopters to land. As the helos approached, one of the security personnel used a strobe light to signal them to the landing zone. As soon as the helos landed, the A-Teams and Charlie quickly loaded up and took off, heading eastward toward Czechoslovakia.

CHAPTER 22

THE EXECUTION

PARDUBICE AIR BASE, CZECH REPUBLIC
19 August, 1991
2140 Hours

As the two-hour flight that covered just over 200 miles drew to an end, the Soviet helicopters landed and taxied toward a hangar at the Czech air base. The helicopters maneuvered adjacent to the hangar where the members of the Spetsnaz Teams came outside and helped the A-Teams offload their equipment and take it inside. The initial meet and greet between the Cold War enemies had been mixed, but within the few minutes it took to get everyone and the equipment inside, introductions started.

The conversations between the American Green Berets and Soviet Spetsnaz were short-lived after Charlie was greeted by Soviet Colonel Provaznik and Captain Stravskoski—time constraints required them to get underway quickly.

Colonel Provaznik, a KGB officer with a Spetsnaz background, went by the name Colonel Karl and it was apparent that he and Charlie knew each other. Quick introductions were made with Captain Stravskoski, Captain Hanna, and Sergeant McDonald. The decision was made that McDonald's team and Charlie would go with the colonel. Captain Hanna and his team would go with Captain Stravskoski.

Colonel Karl gave the word to move out and the Soviet soldiers—who already had their equipment loaded on the awaiting AN-22 Condor—helped carry the Americans' equipment, which included the two coffin-sized oxygen consoles, to the aircraft. As they headed out, Charlie told everyone that the mission details would be covered in flight, and within minutes everyone was loaded up, and the aircraft took off.

It didn't take long after takeoff for the Soviets and Americans to start talking again, and although Cold War enemies, they shared a common bond—as soldiers and brothers-in-arms—and had curiosities about each other. Colonel Karl, Charlie, Captain Hanna, and Sergeant McDonald spent the first fifteen minutes of the flight going over the planning for the operation, and once they settled on the details, they gave the mission briefing to everyone else.

After the briefing and details were completed, everyone got their equipment and parachutes on and then connected to the oxygen consoles in preparation for the ninety minutes of required pre-breathing they had to do for their upcoming jump from 28,500 feet. An hour had already passed by the time the briefings were completed and equipment was on. Conversations ceased once the oxygen masks were on, and the pre-breathing began. The red cabin lights were turned on a few minutes later, in what was the routine procedure for everyone's eyes to adjust for nighttime operations. Everyone sat and waited for the next hour and a half to get to the drop zone inside the Soviet Union.

20 August, 1991
0040 Hours

A time zone change during the flight did not impact the actual flight time to reach the drop zones. At 0040 hours, the loadmasters used hand signals and gave Colonel Karl a ten-minute warning. After ten minutes, the first Soviet team and Captain Hanna's team would jump. Five minutes after them, the other Soviet team and McDonald's team with Charlie and Colonel Karl would jump. The minutes quickly passed as the first two teams stood up and followed the jumpmaster hand signals of one of Captain Hanna's sergeants and one of the Soviet sergeants. Six minutes before drop time, the ramp was lowered, instantly causing the high altitude cold air to circulate inside the aircraft and give everyone a brisk chill. Two minutes before jump, the first two teams disconnected from the oxygen consoles and transferred to the oxygen tanks attached to their parachute harnesses. Huddling close in two groups side-by-side, one American and one Soviet, they made their way toward the edge of the ramp.

The jumpmasters gave a one-minute warning signal. When the go signal was given, both of the teams simultaneously exited the ramp and in a second—vanished in a single motion—silently disappearing into the darkness, which generated muffled, enthusiastic yells from under the oxygen masks of the remaining team members on the aircraft.

Immediately after the first two teams cleared the ramp, one of McDonald's sergeants and one of the Soviet sergeants began their jumpmaster duties, and repeated the previous pre-jump procedures. The two teams disconnected from the oxygen console, and at the two-minute mark, they moved toward the edge of the ramp—just as the previous teams had done. They huddled in their respective teams and waited for the go signal. As the loadmasters watched on from behind the teams, the go signal was given and the two teams left the ramp, silently disappearing into the darkness.

20 August, 1991
0030 Hours
Day 7,722

Ten minutes before the Special Forces teams made their high altitude jump, Jake was awakened in his cell by the sound of voices and commotion in the prison hallway. He got up and went over to the door to listen. He could hear the cell doors being opened and prisoners being moved out. Jake thought for a moment and decided to grab some things—his diary and some other papers—and stuffed them in his clothes. The cell door opened and the guards yelled at Jake to move out to the hallway, where everyone was quickly being lined up—the guards seemed uneasy and nervous—and not much time was given before heading outside. The guards had been quick at getting the prisoners out of the cells and just as quick at rushing them outside to waiting trucks.

As the crowded truck moved out, Jake looked around and saw some familiar faces. At first they whispered quietly among themselves until they noticed that there were no Russian prisoners or guards on the truck. They did a head count—thirty-seven of them—and found that most were Americans except for a German, two English, and one Frenchman. The uncomfortable truck ride dragged on for a few hours. During the ride, there were intense conversations and speculation about what was happening and they did their best to stay optimistic.

REMOTE WOODED AREA

0220 Hours

In a remote wooded area of Russia, a truck loaded with the foreign prisoners came to a stop in where the only illumination was from headlights. The guards began to immediately yell at the prisoners—ordering them off the truck. As the prisoners exited, there were soldiers there who took over giving the instructions and quickly ordered and moved the prisoners toward the edge of a ditch—three feet deep, six feet wide and thirty feet long.

The soldiers then forced the prisoners into the ditch, face down in the dirt. Many of the prisoners wanted to resist and tried to argue, but the soldiers were quick and forceful, hitting them to make them get in the ditch and lie down. It only took the soldiers about a minute to get everyone into the ditch, and within seconds, the soldiers had lined up on one side of the ditch while the guards who brought the prisoners looked on in disbelief.

"Fire!" a voice commanded.

The soldiers fired their weapons into the ditch for thirty seconds—drowning out the yells of the dying prisoners. When the firing stopped, a few more shots rang out, insuring that all the prisoners in the ditch had been executed. The engine of the nearby bulldozer started up, and the process of covering the mass grave began.

REMOTE WOODED AREA
0225 Hours

In another remote wooded area, a truck loaded with thirty-seven prisoners, including Jake, made the bumpy ride down a dirt road. A nervous paranoia had taken over as Jake and the others began to worry. When the truck stopped, the guards began yelling orders at the prisoners to get off the truck. As they followed those orders, waiting soldiers yelled and moved them over to a ditch—three feet deep, six feet wide, and thirty feet long.

As Jake and the others were rushed on—he saw the ditch and his fears quickly became a reality.

"No!" a voice yelled out.

The voices of some of the other prisoners also began to cry out as they saw the ditch and were forced into it. At this point, Jake began to experience a surreal feeling of disbelief. As he was pushed into the ditch, he was hit in the back, forcing him face down on the ground in the crowded ditch. Jake and many of the prisoners tried to resist and argue, but the soldiers were forceful, hitting them and forcing them into the ditch. While the distressed prison guards looked on, the soldiers, just as with the previous group of prisoners at the other location, quickly got everyone into the ditch in under a minute.

As Jake lay in the ditch with the others, he turned his head to the side and saw the back of the head of the prisoner next to him. There was a lot of praying and a lot of yelling, but within seconds of getting the prisoners into the ditch, the soldiers had lined up on one side. Jake said nothing as his mind went into overdrive thinking about his life and asking why this had happened.

Jake closed his eyes as the deafening sound of gunfire began, accompanied by the smell of gun smoke that filled the air. The muzzle flashes of the guns created a flashing illumination over the ditch as Jake grimaced in fear during the thirty seconds of gunfire. A Russian voice yelled out a command to cease fire, and the shooting stopped. Jake lay motionless in the ditch, his eyes still closed during the next few seconds of silence, his ears ringing. Jake heard muffled voices and a few single gunshots, but he kept his eyes closed and wondered if he were dead or alive—afraid to open his eyes as the voices became louder.

Suddenly Jake felt the sensation of being pulled out of the ditch by two sets of hands that had grabbed him. He opened his eyes as he was lifted and fearfully looked around as he was walked a few feet away from the ditch. He didn't understand what he was seeing or hearing as soldiers yelled at him. As his vision and hearing began to clear, he saw a line of dead Soviet soldiers near the ditch—a confusing sight. Jake was also confused by the sight of the men who grabbed him out of the ditch, one a Soviet soldier and the other an American, but the

American-Soviet combination had not yet registered with him.

For Jake, the entire time of being thrown into the ditch and then getting plucked back out felt like a bad dream, and had been a few minutes of a well-executed ambush and rescue operation. Earlier, the Soviet and Sergeant McDonald's teams had completed their free-fall parachute jump and landed about a mile away from where the Soviets were digging the ditch. The noise of the bulldozer used by the Soviets to dig the ditch helped conceal the approach of the teams and allowed them to move in and set up their ambush of what Colonel Karl had earlier briefed were execution squads. The Soviet guards who brought the prisoners had been spared, solely due to the convincing and some financial arrangements made by Colonel Karl.

It was an unlikely and yet fortunate plan that Colonel Karl Provaznik coordinated the rescue of two groups of prisoners. Unfortunately only two groups were rescued out of what Colonel Provaznik estimated to be fifteen groups. Although it was the Soviet Union that kept the prisoners, Colonel Provaznik and a few other officials including someone very high up in the Kremlin had taken it upon themselves to take a chance and try to save some of the prisoners. Provaznik's position along with some others within the Army and KGB gave him practically unlimited access and authority to authorize anything he ordered—without question.

It was not Colonel Provaznik's intention to defect or leave the Soviet Union—he was a loyalist to his native Russia—and arranging the rescue was something he and the others felt was the right thing to do, and represented some of the policies they felt were wrong. Colonel Provaznik's access and position also placed him in a unique position where he was a participant in the weekly and daily operations and intelligence briefings to what would be considered one of the number two KGB chiefs.

During the previous few years and more evident in the previous few weeks was the deteriorating status of the Soviet government, and Provaznik, like many within the government, was practical, realistic, and saw the writing on the wall. Many within the Soviet government knew the end was coming, and with that many were fearful of purges or even prosecution by international courts. Plans were being formulated by those in power to save themselves, and one of the plans was to destroy any evidence of their crimes, included any evidence of the holding of foreign military and intelligence prisoners. The decision had been made to eliminate all evidence of the foreign prisoners; a decision they assumed would eliminate any possibility of any repercussions or prosecutions, and ensure them that they could go on to hold positions in the new government.

The Execution

Colonel Provaznik did not approve of the plan to eliminate the foreign prisoners, which he felt was just another example of what he came to believe was the gross injustice and corruption of the Soviet political system. He realized that many of those in power would go on to hold positions in the new government, but he also knew the he would also hold a position in the new government and realized he was in a position where he could do something about the plans to execute the foreign prisoners.

With little time, Provaznik analyzed and evaluated the situation concerning the prisoners and knew he had to be careful in whom he confided. There was one harsh reality that became too true—he could not save them all. There were several hundred prisoners spread out in more than a dozen prisons. With the time he had, the resources he could acquire, and people he could trust, the reality was that he could only attempt to save two groups, about sixty prisoners. The decision as to which groups to rescue was based more on location and logistics, although Provaznik may have had some personal interest or curiosity about one particular prisoner he had come across almost twenty years earlier.

In 1973, a younger Provaznik was a Spetsnaz soldier on a transport aircraft in North Vietnam when a badly beaten American prisoner was brought on the plane. This brief exposure to Jake instilled a life-lasting impression on Provaznik who had always remembered Jake's name, and as an after-thought, scanned the list of foreign prisoners to look for Jake Walden's name. It upset Provaznik when he saw it on the list, but it also inspired him and gave him a feeling that maybe he could do something to make Jake's lengthy imprisonment right, so Provaznik selected the prison Jake was in as one of the two prisons from which the prisoners would be rescued.

While Jake stood with some of the other prisoners, his head started to clear and the soldiers' voices started to become intelligible, both the Russian and surprisingly the English spoken by the Americans. He and the others could now make out the Americans telling them that they were being rescued, but the moment was still more like a dream than reality as Charlie and Colonel Provaznik were quickly making their way getting the names and checking the list of prisoners. When they got to Jake and asked his name, he responded "Walden." As Charlie continued, the colonel stopped and looked at Jake.

"I know you," the colonel said.

Jake didn't respond.

"It was 1973 in Vietnam, on the plane, we treated your wounds on the flight, remember?"

As Charlie looked on with curiosity, Jake had a slight smile on his face.

"Yeah, you guys fixed me up."

Charlie noticed the interaction and the colonel's brief expression of both pride and satisfaction in Jake's survival. His observations were interrupted by Sergeant McDonald's comment that they had to get going.

The soldiers quickly gathered the prisoners together for Charlie to give them a short briefing about what was happening. The team medic approached Charlie and told him that one of the prisoners didn't make it and was still in the ditch.

"He wasn't shot, looks like a heart attack," the medic told him.

Charlie and the colonel looked on the list and noticed one of the names not checked off. At the same time the prisoners looked around among themselves and also noticed who was missing.

"Hans...Hans," a voice said out loud.

Charlie looked at the list and then looked up at Jake and the group.

"The German Hans Buerger," Charlie said.

"Hans, he had to be in his seventies," a voice from the group was heard saying.

"Sorry about Hans, but right now we have to get going, and we have some things to go over," Charlie told them.

As Charlie gave a quick one-minute briefing, Jake and most of the others tried to listen intently, but some of the prisoners were distracted and anxious, which could be expected. Charlie explained that although they had been rescued, there were conditions. He told them that they would not be able to contact their families, and would instead begin new lives with new identities. While most everyone listened, one of the now ex-prisoners was not in agreement with the conditions of rescue.

"I'm not doing that, I'm going home," a voice yelled out, which became a distraction for Charlie given the immediate urgency of the situation.

"You are one of two groups that have been rescued...out of fifteen groups. The others by now have all been executed...hundreds of them. They're dead, and you're alive, understand?"

He reiterated his point to them a few more times and conveyed an emotional statement to them to not let the death of the others be in vain.

The one outspoken prisoner continued to challenge Charlie and was verbally adamant about going home and didn't care about what happened to anyone else. The rescued prisoners were lined up and began to walk toward the pickup zone as Colonel Provaznik talked quietly to Charlie for a few seconds. Jake observed their conversation and saw that they seemed to be in reluctant agreement. The outspoken prisoner still ranted as Charlie got his attention and told him to help the colonel with Hans's body. The prisoner reluctantly agreed, but he continued to rant toward the colonel as Charlie left to catch up with the group.

The Execution

A few minutes later, an MI-26 helicopter began its descent toward the pickup zone—the group stopped and waited. Charlie stood behind the group with Jake just a few feet in front of him. Although the sound of the helicopter was loud, a faint but distinct sound of a gunshot was heard coming from back at the ditch. The sound was not noticed except for Jake and a few others at the rear of the line. They looked at Charlie—but nothing was said—an unspoken understanding of what just happened was realized. A few moments later, they noticed the figure of Colonel Provaznik as he approached the group alone.

As soon as the helicopter landed, everyone moved out and loaded up. Jake's position in the column put him sitting in the end of the aircraft across from Charlie. After the aircraft took off there were several minutes of silence while the former prisoners sat—still reluctant to believe that they were free. As Charlie and the colonel looked around, they could see the expressions on the faces of the former prisoners as they slowly began to realize they had been rescued. Even though the rescue was a new beginning, no one would ever know about this moment, except for them.

Chapter 23

The Deal

Jake Walden's Home

21 September, 2006

Day 13,233 — 36 Years, 2 Months, 23 Days

Sitting in the living room, Jake abruptly stopped and looked at Charlie and Ted.

"And that's it, Mr. Pratt…here we are."

Ted was excited and had been thoroughly drawn into the story, but his reaction to Jake's statement was disappointment.

"That was what…sixteen…seventeen years ago. So what happened?" Ted asked, almost demanded, as he looked at Jake and Charlie.

"We told you," Charlie said.

"What do you mean you told me?"

"Look, Ted, the conditions of the rescue were classified and kept secret, and frankly, just because you or anyone happens to find out about it doesn't change the fact that it still has to be kept secret."

"That was seventeen years ago, come on!" Ted said to Charlie.

"Yeah, and even though the Soviet Union is gone, the same people are running it with the same secrets they want kept quiet. And the deal was, all or nothing, Ted, all or nothing. That meant that their existence and the condition of their new lives could never be revealed or made public.

"Again, I don't understand, it was so long ago, and people need to know what happened to these guys…it was a crime and people should know about it," Ted argued back.

"You know, Ted, only two groups were rescued, sixty-five altogether, and the other thirteen groups had 283 guys that were executed that night," Charlie said with a slight change in his demeanor.

An uneasy Jake got up from his chair and Charlie paused, looked at Jake and then back at Ted who was not satisfied with the explanation.

"We've got to get going if you're going to get to the airport on time," Charlie told Ted.

"We who?" Ted replied.

"It'll take forever to get a taxi out here, so I just planned on taking you, and I drive right past there anyway on the way home."

"Oh, okay," a disappointed Ted replied.

Charlie got up from the chair, and then Ted, who was still filled with questions realized the interview was over. Jake walked over to the window and looked outside.

"They're leaving," Jake yelled out to his wife in the kitchen.

Ted got an expression on his face like a disappointed schoolboy as he looked at Charlie wanting more answers.

"We've got to go," Charlie told Ted with a sympathetic tone in his voice.

Jake's wife came out of the kitchen, and as she had done previously, angrily walked heavy-footed to the front door and opened it. This time she stood by the door and waited for Ted and Charlie to leave. Ted began to pick up his things from the coffee table.

"I hope you will decide not to do this story, Mr. Pratt," Jake said to Ted.

"You're kidding, right?" An arrogant but exuberant Ted smiled at Jake.

There was an awkward silence for a few seconds.

"This is not what I had thought at first. Yes, I mean there is a conspiracy or cover-up, but not by you. You're the hero of the story, which is much better than I had imagined," Ted blurted out.

"We've got to go," Charlie repeated as he interrupted Ted.

Ted's disappointment just moments earlier had quickly changed to enthusiasm as he looked at Charlie and Jake. They walked toward the door and Ted headed out first.

"It was very nice to meet you," Ted said to Jake's wife, but she did not give him a response, nor did she look at him.

Ted could tell from her attitude and expression that her opinion of him was one of hate or contempt. He walked out followed by Charlie.

"Bye," Charlie told Jake's wife with a reassuring smile and a slight rub on the shoulder, but she just ignored him.

As they walked out to the porch, Ted looked for his bag and noticed it was gone.

"Where's my bag?"

"Oh, the driver probably got it and put it in the car already," Charlie said.

Jake and his wife followed them out to the porch and sat on the bench together. The men started to walk down the steps and as Ted got about halfway down, Jake spoke to him again.

"Mr. Pratt, I know you've probably made up your mind already…and as I've already told you I don't care for you, but I do want you to know that I am truly and sincerely sorry I've ever had to meet you, truly sorry."

"Mr. Walden, I'm not sure what to say. I mean for me it was still very exciting to meet you."

"Not for us."

Ted smiled and ignored the remark, turned, and headed down the steps and followed Charlie to where the car was waiting.

The car was parked in the driveway at the side of the house, facing the road. Charlie walked around the front of the car to the far side as Ted walked to the passenger side. As they arrived at the car doors, Charlie leaned on the roof of the car, throwing his arms over the driver's door—which got Ted's attention.

"So, Ted, you still plan on writing this story, after what we already told you?"

"Look, Mr. Smith, this story is gigantic. It's a once-in-a-lifetime story, and frankly I still don't see why not. So what if fifteen years ago you guys made a deal, the Soviet Union is gone so nothing's going to happen."

Charlie got irritated as he slightly shook his head while staring at Ted. There was a silence for a moment.

"What? What...? What is it?"

Charlie didn't answer at first as he controlled his temper, but finally he answered and angrily fired back at Ted. "That story you did in Iraq, the one you got the Pulitzer for?"

"What about it?"

"What happened to that village, those families?"

"What do you mean?"

"What happened to them? Did you ever go back or follow up to see what they are doing now?"

Ted was caught off guard by the reference to an unrelated story and was a little agitated and confused by Charlie's questioning. Ted didn't know how to answer Charlie's questions.

"Don't know. I've never been back."

Charlie looked at Ted and then reached into the car and got a folder out that he slid across the roof of the car toward Ted. He looked at the folder and asked Charlie about it. Charlie told him that it was the file on the Iraqi village. Ted began to glance through it.

"That village you did that story on, well, after your story was published and you got that award, the Iraqi army went in and wiped it out, killed everyone for cooperating with you, and leveled the village, which isn't even on the map anymore."

Ted listened to Charlie as he looked through the file and the photos, and although it bothered him a little, his ego and arrogance won out.

"You're probably making this up...and if this did happen, it wasn't my fault, I didn't do this, and you can't make me feel guilty!"

"Do you feel guilty?"

"No!" Ted angrily answered, shaking his head as he continued to look through the file.

Charlie watched him as he mumbled to himself saying he didn't do anything wrong and took on a defensive attitude.

"I guess this won't change your mind on Jake's story?" Charlie asked.

"Hell no, no way!" Ted shouted back with increased arrogance and defensiveness.

"You know the only reason you're even here is because Jake's son was killed in that school shooting, and that picture of him carrying his dead son out of the school made a cover; otherwise, we wouldn't be here," Charlie fired back.

Ted did not respond to the last statement. Charlie's patience seemed to be running out while he glanced around for a few moments.

"So, can we go now?" Ted asked, breaking the silence.

"What do you think this is? Look around for Christ's sake! You're not in Kansas or Montana, you're in the middle of central Russia, you dumbass," Charlie yelled as his demeanor drastically changed into one of contempt toward Ted.

Charlie's agitation got Ted's attention. He didn't answer as he continued to watch and listen to Charlie.

"Look over my shoulder, Ted, toward the corner where that little strip mall is located."

Ted looked and saw the intersection and the strip mall, and the two cars parked at the intersection that Charlie was about to point out.

"See those two cars parked at the intersection? Within a hundred miles of here, there are sixteen other houses just like this one with guys like Jake and their families and cars parked outside. Do you know why those cars are there, Ted?"

"No," Ted answered apprehensively.

"Well, that's because you're a dumbass, Ted. We told you that we had to make a deal, all or none, new identity and never to contact their home or anyone."

"What are you talking about?" Ted hesitantly asked.

"Those cars, the men in those cars are waiting for the word on what to do. Whether to call it a day and go home or to make Jake, his family, and those other sixteen families disappear. It's that simple Ted. Some of the people from twenty years ago in Russia still have power, and whether we like it not, that's the deal."

Ted was somewhat ignorantly surprised by Charlie's explanation as he looked at Charlie and the cars at the strip mall.

"I guess if that's the option, I probably shouldn't do the story."

"Yeah, I would say so."

Ted thought for a few seconds as Charlie studied him.

"Look at me, Ted. Look me in the eye and tell me you're not going to do this story. Tell me you're not going to call the senator again, like you did before you came on this trip."

Surprised by Charlie knowing about his call to the senator, a frustrated Ted paused for a few more seconds in disbelief.

"I'm not...I won't do it."

Charlie looked at Ted, studied him, and then glanced at his watch. Noting the time, he pushed himself back off the car.

"Ted, we've got to get going." Charlie walked toward the rear of the car, and on the way, he picked up some tools that were left on the ground by the driver who changed the tire.

"Come around here and help with this stuff."

Ted walked around to the rear of the car as Charlie was putting the tools in the trunk.

"Can you go around there and get the rest of that stuff?"

"Sure."

As Charlie put the tools in the trunk, Ted walked behind.

"You can trust me, Charlie…I won't do the story," Ted not very convincingly said as he walked toward the other side of the car.

"Sorry…I just don't believe you, Ted," Charlie said to himself.

As Ted rounded the corner of the car, he stopped and saw a blue tarp lying on the ground.

"What the…"

Ted quickly turned around toward Charlie, but didn't get the chance to finish his sentence. Charlie stood arm's length distance away from Ted, pointing a 9mm Beretta pistol at Ted's forehead.

The sound of the gunshot startled Jake's wife as she sat next to Jake on the bench, her right hand clutching Jake's left hand as she began to rock slightly, bouncing their hands on her knee. The hand on Jake's right shoulder released its grasp as the driver walked around to the front of Jake and his wife. The driver, Colonel Karl—squatted down in front of them and got on one knee—with both of his hands, clasped their clutched hands. He looked first at Jake and then to his wife.

"It's all right, Nadya. It's over."

Jake's wife—Nadya, the nurse he had first met in prison over thirty years earlier—understood, but she still had difficulty holding back her tears and fear.

"I know, I know," Nadya tearfully told Karl.

Jake didn't say anything and just acknowledged Karl's comments. Karl got up and again reassured Jake and Nadya that everything was all right as he walked down the steps, accidentally brushing his head against the flag hanging from the post next to the steps. Nadya continued to clutch Jake's hand as the colonel walked around the side of the building.

While they sat on the bench, they heard the trunk of the car slam, then the car doors, and then the start of the engine. As the car drove out of the driveway, Charlie and Karl waved to Jake and Nadya. They continued to sit and just stared out past the porch.

Back at the Washington Post building, Kyle was sitting in his office when his cell phone rang. He looked at the phone and for a moment was excited when he saw Ted Pratt on the caller ID.

"Ted! How's it going?"

"Sorry, Kyle, not Ted. He decided he's going to stay here awhile"

Kyle was silent.

"Look, Kyle, we were right about Ted, no doubt."

Kyle didn't say anything as Charlie talked to him from the car driving away from Jake's house.

"Kyle, have you checked your e-mail?"

"No."

"Check it. I sent you a new photo for the wall, you can hang next to the other one."

"Just a minute, let me check."

The photo Charlie talked about was a framed 11x16 group photo Kyle had hanging on the wall in his office, one of the few things Kyle had on the wall. Had Ted ever taken notice, paid closer attention to his boss's achievements, he may have noticed the group photo. He might have noticed that the photo in the magazine of the man carrying his dead son from a school massacre in central Russia was Jake, and was also one of the people in the group photo on Kyle's wall. Had Ted taken notice, when he arrived at Jake's house, he would have definitely noticed that the same photo on Kyle's wall was also on Jake's wall and that Jake and Nadya and their two children were in the photo.

"That picture on the wall, you and I both know that those people are alive because you made a decision, you made a choice twelve years ago, the same choice Ted could have made. You had a choice, Kyle, and believe me when I tell you, you made the right choice. You didn't have to think about it, and you did it instinctively to save those people, not to get a story," Charlie told Kyle with sincerity.

While Charlie talked, Kyle got the e-mail and opened the attached photo.

"Okay, got the e-mail."

"Second row from the bottom right, fourth and fifth person in, see them?"

"Yeah…that's Jake and his wife?"

"Yes, and the boy and girl in front of them are their kids. The boy is the one Jake carried out of that school. So except for the boy, everyone else in the picture is alive. There's a lot more of them now, more family than twelve years ago."

"Looks like it's almost double."

"Kyle, if you ever start to doubt that you did the right thing, look at that picture and know that fifty-plus people are alive because of you and not dead because of you or something Ted did. Remember that and never forget that, Kyle."

"I know, Charlie, I know…it's just hard."

"They're having their Fourth of July picnic again next summer. Maybe you can come over and visit, meet the rest of them in person. It might help, to see Jake again and meet some of the others."

"Maybe, that might be good."

"Sorry, Kyle, but I've got to go."

Charlie closed up the cell phone as the car turned the corner. Karl gave a hand signal and called out the window to the two waiting cars at the corner and told them to leave.

As Jake and Nadya sat on their front porch bench, they could see the cars drive off down at the corner. They continued to sit in silence for a few minutes. Then Nadya closed her eyes for a second, rolled her shoulders back, and took in a deep breath. She opened her eyes, let go of her tight grip on Jake's hand and slowly stood up. She looked out on the rural scenery in front of their house and then walked over to the door and slightly opened it. She reached inside and grabbed a four-foot flagpole with a Green Bay Packers football flag attached. Nadya walked to the front of the porch steps, took down the Cardinals Baseball flag, and put up the Packers flag.

"Anna will be home soon. I'll cook an early dinner," Nadya said as she swapped the flags.

Jake nodded as Nadya went inside the house.

Five minutes later, Jake continued to sit in silence when he noticed two cars quickly approaching the house. He watched the cars as they pulled up to the front of the house and stopped. Four men armed with AK-47 assault rifles got out of the first car, surveying the area as they exited and then spread out. Two more armed men got out of the second car as Jake watched.

"Everything okay, Jake?" one of men asked in Russian.

Jake nodded but did not say anything to the man he knew from his years in the gulag. The man was Jake's friend, Alex.

Jake's fourteen-year-old daughter Anna got out of the back of the second car where two other teenage girls were also sitting.

"You sure, everything is good, yes?" Alex asked while the armed men with him cautiously kept watch.

"It's all right, Alex. Thank you for picking up Anna."

"You are welcome, my friend, you are welcome."

Alex smiled, happy to hear that everything was okay. Alex and the others got back into the cars and drove away as Anna stood at the bottom of the steps and watched the cars drive off. Anna then walked up the porch steps and looked at her father.

"How was school?" Jake asked.

"Good, half day today, remember?"

"Oh, so where have you been?"

Anna paused a moment as she looked at her father, studied him, and felt some concern while she noticed that he was somewhat distraught and not fully involved in the conversation. Anna, however, was not a typical fourteen-year-old girl and picked up on that; she was intelligent, observant, sympathetic, and more importantly, knowledgeable of her parents' past. Jake finally noticed Anna's pause.

"What?"

"Uncle Charlie, why was he here?"

Jake turned his attention to Anna, a little concerned about her question.

"Charlie, what do you mean?"

"He was here...he just left. Alex came and picked us up, that's not normal. We've been over at the store waiting for the flag."

As Anna talked, she motioned toward the corner strip mall and the flag hanging off the porch. Jake had been so preoccupied with memories and telling his story to Ted that he had not realized that Anna may have seen what happened to Ted at the side of the house.

That thought started to bother him, but Anna was also aware of the situation that her father was in. Although Charlie had instructed Jake and the other prisoners not to tell their children about their past and circumstances, Jake and the others secretively and effectively told the children about their situation when they became old enough to understand. Anna had just told her father that she was waiting for the flag, which had been established years earlier and was part of a detailed system to help family members if the need for escape ever arrived. The flags were simple, red to stay away and green was for all clear.

Over the years, Jake and the other ex-prisoners had become very close. Many of them worked at the same places and all of them, including the families, grew to know each other and got together several times a year for holidays, gatherings, and picnics like the ones in the group photo that Kyle had. The contacts made in the prison camps with people like Alex helped in setting up a complex network system. Alex had the military connections, but he also had the connections in the Russian crime circles. Jake and the others realized that escape by anyone would jeopardize everyone; however, they also realized that if something should ever happen, escape would be necessary. Their concern caused them to establish plans that they hoped would at least save most of the children if escape became necessary.

As Jake looked at his daughter standing on the porch, he realized that she had to have seen what happened. He wanted it not to be true, but he knew in his heart she had to have seen. Anna could see on her father's face his frustration as his eyes teared up. The intuitive Anna walked over to her father, reached out with her right hand, and gave him a quick head scruff, like a parent would give a child. She quickly embraced his head and pulled him to her chest, giving him a tight hug while he held back his tears.

"You're a good papa," Anna whispered to him in English as she bent down and gave her father a kiss on the top of his head. Anna then gave her father another head scruff and went inside.

As the screen door closed, Jake was overcome with emotion. His daughter saying "You're a good papa" did it, and he tried to hold back his tears. With both hands, he grabbed his pant legs and clutched them as tears rolled down his face as he thought about how close his family had come to death.

He didn't get the privacy he wanted very long as his yellow Labrador ran up the steps and tried to get up in his lap. The dog instinctively started to lick Jake's face as he gently tried to wrestle back the dog, who was persistent and continued to give him kisses and licked at the tears on his face. Although Jake was resistant, the dog's instinct gave him some comfort, and the dog's actions forced him to reluctantly change his mood as he gave in to the dog's affection.

"Okay, okay, get down," he told the dog as he stood up. Jake wiped the tears away and took another minute to gain his composure. The dog paced and gave a couple of barks. "All right, all right."

He opened the screen door and let the dog go inside. He took a few more moments staring out into the countryside to the front of the house. He then opened the screen door, went inside, slowly walked into the living room and glanced at some of the pictures on the wall. As he heard his wife and daughter talking in the kitchen, he paused momentarily and looked at the group photo of himself with the other former prisoners and their families, a copy of the same one that was in Kyle's office. He then walked toward his desk in the corner and sat down.

Jake leaned forward, closed his eyes, and put his head in his hands for a few seconds. He then sat up and opened his eyes, looked at the computer screen and pulled up a music playlist. He scrolled through it for a few seconds until he found a song he liked—"Take me Home" by Phil Collins. Jake found a sort of irony in the parallels of his life and the lyrics of the song, as he had with many songs since being out of prison. Listening to music had become a relaxing hobby.

As the song began, Jake sat back in his chair, looked up and saw his wife and daughter standing at the kitchen doorway looking at him. Still with eyes a bit red and watery, he looked at them, smiled, and asked, "Want to go out?"

GLOSSARY OF TERMS
(COLD WAR AND MILITARY)

Agency: A term commonly referred to for the Central Intelligence Agency or CIA.

An-22 Antel: The Antonov An-22 Antei (NATO reporting name "Cock") was the world's heaviest aircraft, until the advent of the American C-5 Galaxy and later the Soviet An-124. Powered by four pairs of contra-rotating turboprops, the design remains the world's largest turboprop-powered aircraft.

AO: Area of operations.

Arms race: Massive military buildup by both the Soviet Union and the United States in an effort to gain military superiority.

A-Team: U.S. Army Special Forces twelve-man teams organized to conduct unconventional warfare, foreign internal defense, and direct action missions (see Green Berets).

B-52: The B-52 is a long-range, heavy bomber that can perform a variety of missions. The bomber is capable of flying at high subsonic speeds at altitudes up to 50,000 feet (15,166.6 meters). It can carry nuclear or precision guided conventional ordnance with worldwide precision navigation capability.

http://www.af.mil/information/factsheets/fact-sheet.asp?id=83

Bad Tölz Germany: Bad Tölz is located in the Bavarian southern edge of Germany. In 1937, the SS-Junkerschule Bad Tölz was established at Flint Kaserne near the town Bad Tölz. The SS-Junkerschule (SS Officer Candidate School) operated until the end of World War II in 1945. During the early 1950s, Flint Kaserne became the base of the U.S. Army's 1st Battalion, 10th Special Forces Group.

Base Camp: A resupply base for field units and a location for headquarters of brigade or division size units, artillery batteries and air fields. Also known as the rear area.

Berlin Wall: The Berlin Wall was a barrier constructed by the German Democratic Republic (GDR, East Germany) starting on 13 August 1961, which completely cut off West Berlin from surrounding East Germany and from East Berlin. The barrier included guard towers placed along large concrete walls which circumscribed a wide area (later known as the "death strip") that contained anti-vehicle trenches, "fakir beds" and other defenses. The Eastern Bloc claimed that the wall was erected to protect its population from fascist elements conspiring to prevent the "will of the people" in building a socialist state in East Germany. In practice, the Wall served to prevent the massive emigration and defection that marked Germany and the communist Eastern Bloc during the post-World War II period. In 1989, a radical series of political changes occurred in the Eastern Bloc, associated with the liberalization of the Eastern Bloc's authoritarian systems and the erosion of political power in the pro-Soviet governments in nearby Poland and Hungary. After several weeks of civil unrest, the East German government announced on 9 November 1989, that all GDR citizens could visit West Germany and West Berlin. Over the next few weeks, a euphoric public and souvenir hunters chipped away parts of the Wall; the governments later used industrial equipment to remove most of the rest. The fall of the Berlin Wall paved the way for German reunification, which was formally concluded on 3 October 1990.

Blood trail: A trail of blood on the ground left by a fleeing man who has been wounded.

Blue Room: The Blue Room was one of several terms used by American POWs in the Hanoi Hilton for a room where prisoners were tortured by the North Vietnamese captors.

Body bag: Plastic bag used to transport dead bodies from the field.

Body count: The number of enemy killed, wounded, or captured during an operation. The term was used during the Vietnam War by Washington and Saigon as a means of measuring the progress of the war.

C-130 Hercules: The C-130 Hercules primarily performs the tactical portion of the airlift mission. The aircraft is capable of operating from rough dirt strips and is the prime transport for air dropping troops and equipment into hostile areas.

C-141 Starlifter: The C-141A, built between 1963 and 1967, was the USAF's first jet aircraft designed to meet military standards as a troop and cargo carrier. For more than forty years, the C-141 Starlifter performed numerous airlift missions for the U.S. Air Force. Its great range and high speed enabled the Starlifter to project American military power and humanitarian efforts rapidly across the globe.

C-17 Globemaster: The Boeing (formerly McDonnell Douglas) C-17 Globemaster III is a large military transport aircraft. Developed for the United States Air Force (USAF) from the 1980s to the early 1990s by McDonnell Douglas, the C-17 is used for rapid strategic airlift of troops and cargo to main operating bases or forward operating bases throughout the world. It can also perform tactical airlift, medical evacuation, and airdrop missions.

Cessna 0-1 Bird Dog: The Cessna L-19/O-1 Bird Dog was a liaison and observation aircraft. During the Vietnam War, the aircraft were used for reconnaissance, forward air control (FAC), and search and rescue.

Checkpoint Charlie: A crossing point between West Berlin and East Berlin when the Berlin Wall divided the city.

Cherry: Slang term for youth and inexperience.

Code of Conduct: Military rules of conduct for U.S. military personnel.

Cold War: The Cold War was the continuing state from roughly 1946 to 1991 of political conflict, military tension, proxy wars, and economic competition between the Communist World — primarily the Soviet Union and its satellite states and allies — and the powers of the Western world, primarily the United States and its allies. Although the chief military forces never engaged in a major battle, they expressed the conflict through military coalitions, strategic conventional force deployments, extensive aid to states deemed vulnerable, proxy wars, espionage, propaganda, conventional and nuclear arms races, appeals to neutral nations, rivalry at sports events, and technological competitions such as the Space Race.

Communism: A theoretical economic system characterized by the collective ownership of property and by the organization of labor for the common advantage of all members. A system of government in which the state plans and controls the economy and a single, often authoritarian party holds power, claiming to make progress toward a higher social order in which all goods are equally shared by the people. The Marxist-Leninist version of Communist doctrine advocates the overthrow of capitalism by the revolution of the proletariat.

Concertina wire: Coiled barbed wire used as an obstacle.

Containment: Fundamental U.S. foreign policy during the Cold War in which the United States tried to contain Communism by preventing it from spreading to other countries.

DEFCON: An acronym for "Defense Readiness Condition." The term is followed by a number (one to five) which informs the U.S. military to the severity of the threat, with DEFCON 5 representing normal, peacetime readiness to DEFCON 1 warning the need for maximum force readiness, i.e. war.

Détente: The relaxing of tension between the superpowers.

Deterrence Theory: A theory that proposed a massive buildup of military and weaponry in order to threaten a destructive counterattack to any potential attack. The threat was intended to prevent, or deter, anyone from attacking.

DMZ: Demilitarized zone. The dividing line between North and South Vietnam established in 1954 at the Geneva Convention.

Dog tag: A dog tag is the informal name for the identification tags worn by military personnel, named such as it bears resemblance to actual dog tags. The tag is primarily used for the identification of dead and wounded and essential basic medical information.

EB-66C: The EB-66C (earlier version was RB-66C) was a specialized electronic reconnaissance and ECM aircraft with an expanded crew of seven, including additional electronics warfare experts.

EC-21: The Lockheed EC-121 Warning Star was a United States Navy and United States Air Force airborne early warning radar surveillance aircraft. The EC-121s were also used for intelligence gathering (SIGINT). EC-121s were used extensively in Southeast Asia between 16 April 1965, and 1 June 1974 to provide radar early warning and limited airborne control of USAF fighter forces engaging MiG interceptors.

Ejection: Escape from an aircraft by means of an independently propelled seat or capsule.

F-4: Phantom jet fighter-bombers. Range: 1,000 miles. Speed: 1400 mph. Payload: 16,000 lbs. The workhorse of the tactical air support fleet.

FAC: Forward air controller; a person who coordinates air strikes.

Fall of Soviet Union: The dissolution of the Soviet Union was the disintegration of the federal political structures and central government of the Soviet Union, resulting in the independence of all fifteen republics of the Soviet Union between March 11, 1990 and December 25, 1991.

Fallout shelter: Underground structures, stocked with food and other supplies, that were intended to keep people safe from radioactive fallout following a nuclear attack.

Firefight: A battle, or exchange of small-arms fire with the enemy.

First Indochina War: The First Indochina War (also known as the French Indochina War) was fought in French Indochina from

December 19, 1946, until August 1, 1954, between the French Union's French Far East Expeditionary Corps, led by France and supported by the Vietnamese National Army against the Việt Minh, led by Hồ Chí Minh and Võ Nguyên Giáp. Most of the fighting took place in Tonkin in Northern Vietnam, although the conflict engulfed the entire country and also extended into the neighboring French Indochina protectorates of Laos and Cambodia.

First Strike Capability: The ability of one country to launch a surprise, massive nuclear attack against another country. The goal of a first strike is to wipe out most, if not all, of the opposing country's weapons and aircraft, leaving them unable to launch a counterattack.

FRAG: Fragmentary order (FRAGO JP1-02) — An abbreviated form of an operation order, usually issued on a day-to-day basis, that eliminates the need for restating information contained in a basic operation order. It may be issued in sections. (Army) — A form of operation order that contains information of immediate concern to subordinates. It is an oral, a digital, or a written message that provides brief, specific, and timely instructions without a loss of clarity. It is issued after an operation order to change or modify that order or to execute a branch or sequel to that order.

Freedom Bird: The plane that took soldiers from Vietnam back to the world.

French Fort: A distinctive triangular structure built by the French by the hundreds.

Glasnost: A policy promoted during the latter half of the 1980s in the Soviet Union by Mikhail Gorbachev in which government secrecy (which had characterized the past several decades of Soviet policy) was discouraged and open discussion and distribution of information was encouraged. The term translates to "openness" in Russian.

Green Berets: U.S. Army Special Forces also known as Green Berets. Twelve-man teams to conduct unconventional warfare, foreign internal defense, and direct action missions. During the Vietnam War, Special Forces individually and as teams organized and led irregular military units such as the *Montagnards.* This same mission has been replicated numerous occasions up to the most recent operation in Afghanistan.
http://www.soc.mil/USASFC/USASFC%20History.html

Gulag: The gulag was the government agency that administered the main Soviet penal labor camp systems.

Gunship: Armed helicopter.

HAHO: High-altitude, high-opening parachute jump for insertion of troops behind enemy lines. These jumps are typically conducted from altitudes 15,000 feet and higher where jumpers deploy their parachutes at high altitudes and fly their parachutes for extended distances.

HALO: High-altitude, low-opening parachute jump for insertion of troops behind enemy lines. These jumps are typically conducted from altitudes 15,000 feet and higher similar to HAHO jumps, but the jumpers free-fall and open their parachutes generally between 1000 and 3000 feet.

Hanoi Hilton: The Hoa Lo Prison located in Hanoi Vietnam sarcastically known to American prisoners of war as the "Hanoi Hilton," was a prison used by the French colonists in Vietnam for political prisoners and later by North Vietnam for prisoners of war during the Vietnam War.

Hotline: A direct line of communication between the White House and the Kremlin, established in 1963. Often called the "red telephone."

ICBM: Inter-continental ballistic missiles were missiles that could carry nuclear bombs across thousands of miles.

Immersion foot: Condition resulting from feet being submerged in water for a prolonged period of time, causing cracking and bleeding.

Iron curtain: A term used by Winston Churchill to describe the growing divide between Western democracies and Soviet-influenced states.

JPAC: The Joint POW/MIA Accounting Command (JPAC) is a joint task force within the United States Department of Defense (DoD) whose mission is to account for Americans who are listed as prisoners of war (POW), or missing in action (MIA), from all past wars and conflicts. It has been especially visible in conjunction with the Vietnam War POW/MIA issue. The mission of the Joint POW/MIA Accounting Command (JPAC) is to achieve the fullest possible accounting of all Americans missing as a result of the nation's past conflicts. The motto of JPAC is "Until they are home."

K-bar: Combat knife.

KIA: Killed in action.

Korean War: The Korean War (25 June 1950 – armistice signed 27 July 1953) was a military conflict between South Korea supported by the United Nations, and North Korea supported by the People's Republic of China (PRC), with military material aid from the Soviet Union. The war was a result of the physical division of Korea by an agreement of the Allies at the conclusion of the Pacific War at the end of World War II.

LZ: Landing zone. Usually a small clearing secured temporarily for the landing of resupply helicopters. Some become more permanent and eventually become base camps.

Machete: The machete is a large cleaver-like cutting tool. The blade is typically 32.5 to 60 centimeters (12.8 to 24 in) long and usually under 3 millimeters (0.12 in) thick. In various tropical and subtropical countries, the machete is frequently used to cut through rain forest undergrowth and for agricultural purposes.

Mi-17: The Mi-17 (also known as the Mi-8M series in Russian service, NATO reporting name "Hip") is a Russian-designed helicopter currently in production at two factories in Kazan and Ulan-Ude. Mil Mi-8/17 is a medium twin-turbine transport helicopter that can also act as a gunship. The Soviet Union specifically designed the Mi-17 for the Soviet war in Afghanistan.

Mi-26: The Mil Mi-26 (NATO reporting name "Halo") is a Soviet/Russian heavy transport helicopter. It is in service with civilian and military operators. It is the largest and most powerful helicopter ever to have gone into production.

MIA: Missing in action.

Montagnard: A Vietnamese term for several tribes of mountain people inhabiting the hills and mountains of central and northern Vietnam. The term *Montagnard* means "mountain people" in French and is a carryover from the French colonial period in Vietnam for the indigenous peoples of the Central Highlands of Vietnam.

Mortar: A muzzle-loading cannon with a short tube in relation to its caliber that throws projectiles with low muzzle velocity at high angles.

Mutually assured destruction: MAD was the guarantee that if one superpower launched a massive nuclear attack, the other would reciprocate by also launching a massive nuclear attack, and both countries would be destroyed. This ultimately became the prime deterrent against a nuclear war between the two superpowers.

NVA: North Vietnamese Army.

Pardubice Air Base: Pardubice Air Base was a military base near the city of Pardubice, Czech Republic. During World War II the airport served for training of Luftwaffe pilots and toward the end of the war it was used for combat operations and was destroyed by bombing. Since 1950, the airport was used only for the military. The airport hosted 4th and 18th Fighter Air Wings equipped with S-199, MiG-15, C-2, C-5, C-11, MiG-19S, MiG-19PM, MiG-21F and Mi-1 helicopters, 47th Reconnaissance Wing with MiG-21R, Il-28L, Il-14 and later with Su-22 and since 1986 the 30th Strafer Wing with Su-25K.

People's Republic of China: People's Republic of China (PRC), commonly known as China, is the most populous state in the world. Located in East Asia, it is a single-party state governed by the Communist Party of China (CPC). The PRC exercises jurisdiction over twenty-two provinces, five autonomous regions, four directly administered municipalities (Beijing, Tianjin, Shanghai, and Chongqing), and two highly autonomous special administrative regions (SARs) — Hong Kong and Macau. Its capital city is Beijing.

Perestroika: Introduced in June 1987 by Mikhail Gorbachev, an economic policy to decentralize the Soviet economy. The term translates to "restructuring" in Russian.

Perimeter: Outer limits of a military position. The area beyond the perimeter belongs to the enemy.

Platoon: A subdivision of a company-sized military unit, normally consisting of two or more squads or sections.

POW: Prisoner of war.

Pulitzer Prize: The Pulitzer Prize is a U.S. award for achievements in newspaper and online journalism, literature and musical composition. It was established by American (Hungarian-born) publisher Joseph Pulitzer and is administered by Columbia University in New York City.

RPG: Rocket-propelled grenade. A Russian-made portable anti-tank grenade launcher.

Sabre: The North American F-86 Sabre (sometimes called the Sabrejet) was a transonic jet fighter aircraft. Produced by North American Aviation, the Sabre is best known as America's first swept wing fighter which could counter the similarly winged Soviet MiG-15 in high-speed dogfights over the skies of the Korean War. Considered one of the best and most important fighter aircraft in the Korean War, the F-86 is also rated highly in comparison with fighters of other eras. Although it was developed in the late 1940s and was outdated by the end of the 1950s, the Sabre proved versatile and adaptable, and continued as a front-line fighter in numerous air forces until the 1990s.

Glossary of Terms

Search and Rescue: The use of aircraft, surface craft, submarines, and specialized rescue teams and equipment to search for and rescue distressed persons on land or at sea.

Sharashka: Sharashka (sometimes Sharaga or Sharazhka) was an informal name for secret research and development laboratories in the Soviet Gulag.

Son Tay Prison: The Son Tay prison camp was a POW camp operated by North Vietnam near the town of Son Tay the late 1960s through late 1970.

SOP: Standard operating procedure.

Soviet Union: Also called the U.S.S.R. A former country of eastern Europe and northern Asia with coastlines on the Baltic and Black seas and the Arctic and Pacific oceans. It was established in December 1922 with the union of the Russian SFSR (proclaimed after the Russian Revolution of 1917) and various other Soviet republics. In 1991, a number of constituent republics declared their independence, and the U.S.S.R. was officially dissolved on December 31, 1991. Moscow was the capital.

Special Forces: U.S. Army forces organized, trained, and equipped to conduct special operations with an emphasis on unconventional warfare capabilities.

Squad: Small military unit consisting of less than ten men.

Star Wars: Nickname (based on the *Star Wars* movie trilogy) of U.S. President Ronald Reagan's plan to research, develop, and build a space-based system that could destroy incoming nuclear missiles. Introduced March 23, 1983 and officially called the Strategic Defense Initiative (SDI).

Superpower: A country that dominates in political and military power. During the Cold War, there were two superpowers: the Soviet Union and the United States.

Survival, evasion, resistance, and escape: Actions performed by isolated personnel designed to ensure their health, mobility, safety, and honor in anticipation of or preparation for their return to friendly control. Also called SERE.

U.S.S.R.: The Union of Soviet Socialist Republics (U.S.S.R.), also commonly called the Soviet Union, was a country that consisted of what is now Russia, Armenia, Azerbaijan, Belarus, Estonia, Georgia, Kazakhstan, Kyrgyzstan, Latvia, Lithuania, Moldova, Tajikistan, Turkmenistan, Ukraine, and Uzbekistan.

UH-1H: Huey helicopter.

VC: Viet Cong, the National Liberation Front.

Victor Charlie: The term used to identify Viet Cong.

Viet Cong: Communist-led forces fighting the South Vietnamese government. The political wing was known as the National Liberation Front, and the military was called the People's Liberation

Armed Forces. Both the NLF and the PLAF were directed by the People's Revolutionary Party (PRP), the southern branch of the Vietnamese Communist Party, which received direction from Hanoi through COSVN, which was located in III Corps on the Cambodian border. After 1968, as negotiations began in Paris, the NLF established the Provisional Revolutionary Government.

Viet Minh: Viet Nam Doc Lap Dong Minh Hoi, or the Vietnamese Allied Independence League. A political and resistance organization established by Ho Chi Minh before the end of World War II, dominated by the Communist Party. Though at first smaller and less famous than the non-Communist nationalist movements, the Viet Minh seized power through superior organizational skill, ruthless tactics, and popular support.

Vietnam Veterans Memorial: The Vietnam Veterans Memorial is a national memorial in Washington, D.C. It honors U.S. service members of the U.S. armed forces who fought in the Vietnam War, service members who died in service in Vietnam/South East Asia, and those service members who were unaccounted for (Missing In Action) during the war.

Vietnam War: The Vietnam War was a Cold War-era military conflict that occurred in Vietnam, Laos, and Cambodia from 1 November 1955 to the fall of Saigon on 30 April 1975. This war followed the First Indochina War and was fought between North Vietnam, supported by its communist allies, and the government of South Vietnam, supported by the United States and other anti-communist nations. The Viet Cong (also known as the National

Liberation Front, or NLF), a lightly armed South Vietnamese communist-controlled common front, largely fought a guerrilla war against anti-communist forces in the region. The Vietnam People's Army (North Vietnamese Army) engaged in a more conventional war, at times committing large units into battle.

WARSAW PACT: Military alliance of the Soviet Union, Albania (until 1968), Bulgaria, Czechoslovakia, East Germany, Hungary, Poland, and Romania, formed in 1955 in response to West Germany's entry into NATO. Its terms included a unified military command and the stationing of Soviet troops in the other member states. Warsaw Pact troops were called into action to suppress uprisings in Poland (1956), Hungary (1956), and Czechoslovakia (1968). The alliance was dissolved in 1991 after the collapse of the Soviet bloc, and Soviet troops departed. Several Warsaw Pact members later joined NATO.

WIA: Wounded in action.

World War II: World War II, or the Second World War (often abbreviated as WWII or WW2), was a global conflict lasting from 1939 to 1945, involving most of the world's nations in which Great Britain, France, the Soviet Union, the United States, China, and other allies defeated Germany, Italy, and Japan. It was the most widespread war in history, with more than 100 million military personnel mobilized.

REFERENCES AND RESOURCES

American Cold War Veterans (ACWV) http://www.american-coldwarvets.org/

Applebaum, Ann. (2003). *Gulag: A history*. New York, NY. Doubleday. Retrieved from: http://www.anneapplebaum.com/gulag-a-history/ Winner of the 2004 Pulitzer Prize and Britain's Duff-Cooper Prize.

CIA Historical Collection Publications. https://www.cia.gov/library/publications/historical-collection-publications/

Coram, Robert. (2007). *American Patriot: The Life and Wars of Colonel Bud Day*. New York, NY. Hachette Book Group. http://www.robertcoram.com/home.html

CRS Issue Brief for Congress: POWs and MIAs Status and Accounting Issues (June 2005). Washington D.C., Library of Congress. Retrieved from www.fas.org/sgp/**crs**/natsec/IB92101.pdf

Defense Prisoner of War Missing Personnel Office (2011). Retrieved from http://www.dtic.mil/dpmo/russia_europe/gulag_study/

GARF: The Gulag Study. http://www.nationalalliance.org/gulag/5gulag.htm

Gargus, John. (2007). *The Son Tay Raid: American POW's in Vietnam were not forgotten*. College Station, Texas. Texas A&M University.

National Alliance of Families: http://www.nationalalliance.org/

National Archives: http://www.archives.gov/

POW Network: http://pownetwork.org/

Rescue Attempt: The Son Tay Raid. http://www.nationalmuseum.af.mil/factsheets/factsheet.asp?id=14410

Schemmer, Benjamin J. (2002). *The Raid: The Son Tay prison rescue mission*. New York, NY. Random House.

Son Tay Raid: http://www.psywarrior.com/sontay.html

Son Tay Raider Association: http://www.sontayraider.com/

Soviet and Warsaw Pact Military Journals. http://www.foia.cia.gov/Soviet_and_Warsaw_Pact_Military_Journals.asp

Soviets held U.S. POWS after WWII: Yeltsin aide says some Americans still live in Russia. November 12, 1992|By New York Times News Service. http://articles.baltimoresun.com/1992-11-12/news/1992317203_1_volkogonov-soviet-union-prison-camps

References and Resources

Special Operations.com: http://www.specialopera-tions.com/Operations/sontay.html

The Soviet Union: Barbaric History. http://markhumphrys.com/soviet.html

Time magazine, May 12, 1975. What next in Asia. Vol. 105 No. 19

Vietnam POW Homepage: http://www.nampows.org/

Photo Images

Book Cover Photo by Warren Martin

Image 1 POW Logo Image. http://www.google.com/imghp

Image 2 Aircraft Training in Florida for Raid 1970. http://com-mons.wikimedia.org/wiki/Main_Page

Image 3 Son Tay Prison Camp 1970. http://commons.wiki-media.org/wiki/Main_Page

Image 4 Remains of Helicopter inside Son Tay Prison. http://commons.wikimedia.org/wiki/Main_Page

Image 5 Vietnam Memorial Wall. http://www.google.com/imghp

Image 6 Hoa-Lo Prison a.k.a. The Hanoi Hilton. http://com-mons.wikimedia.org/wiki/Main_Page

Image 7 Time Cover. https://www.google.com/

Image 8 Soviet Prison Camp a.k.a. The Gulag. http://www.nationalalliance.org/gulag/5gulag.htm

Image 9 The Berlin Wall – November 9, 1990. http://commons.wikimedia.org/wiki/Main_Page

Image 10 Flint Kaserne in Bad Tölz Germany. http://commons.wikimedia.org/wiki/Main_Page